Straight for the Kill

STRAIGHT FOR THE KILL

A BENOIT AND DAYNE MYSTERY

WINTER AUSTIN

TULE
PUBLISHING

DEDICATION

This book is for Lisa.
We became sisters when I married your brother;
it's a bond cemented by years, love, and strength.
I will always have your six.

PROLOGUE

Prelude: Twenty-five years ago

EARL JOHNSON HATED snow.

Every year he wished he could move south during the winter like all the other snowbirds. But he couldn't afford it. Not on the meager earnings he made as a farmer, and even that was barely enough to keep him alive. No family, no spouse, and no children, Earl was on his own.

Oh, how he detested snow. Especially when it covered this winding, snaking road that cut a swath through a thick wooded area. In the dark, Earl barely made out the tracks of a vehicle that had gone before him. The beams of his headlights bounced off the large flakes tumbling from the sky. Driving in this was utter nonsense and yet he had to do it. Someone had to check on the cows and make sure they found a good place to bed down during this freak autumn snowstorm.

"Dad-burn snow."

As he navigated his twenty-year-old Ford around a tight curve, Earl squinted through the murky night. Movement off to the right side of the road caught his attention. He took his foot off the gas and shifted it to tap the brake. The Ford straightened, the headlights cut through the dark and landed on an odd shape that tottered out of trees and right into the roadway. Earl slammed his foot down on the pedal.

He should have known better. The old beast wasn't prepared for quick stops, especially on snow.

The tires locked and the vehicle slid into a spin. The truck did a full three-sixty. As the lights slashed over the figure frozen in the middle of the road, Earl glimpsed the sight of … a bride? In the next instant, there was a sickening crunch before the tires left the road and the truck rolled several times before coming to rest on its top.

Hot radiator fluid hit the snow, steam hissing in the chilled air. Earl struggled to keep his eyes open. His head throbbed, a tickling sensation crept along his neck and cheek. *I shouldn't have left the house* was his last thought as he succumbed to the blackness.

But she had watched the accident from the tree line. She took a tentative step back, her hands clasped over her mouth to stuff back the screams clawing at her throat.

A hand clamped down on her shoulder and whipped her around. She stared into the two, black orbs glaring back at her.

"This is your fault."

The finality of that statement seared a place in her mind. Her fault.

CHAPTER ONE

Day 1: Thursday evening, two days before Halloween

THE CHATTER AND laughter of trick-or-treaters drifted in through the open windows. A mild autumn breeze lifted the gauzy curtains bracketing the windows. It was a perfect evening for late October, and the kiddos took advantage of the nice weather to beg for their wares. Juniper was holding its trick-or-treat night early this year so parents of the high school football players could watch their boys play in the district playoffs. Eckardt County stood a chance to go far in their division.

Sheriff Elizabeth Benoit, one day post-emergency appendectomy surgery, was stationed near the bay window that afforded her a better view of her visitors. She shifted in her recliner and pulled the ARMY STRONG fleece throw up to her shoulders as she watched a pair of Marvel superheroines march past the glowing jack-o'-lanterns lining the porch steps.

"Trick or treat," their voices singsonged to the man perched on the porch swing.

"Well, it's Ms. Marvel *and* Captain Marvel," Undersheriff Raphael "Rafe" Fontaine said. "Out saving the world one candy bar at a time."

The girls giggled and held up their Marvel-themed buckets. Rafe tossed in a few fun-sized chocolate bars. From somewhere in the yard, Elizabeth heard a mother holler, "What do you say?"

"Thank you," the girls chimed as one. Together they skipped down the steps and disappeared from sight.

Elizabeth sighed, wincing when her tender abdomen twinged. As advanced as surgery had become, needing only three tiny incisions to remove a festering, dying organ, it still left the patient in pain and fatigued. A warm, wet nose nudged her hand. She slid her palm up and along her faithful companion's head and rubbed the silky ears. Bentley, Elizabeth's red border collie, huffed in contentment, laying her muzzle on Elizabeth's lap.

Darkness pressed down on the vestiges of daylight, bringing to life the streetlamps lining the sidewalks. In a month's time, the homes along her block and stretching all the way to the town square would be decked out in their best Christmas lights. But for now, Elizabeth's neighbors' yards were a cascade of spooky to goofy.

Just two doors down, The Watering Hole, Marnie's bar, was a kaleidoscope of green, white, blue, and orange from the strobe lights she turned on for the kids to stop and get their candy. When tonight's citywide trick or treat ended, Elizabeth's sister would resume her duties as bartender and owner with her usual crowd. Her annual All Hallows Eve party would happen Saturday night. Elizabeth doubted she'd make it.

Such a shame. She'd been looking forward to it this year. In a weird turn of events, Elizabeth had managed to convince Rafe to do a couples costume—despite the fact they were not a couple—and go as two of her favorite characters in Craig Johnson's mystery series. But alas, that pairing would have to wait until next year.

A family of five tromped onto the porch, the youngest crawling up the steps dressed as a ladybug with her momma right behind. The older kids declared their intents, Rafe paid reparations, and Elizabeth's home was saved once more from tricks. One of the older girls spotted Elizabeth through the window and waved her sparkly wand. Elizabeth waved back.

Rafe rose from his post and came into the house. He held up the empty bowl. "We're out."

"That was the last of the candy."

"Looks like we're done for the night." He turned off the porch light and took the bowl into the kitchen. "Do you want anything?"

Elizabeth waited for him to circle back around the counter partition. He leaned a shoulder into the wall and crossed his arms. Her undersheriff made quite the picture standing like that, giving her drugged up, hurting body a little thrill. The mutual attraction burned between them, yet they'd never acted on it. Elizabeth was reaching the point where her give a damn was busted and she didn't care what anyone thought about the two of them together. With the narcotic leaving her giddy, she just might take the plunge. Except her surgeon had warned her—no extraneous activities for a few weeks.

Alas, any thoughts of doing more than kissing Rafe would have to be tabled for now.

Sitting here and staring out the window was driving her batty. She clumsily—*man, these drugs are a doozy*—shoved the fleece blanket aside. "I want to sit outside for a bit."

Bentley danced aside, ears perked at the prospect of getting to run outside and greet lagging treaters as they passed the house.

Rafe strode across the hardwood floor in a few steps and caught Elizabeth's elbow as she attempted to stand. "Hold on there, High Speed. Let me help."

The nickname was a familiar, untimely reminder of her ex-husband and Rafe's older brother. It was a vernacular she'd picked up from Joel, who'd heard it for more than a decade as a soldier in the army and as a Delta Force operative. He used it to describe Elizabeth because of her tendency to want to be the one to do it herself, lightning fast. Rafe had picked up on the moniker.

She wagged her hand, a smile playing at the corners of her mouth at her appendage flapping like a rag in the wind. "I got it."

Rafe took a firm hold of her. "No, you don't."

Her protests died once they reached her dried-out mouth. Argh, another icky side effect of the narcotic. "Water."

"I'll get you a glass once we're outside."

With measured steps, keeping her back ramrod straight because it eased the pressure on her abdomen and the surgical points, she and Rafe shuffled outside. Once she was seated on the porch swing, she sagged into the plush cushions. Bentley gave a nose tap to her hand, received an assuring pet that all was okay, and the border collie scuttled off the porch to have run of the yard. Rafe stepped inside and was back shortly with a lidded travel cup, ice clinking against the sides.

Elizabeth took a drink, relishing the cooling sensation it had on her body. Man, that brief walk out here had caused her to break out in a sweat. Or was this menopause setting in? Couldn't be—she was too young for that, right? Had to be the narcotics. It was a known side effect, this extra warmth.

"No more drugs," she muttered.

Beside her, Rafe chuckled. "You'll regret that declaration the instant the pain really hits."

"I feel like I'm tripping. I don't like it."

"You're not going to like hurting more. Give it another day to heal, and then you can just take regular pain meds."

She took another long swallow. "How are things at the fort?"

"Fine. You need to stop worrying about it. I've … we've got everything handled."

"We? As in you and Lila?"

"As in all of us." He took her hand and gave it a gentle squeeze. "Been at this long enough we've got the routine down pat. Don't forget, most of us have been in law enforcement far longer than you. Just focus on getting better."

Elizabeth let it be. Rafe knew what he was doing, had been chosen as her undersheriff for a reason. She twined her fingers with his and laid her head on his broad, capable shoulder. They sat there watching the candles in her jack-o'-lanterns flicker while Bentley zoomed around the yard, greeting the kids who walked past with joyous barks.

A while later, a midsized sedan crawled along the street and pulled into the drive. Rafe tensed under her.

Elizabeth lifted her head. "Who is that?"

"I don't know," he answered softly.

Bentley changed course and ran to the bottom of the porch steps. She sat; her shoulders hunched as she lowered her head. The border collie was usually friendly to all save one person, but she had been extra protective of Elizabeth since her surgery.

Rafe stood, slipping free of her hold, and moved to the top of the steps. Elizabeth noticed his hand twitching toward his sidearm. Bentley wasn't the only one in protector mode.

After a moment, the car's owner stepped out. Even with Rafe blocking part of her view, Elizabeth recognized her visitor.

"Seraphina? Is that you?"

Seraphina Russell, a long-ago friend of Marnie's, closed the sedan door and strolled up the drive. "It is. Hey there, Rafe. Is that a costume, or are you really a sheriff?"

"Deputy. Undersheriff actually." His hand fell away from his weapon.

All five-feet-eleven inches of lithe woman came to a stop before Bentley. Seraphina looked down at the dog. "Will she let me pass?"

"Bentley, off."

The collie chirped at Seraphina, then hightailed it up the steps and scuttled down to her dog bed beside the door.

"Guess she approves." Seraphina tossed a long, strawberry-blonde braid over her shoulder as she joined them on the porch.

"She does," Elizabeth said.

Seraphina patted Rafe's arm. "Lookin' good there, Raphael."

He grunted his response and remained standing at the end of the swing.

"Mom mentioned you had come home a few years back." Seraphina took a seat on the porch railing across from Elizabeth. "Said you and Joel divorced."

"Ancient history."

Seraphine smiled. "Hard to believe. Joel Fontaine and Elizabeth Benoit were high school sweethearts destined for greatness. Didn't think the two of you would ever split."

"Not every relationship can survive on sweetness alone." Elizabeth listed to her left to ease the ache on her right side.

"Mom also told me you were the sheriff now."

"I am. Two years next month. I see your mom every now and again. How is she doing?"

"Okay, all things considering. I wish she'd move closer to me, but she refuses to leave that old house and the memories. Even the prospect of a nice, assisted living facility that gives her access to disability services isn't enough to make her move."

Caroline Russell had been paralyzed in an accident that had taken her husband's life, Seraphina's father, when Seraphina was a girl. For a decade, it had been a hard slog as Caroline coped with the loss of not only her husband and his steady income but her inability to care for her two young children. About the time things were looking up for Caroline, tragedy struck again.

"What brings you to Juniper, Sera?" Elizabeth asked.

The other woman hugged the porch support and leaned into it. "I had vacation time the company told me to take.

Oh, the glamorous life of a pharmacist. Decided I should spend it with Mom. Maybe, finally, I could convince her to come with me."

"Does Marnie know you're here?"

"Not yet. I drove past her bar and noticed it was hopping with kids. You allow kids to trick-or-treat at a bar?"

Elizabeth chuckled. "She has the bar part shut down while it's going on. She's usually outside passing out the candy. Believe me, I've gotten an earful from some of our religious community on allowing it. But it was a tradition started before I ever took office, and no one seems to want to cross swords with the man who okayed it in the first place."

The growing shadows covered part of Seraphina's face. Elizabeth noticed a shift in the atmosphere.

Rafe's radio crackled with a report from Alexis. It broke the odd mood.

"You look like you're recovering from something," Seraphina mentioned.

Elizabeth placed a hand on her tender abdomen. "Emergency appendectomy. Not fun all around. In fact, it kinda sucks."

"I bet. Well." Seraphina slid off the railing. "I should let you get some rest."

"It was nice of you to stop."

She smiled, lifting a shoulder. "Thought I'd say hi, let you know I was in town."

"How long you here for?" Rafe asked, his gruff voice rumbling through the dark.

"Oh, for a few days I 'spect." Seraphina skipped down the steps, turned back, and waved at them. "Later, you two."

Rafe lingered at the edge of the porch. Once her sedan had disappeared down the street, he resumed his seat beside Elizabeth.

"You should probably go back inside and sleep," he said.

She sighed and rested her head on his shoulder once more. "Five more minutes. Then you can boss me around."

Before she took more narcotics to ease her into sleep, she needed a clear head to mull over why Seraphina Russell was back other than the reasons she'd given. Elizabeth wasn't the only one to mark this anniversary.

CHAPTER TWO

ECKARDT COUNTY DEPUTY Lila Dayne located the spot fellow deputy Ben Fitzgerald told her was a good place to park and watch for underage partiers. Homecoming and Halloween were favorite times for the high schoolers and visiting college students to get drunk and lit up. This piece of land with acres of timber and rolling fields was rented out as prime hunting property and left unsupervised for most the year. The perfect spot for rebelling teens to get away from adult supervision and let loose. Who cared that tomorrow was a school day?

Lila picked a nice hidey spot that gave her a view of the gravel road to her left, where she could see everyone coming and going and the entrance to the field to her right. The autumn foliage hadn't completely shed back here in the boondocks, and her unmarked, dusky squad car blended in with nature. Positioning the car as she had ensured the oncoming headlights wouldn't bounce off the frame and alert the wayward kids to her presence, but for extra precaution, she'd fixed a special camouflage blind several feet in front of the car. A little something special her boyfriend—could she really call him her boyfriend?—Deputy Kyle Lundquist had cooked up. Avid game hunter that Kyle was, he knew exactly what would keep those kids from spotting her.

Settled deep in the car seat, Lila rolled her windows down halfway to get a breath of the fresh autumn air and hear approaching vehicles. The partygoers wouldn't arrive until the evening's festivities in town were over and their parents were in bed. She glanced at her phone. A few minutes past eight, which meant she had about an hour before anyone showed up. Enough time to review the case she'd squirrelled out of the department.

The timing of Sheriff Benoit's emergency surgery and this anniversary couldn't have been better. With Elizabeth gone and Fontaine busy in his caretaker duties, Lila had, with the night dispatcher's help, snuck the case file box out of the sheriff's office. Alexis nearly swallowed her tongue when Lila told her what she was doing, but the last thing Lila needed was for Kyle to find out. They were both on duty tonight, and all it would take was for him to walk in and catch her and the jig was up. Alexis did her job as lookout; Lila loaded up and got the heck out of Dodge.

Lila turned on her phone flashlight and flipped the lid off the banker's box. She grabbed out the top two files; beneath lay a costume encased in a plastic bag. After setting the files on the passenger seat, Lila pulled out the evidence bag and examined the black and red costume.

"Pirate?" Shaking her head, she went to drop it back in the box, but a glint at the bottom gave her pause.

She set the costume aside and lifted out two evidence baggies with identical black velvet chokers. Dangling from the center of the chokers were clear oval stones with a red symbol that looked like a diamond with tails. Odd. Lila replaced the baggies and the costume in the box.

A quick check of her surroundings revealed she was still alone. She set the files in her lap and dove in.

Twenty-five years ago, nearly to the day, after a freak autumn snowstorm, one Brendette Lundquist was found dead in a field. Preliminary ruling was she had accidentally overdosed, and then succumbed to the elements to die of exposure. Notes in the margins, distinctly in Elizabeth's handwriting, stated this ruling was too pat, that the autopsy didn't give any solid indication of how she actually died. Several photos of the young woman as she'd been found in the middle of nowhere on the snow were paper-clipped to the back of the report. By these photos alone, one would surmise the same thing as the coroner at the time. Elizabeth knew something that wasn't stated in these reports or by her own hand.

Lila read over the rest of the file. It was no secret Elizabeth had it out for Sheehan when she took office. Recently, Lila had learned—from a slipup on Kyle's part—that the sheriff's friend's death was the catalyst for her grudge against the old codger. But former sheriff Kelley Sheehan kept a pocketful of backup plans to protect himself. Unfortunately, no one, save for the disgraced sheriff, knew what those were.

The slippery snake had managed to confuse Elizabeth, and her desire to see him behind bars had dimmed.

On the flipside, if Kyle knew Lila was reading this, he'd burst a blood vessel. Brendette was the sister he never spoke of, the one who set him on a path to what he became, and the one whose death had left his younger sister with a severe case of anxiety. The only reason Lila knew his sister's name was because in moments of extreme exhaustion, Kyle would talk in his sleep. Investigator that she was, Lila did some digging in newspaper archives and put two and two together to make four. He, like Elizabeth, kept this part of his life sequestered away. The hypocrite. Lila's brush with a serial killer and her losses were favorite topics Kyle liked to pursue instead of allowing her to pick apart his own.

Flapping the file shut, Lila leaned her head against the headrest and checked her surroundings. The distant chatter of canines carried through the window. Either those were coyotes or a pack of feral dogs out hunting. If those bone-headed kids knew about the dogs, why the hell would they ever come out to a place like this? She peeked into the back seat. Yup, her rifle and shotgun were there. Hopefully, there wouldn't be a need for either one.

After letting a few moments slip by—still no sounds of wayward partiers arriving—Lila picked up the other file and opened it.

This report had nothing to do with Brendette's death. Yet maybe it did. It was unusual in that it was an accident report. On the same night of the snowstorm, a young woman, dressed in a zombie bride costume was struck by an oncoming truck when she ran into the middle of the road. The truck flipped off the road, coming to rest on its roof. The driver of the truck, one Earl Johnson, was severely injured in the accident and two days later died from his injuries. The young woman—

A sound outside the car brought Lila's head up. She doused the flashlight on her phone and peered out the window.

"Help!" A pair of hands slapped against the window.

Lila jolted hard, throwing the file and her phone to the car floor. "What the hell!"

Fingers, coated red, grasped the edge of the window and clung. "Please! Help!"

Her weapon drawn, Lila aimed the pistol at the intruder as she grabbed the door handle. "Back away from the car!"

"Oh my God, please." The begging broke into sobs as the female backed away.

Lila bolted from her car, her sidearm still pointed at the kneeling girl. The dome light caught on the shiny black fabric the girl wore.

"What the ever-loving …?"

She lifted her face. Lila choked on her orders. The girl's heavily made up face was streaked with dark stains, her tears making the cat eyes run.

"What happened to you?" Lila asked as she holstered her service weapon.

"I …" She yanked the fake vampire teeth out. "I tried to help. But she … You have to help her."

A cacophony of yowling and barking cut through the night air.

What the girl was trying to say penetrated Lila's frozen brain. She spun back to the car, yanked open the back door, and pulled out the shotgun and a Mag light. After loading the firearm, she pocketed more shells, then faced the cowering female.

"Show me."

The girl lifted a trembling hand and pointed back toward the thicker part of the timber. Lila gaped at the darkened maw.

"Aww, hell." She grasped her radio. "Alexis, I'm leaving my vehicle to investigate a possible emergency. Send backup to my location."

"Copy."

"Send a bus too."

"Copy."

Lila grabbed the girl's arm and hauled her to her bare feet. No way was she leaving this girl alone with her car. She pushed her forward. "Take me there."

Sobbing as she moved, the girl tripped forward, following the gravel road. Lila hefted the shotgun to rest on her shoulder as she scanned the road and their path with the flashlight. Creepy crawlies skittered down her back as they went farther into the woods.

This was a huge mistake.

The girl veered left and started trotting. Lila followed suit. The racket of the animals grew louder.

The flashlight beams reflected off the canines' eyes, casting a yellowish-red glow. The light brought a momentary halt to the fight—coyotes, not dogs. Lying on the ground among them was a human form. One that they had feasted on, the bloodied snouts a glaring indication.

"Shit."

"Help her," the girl sobbed.

Her shotgun settled in her hands, Lila flipped off the safety. "I'll try."

The first blast sent the pack shrieking and scattering, but they refused to leave the body. Lila leveled her sights on the one she deemed the pack leader and fired. The leader went down, and the rest fanned out, but still refused to leave. Lila had her sights on another and put it down as well, sending the remaining animals fleeing for their lives. As the coyotes ran off, she reloaded.

"How did this happen?" she demanded.

"I don't know!" the girl shrieked. She slapped her hands to her face and cried harder.

With a shake of her head, Lila drew her sidearm and approached the corpse of the first coyote. Assured it was dead, she checked the other, scanning the area to make sure the rest didn't come back. They probably hadn't gone far, not when they had an easy meal waiting for them.

"Deputy Dayne, report?"

"Alexis, ETA on my backup?"

"Deputy Fitzgerald is almost there. Ambulance is ten minutes out."

"Fitzgerald?"

"I'm at your car," he answered.

Lila rotated the flashlight back the way she and the girl had come. "Head west about four to five hundred yards and hang a sharp left into the trees. We're nearly fifty to eighty yards in."

"We who?"

"Just hustle your ass. We've got an injured woman. And have a shotgun handy. We got predators."

Ignoring his rants, Lila turned the flashlight on the barefoot woman on the ground, dressed in a black-and-red pirate costume.

Her heart took on a different pace.

"I'm not liking this," she muttered.

The coyotes had managed to mangle the body, the costume she wore ripped open at the abdomen, leaving a gaping wound where her stomach should have been. There were bite marks on her arms and the exposed, fleshy part of her legs, but it didn't appear she had been alive when they had started in on her. She flicked the beam up to the woman's face and grimaced. The young woman's blue eyes were open, wide, frozen in horror, her mouth ajar as if she'd tried to scream. A bloodred wig was barely attached to her dark brown hair. Lila gulped. If she didn't know any better, she'd swear she was staring at one of those photos in the Lundquist file. The beam glinted off a clear stone lying in the hallow of the woman's throat.

A whining chatter from the trees made her lift the shotgun. "Come at me, you freaking bastards."

"Dayne?"

She swiveled around on the balls of her feet. Fitzgerald jogged past the hysterical girl and headed toward her.

Lila grasped her radio once more. "Alexis. Call Dr. Remington-Thorpe. And patch me through to Fontaine."

"Any message you want me to give the doctor?"

"We've got a DOA."

Fitzgerald came to a stutter-step stop. He dropped to his knees and gaped at the body on the ground.

"Alexis, I want Deputy Lundquist and Sheriff Benoit left out of the loop on this one for now. Copy?"

"Deputy Lundquist was paged about the call out."

"Turn him around."

Fitzgerald met Lila's gaze. He shook his head.

"Alexis, turn him around."

CHAPTER THREE

"F ROM MY PRELIM, I can tell you she was strangled. Whether that's what killed her or not remains to be seen."

Lila nodded at the medical examiner's frank statement. Under a slew of LED spotlights, she kept a steady watch on the man striding toward them.

"The coyotes did a lot of damage to her torso. It's a mess."

Lila peeled her gaze from the undersheriff to meet Dr. Olivia Remington-Thorpe's. "Is it going to make it difficult to pinpoint her time of death?"

Olivia still wore orange and purple scrubs, having rushed here from her office. "Hard to say at this point. I'll have a better idea when I get her on my table."

"Do you recognize her?"

"I do. Her name is Kerri Peterson. The girl you sent to the hospital is Andrea O'Ryan. They were friends."

Lila groaned. "This is not my night." She turned to Olivia. "Are you aware of a twenty-five-year-old case the sheriff might have connections to?"

Olivia's face scrunched. "I think I know what you're referring to. Does it have something to do with Kyle's sister?"

"Yes." Lila gripped Olivia's arm. "Do not say a word to

Elizabeth or Kyle."

The doctor nodded. "Ellie won't find out from me. You're going to have a harder time with Kyle."

Lila couldn't have been more grateful for a two-vehicle accident on the other side of the county drawing him away. It would keep him preoccupied and give her time to come up with a good excuse for what she was going to do.

Olivia departed as Fontaine strode in and came to a halt before Lila. He towered over her by a good foot, but Lila never let it hinder her. She accepted him as her superior at the sheriff's recommendation, but the two of them were like water and oil. Or more accurately, fire and gasoline.

"Where's the body?" he demanded.

"Olivia's crew has it processed and loaded."

He turned to the ME's van and made to move in that direction. Lila reached out and snagged his arm, jerking him to a stop.

"No."

He rotated slowly, anger rolling off him. "Excuse me."

She drew back her shoulders and jutted her chin up. "I said no. I can't in good conscience allow you to see the body. I asked you out here against my better judgment."

Fontaine's eyes narrowed. "You have no authority to order me around, Dayne."

"I don't. But in this case, during this investigation, I'm in charge. You're here, so I can tell you to keep Elizabeth out of it. She, you, and Kyle will have no involvement whatsoever in this case."

"Dayne, you're treading a dangerous line here."

"That's exactly the reason I'm pulling rank. Until such

time I deem necessary, I will be heading this investigation and I'll handpick my team to aid me. Do as I say, and I'll keep you apprised. Ignore me, and I will turn this over to outside investigators."

"What the hell is going on? What the *hell* happened out here?" he snarled.

"I know you don't trust me; you have made that loud and clear. But I would never do anything that would jeopardize a case. Do I have your word you will not interfere?"

He glared at her, his chest rising and falling in rapid succession. Well, he could snarl and huff all he wanted; she wasn't going to back down.

Fontaine watched the ME's van, his shoulders sagged. He turned to Lila. "You have my word."

Okay, that went easier than she expected. "A young woman was found deceased out here. A pack of coyotes feasted on her. Her friend stumbled on the situation, then came to find me."

"Why does this ordeal constitute banning me, the sheriff, and Deputy Lundquist from the investigation?"

"Because both young women were dressed in similar fashion to two other incidents from twenty-five years ago."

"It's Halloween time, Dayne. Everyone is dressing up."

Lila pulled the evidence baggie from her pants pocket and held it out. "How many girls do you know wear a black velvet choker with a clear oval pendant with a red-inked symbol inside?"

He gaped at the evidence, then thrust it back at her. "I don't get it."

"Neither did I, until I realized I'd seen it before."

"How would you have seen it?"

"Long story. The deceased was wearing it. Just like Denise Russell and Brendette Lundquist." Lila shoved the baggie back into her uniform pocket. "See where I'm going with this?"

Sighing, Fontaine crossed his arms. He remained close-mouthed, looking around.

Lila had ordered the coyote bodies left until the vet could get out here to gather them. On the off chance the beasts had ingested any flesh, Lila wanted to have it added to the evidence. Also, to check for any diseases, because they'd attacked Andrea, too.

Insects were swarming the area, the scent of blood and death strong attractants. Those that ventured too close to the spotlights were zapped, the sound of their sizzling bodies adding to the eeriness of the area.

Not knowing how Lila wasn't losing her mind surrounded by trees and nature out here in the middle of nowhere was probably driving Fontaine nuts. True, she should have some residual post-traumatic stress from her ordeal last summer after her clash with a serial killer. A year's worth of therapy and sheer will had shored up her cracks. She refused to be defined by her tragic past any longer. It still didn't mean she wasn't compartmentalizing the situation.

"When do you want me to tell the sheriff?" Fontaine asked moments later.

"I haven't decided yet. Let Olivia get the autopsy finished and give me a chance to evaluate the results."

"What do you want me to tell her now?"

Lila bit her lips. This would be the tricky part. The fact

she'd gotten Fontaine to agree to her demands was a miracle. Keeping Elizabeth out of the loop would prove harder still. But Fontaine could handle her. Kyle, on the other hand, was going to be far from a cakewalk.

"Have any ideas?" she asked.

Fontaine shook his head, letting his arms drop, and he hooked his thumbs behind his duty belt. "You're opening a big-ass can of worms here by overstepping your authority and keeping her in the blind. If your theory about this being related to the death of her best friend pans out, she's going to come unglued."

"I'm a big girl."

"Your shoulders aren't that broad." He pointed at her. "The minute Lundquist finds out you were hiding this from him, Elizabeth will be the least of your worries."

"Aware of that."

"I'll figure something out to tell her. Who are the girls?"

"Deceased is Kerri Peterson. The traumatized friend is Andrea O'Ryan."

"Shit, Dayne, you're in for it."

"What's that supposed to mean?"

"You'll soon find out." He moved as if to leave. "I'll check in with Lundquist at the accident scene."

"Please let me be the one to talk with Kyle about it." Lila twisted the hem of her Eckardt County Deputy jacket. "I really think he needs to hear it from me."

Fontaine scrubbed the side of his face. "He won't hear it from me. Who are you picking to work this with you, since you've banned your forensics guy?"

"DCI is here to help with that part." In fact, Iowa's Department of Criminal Investigations had a local team already at work, freeing Lila and Dr. Remington-Thorpe to do their jobs as investigator and ME. "I'll have Young and Meyer with me on this. Fitzgerald can help if he can keep it together."

Fontaine's features tightened. "Fitzgerald might not be a good choice."

"Why not?"

"He's a pain in the ass. Do what you want, but I'd advise you to keep him out of it or you're going to have a bigger headache trying to keep him in line. Young and Meyer will do. Brent was too young to remember what happened."

He was right about Fitzgerald. Did she really want the headache of dealing with an usually obstinate deputy? "You're being awfully cooperative about this," Lila said.

"You didn't give me much of a choice." He stalked off to his squad car.

Lila waited until he'd driven off before heading to her own car. She wanted to get to the hospital and interview Andrea before anyone had a chance to intervene, like her parents. Lila didn't recognize either girl and wouldn't know who their parents were if she stood right next to them. But then she wasn't known to hang out in places where the younger generations of Eckardt County tended to congregate, and the older generations treated her as an outsider.

The head of the DCI team cut her off halfway to her vehicle. He let her know what they'd found and how much longer they'd remain at the scene. Lila gave the okay for the team to wrap up and contact her when they had results.

Fitzgerald met her at the driver's side. "I need in on this,

Dayne."

Resting her hand on the car door handle, she tilted her head to get a good look at him. "Why?"

"You're going to need someone who has connections."

Her stance slackened. Slowly, she faced him. "Connections?"

Fitzgerald ducked his head as he inched closer to her. "I know those girls' families. You go walking in there to interview them you're going to be stonewalled."

"Let me guess. They're influential people?"

"No." He lifted his gaze to her. "They're not."

"Are we talking a Kauffmann deal? Or a Pratt Meyer deal?"

"More like a Benoit or Fontaine deal. Middle-of-the-road people. What you might call middle class if you were in Chicago. The type of people who can cause a big stink if given the right motivation. A murdered child is all the motivation they'll need."

"Meyer can handle them."

Fitzgerald's laugh sounded more like a choking cough. "You send that rookie or Young into those people's houses and all hell will break loose. Meyer is looked at as a rich snob and Young ... well, you get my drift."

Lila sighed, leaning against her car. She got his drift. Deputy Corey Young was Sioux. There were some nasty individuals who hadn't gotten their heads out of their asses when it came to her heritage. Speaking of which, Lila needed to get to the hospital now. She'd sent Young to keep watch over the girl. If what Fitzgerald was alluding to was correct, there might be a fight.

"What makes you so certain I can't get them to cooperate with me?"

"Are you kidding me? You honestly think any of those people will give you a straight answer? You're not one of us. No matter how long you've been here. Face it. You need me on this. If you plan on keeping Benoit, Fontaine, and Lundquist out of it, you need me."

Lila waved her hand. "Fine. The minute you give me any shit, you're gone."

His shoulders sagged as if he'd been holding himself together by sheer will. "I won't."

Lila slapped the side of her car. "I'm going to the hospital. You should stay with the DCI team until they leave."

"If the parents are there, don't engage," he warned.

"The girl is over eighteen; there's nothing they can do."

"That won't mean jack shit with them."

"What do you expect me to do?" she asked his backside.

He simply shrugged and kept on walking.

CHAPTER FOUR

L OUD, COMBATIVE VOICES greeted Lila as she entered the ambulance bay area of the ER wing. She picked out Dr. Dominic Thorpe's and Deputy Corey Young's—the others she was not familiar with.

"Damn it," she muttered and sped up.

The closer she got, the clearer the argument became. One woman seemed to be leading the charge in arguing with Dominic. Lila rounded a corner and the cluster of people came into view, standing in the middle of the ER hallway. Young was backed into a wall by a furious man wagging his finger in her face. Condescension twisted his features. Young, on the other hand, looked red-faced and strained, like she was barely keeping her professional composure, her hand resting on the butt of her sidearm.

Long years of living among a mix of races and working the inner-city streets of Chicago had ingrained Lila with a sixth sense when she was facing a bigot. Ice raced through her veins; white noise roared in her ears. She stalked down the hall, her hand settling on her service weapon.

"Hey!"

Everyone involved with this ruckus jolted and froze in place. Lila marched up to the man cornering her fellow deputy, grabbed his arm, and jerked him away from Young.

"You, sir, will be detained for police harassment if you continue. This is your only warning." She shoved him toward the opposite wall. "Stay there."

He opened his mouth, pinkish-red blotches peppering his face.

"You say one more word and you will leave here in cuffs."

He shut his mouth.

"You can't do that."

Lila turned her focus on one of the women that had been badgering Dominic. "My badge says otherwise."

The dark-haired woman sneered. "Who do you think you are?"

"Deputy Dayne," Dominic warned.

The woman's eyes flashed. Lila drummed her fingers on the pistol butt. The bully took a step back.

"Deputy Young, Dr. Thorpe, what is going on here?" Lila glanced at Young. "Other than what I gathered on my walk down here."

Dominic slipped between the two women and came to stand between Lila and Young. "Deputy Dayne, this is Erin and Rick O'Ryan and Hillary Peterson. They are the parents of the two young women."

Lila gave props to the doc for keeping his composure. Ever the compassionate healer, Dominic Thorpe. He was by no means a small man, quite capable of handling himself in any situation, but his unpretentious nature left many people to assume he was a pushover. Still others became fixated on his race. From the vibes filling the atmosphere, Lila sensed Young wasn't the only one feeling the heat.

"Mind explaining to me what the issue is here?" Lila pressed.

"We want to see our daughters," Erin O'Ryan snapped.

Lila looked to Dominic for the explanation, knowing what the answer was before he said it.

"Miss O'Ryan has asked for her parents not to be with her."

"This hack job won't answer us one way or the other on what Kerri wants," Erin added. Apparently, no one else could talk in this little entourage.

Dominic shifted, most likely to rebut O'Ryan, but Lila laid a hand on his arm. He stiffened under her touch. When it came to medicine, Dominic was far from a hack, and he was not one to let insults slide. Fitzgerald's warning echoing in the back of her mind, Lila squeezed Dominic's arm then released him. He seemed to catch her drift and let his shoulders drop.

No words. Only silence. That was how they would regain control of this situation.

Lila studied the three people, her perusal ending on Hillary Peterson. The woman stood ramrod straight, like she was being held up by invisible wires. Despite her attempt to hold her own, fear flickered in her semi-glazed eyes. She put on a good show. Lila knew her kind. Had been raised by a woman like her. Single mother. No steady male influence in her daughter's life. A woman on the edge, the type most likely to resort to recreational use or abusing some form of drug.

A prime target for predators. Which, in turn, made her daughter prey.

The O'Ryans practically vibrated. Lila could read their minds by their wavering facial expressions of indignation, self-righteousness, and worry. Never fear. No, not for these two. Because fear in the face of people they deemed below them was sacrilege. They were aware their daughter was alive and here. Their show was for Hillary's sake.

"Are you going to do anything about this, *Deputy*?" Erin demanded.

Yep, no patience for that one. The mouthpiece. Would probably go to the sheriff or higher up if she didn't get her way. Lila narrowed her gaze on Erin. The woman shouldered her way in front of her husband.

Interesting.

"Dr. Thorpe, is there anything you can relay to the O'Ryans?" Lila asked.

"Unfortunately, no. Miss O'Ryan has not given consent."

"What about Kerri?" Erin demanded.

"She's not your daughter nor your concern." Dominic's words dripping with venom.

Lila watched Hillary. The woman didn't flinch or open her mouth. Her gaze remained locked on a spot somewhere above Lila's head. Lila glanced up. A quote from some long-dead doctor was painted on the wall. A fitting place to keep her attention.

"Deputy Dayne," Dominic broke in. "I must attend to my patients." He was a surgeon but kept ER rotations to ease the burden from a lack of medical practitioners in the county. A sad reality for rural areas in the Midwest where doctors were scarce and hospitals were shutting down.

"Go."

Erin made a noise from her throat. Lila jabbed a finger at the woman, and she stayed quiet.

Once Dominic disappeared into a room—presumably Andrea's—Deputy Young moved to stand next to Lila. Despite Young having worked in the Eckardt Sheriff's Department for more than a year, the two of them still had not meshed. Lila chalked it up to her penchant for keeping people at bay. The fewer people she became entangled with, the less likely she would get hurt. She'd lost enough people in her life.

"Now, Mrs. and Mr. O'Ryan." Lila noted Rick's wince at her purposeful flip of status. "You will take a seat in the waiting room. You will remain there until such time as your daughter wishes to see you or we"—she pointed to herself and Deputy Young—"tell you to go home."

"We will go nowhere," Erin snarled.

"Mr. O'Ryan, you can speak now," Lila said. "I won't cuff you."

The man glared at her, his lips thinning.

"Excuse me?" Erin screeched.

Rick slipped back. The power dynamics of this couple was a study in what not to be. His bigoted bravado was either an act for his wife or the man really was a prick and let everyone know when she wasn't around.

Lila focused on Erin, her current threat. "Mrs. O'Ryan, you can do as you're told, or you can spend the rest of this night cooling your heels in lockup. Choice is yours. Right now, I'm short on patience and long on reasons to have Deputy Young escort you to her car."

Fury rolled off the woman. "I'll have your badge for this."

"Stand in line."

Erin O'Ryan took a step toward Lila. Her husband grabbed her arm and dragged her back at the same time Young moved to intervene.

"We're going to the waiting room," Rick said and hauled his wife off.

Lila tracked their movements until they rounded the corner at the nurse's station. Once they were out of view, she motioned to Young to follow.

Out of earshot of Hillary Peterson, Young said, "You're going to pay for that."

"Too bad, so sad." Lila stopped in front of the room she suspected was Andrea's. "You're on post. No one is to enter this room unless it is me, Dr. Thorpe, or a nurse. You have any problems, you radio me ASAP."

Young nodded. She frowned, staring at Lila in a way that had long unnerved her, as if Young could read into her soul and see what was hidden beneath. "Are you going to be okay to handle telling the Peterson woman? I know death notices aren't your thing."

A cascade of tremors quivered through Lila's internal organs. God, how she hated this part of the job. Since her second day on the job as an Eckardt County deputy, when she had a panic attack at a death notice, the duty had landed on the sheriff's and Fontaine's shoulders. Neither one was here to bail Lila out this time. And whose fault was that? Hers, of course, because she told them to stay clear. She lifted a trembling hand, fisted it to stop the shaking, and dropped it back to her side.

"I don't have much choice in the matter," she said, glancing at Hillary. "If I wait for Fontaine to get here, the O'Ryans will cause another stink and it will get blurted out. She doesn't deserve that."

"It's a bad deal all around."

"Murder always is." Lila tapped her radio. "Trouble, call."

With Young in position by the door, Lila turned her attention on Hillary Peterson. Her steps were slow and purposeful, dragging herself more or less toward the woman.

"Ms. Peterson ..."

"It's Mrs.," the woman stated.

"Is there a Mr. Peterson?" Oh God, let there be one. If they could wait for him to arrive, Lila might have the opportunity to pawn this awkward situation off to Fontaine. That was if she could get him here in time. Far as she knew, Fontaine was with Kyle at the accident scene, and it could be a long wait for that to wrap up.

Hillary shook her head. "Kerri's father ..." She released a shaky sigh. "He was killed in Afghanistan. So, no, there isn't a Mr. Peterson."

Strike out. No breaks for Lila Dayne this night.

Killed in Afghanistan. Military. Meaning Hillary had experience with death notices. Maybe the glossed-over eyes weren't a sign of drug use but of a woman who was all too aware of what was coming and she was holding herself together by a thread.

This could go one of two ways: Hillary became hysterical. Or she buried her pain and soldiered on. Either way, it wouldn't be good for Lila.

She held out her hand. "Please come with me, Mrs. Peterson."

Together they walked down the hall in the opposite direction the O'Ryans had gone, toward Olivia's morgue, the cloaking silence punctuated by the sharp click of Hillary's shoes against the flooring. Her body running on auto, Lila's brain swam with the white noise of past experiences, her doubts, and trepidation. Maybe escorting her to the morgue to view the body would be easier. Olivia—a doctor with longtime experience dealing with emotional patients—could take over when Hillary broke down.

After they bypassed the entrance to the main hospital wing, Hillary slowed. She caught Lila's arm and dragged her to a stop. Hillary fiddled with adjusting her purse strap over her shoulder, her gaze darting from Lila to the floor and back. A sigh of resignation preceded her shoulders slumping.

"Deputy Dayne, just tell me. My daughter is dead. Isn't she?"

"Mrs. Peterson, I really think we should—"

"Please don't. Don't placate me. I know where we're heading." She crossed her arms then pressed her right hand to her forehead and rubbed it. "Kerri's dead." Her voice cracked on her daughter's name.

Lila rolled her lips back over her teeth and bit down, averting her attention to the open hallway from where they'd come. She couldn't do this. Not here. Not now.

"By your silence, I'm right."

Lila's focus snapped back to Hillary.

"How?"

Lila gulped. Balling her hands into fists and squeezing helped. "We aren't completely certain ..." She winced. "It looks like ... homicide."

The woman released a shuddering sigh, broke on a sob, and sank to the floor. Hillary bowed her head between her bent knees and cried. Squeezing her eyes shut, Lila, too, bowed her head and listened to the woman grieve.

Seconds crawled as Lila grappled with what to say. Everything that came to mind felt insincere, mere words served up on a silver platter, lacking heart. Yet Lila knew exactly what Hillary was experiencing. Lila's own grief over her losses had yet to subside.

Looming over this poor woman was pointless. If Elizabeth were here, she'd sit down beside Hillary and offer comfort. Lila winced. She was not the comforting type. She could barely muster up enough for Kyle.

Throwing aside her gruff, cynical persona, Lila moved to sit beside Hillary. When their shoulders bumped, Hillary lifted her head and blinked dripping eyelashes at Lila.

Lila looked away, finding a point on the opposite wall to hold her interest. She draped her arms over her knees then started rubbing her fingers and thumb together. The circular motions soothed her.

"I know what I'm about to say will sound hollow, but it's the truth."

Hillary sniffed. From the corner of her eye, Lila saw the woman wipe at her nose.

"I know exactly what you're going through. I've lost loved ones." Lila swallowed. "My own child died." She tilted her head to look at Hillary. "I feel your pain."

Through her grief-stricken features, Hillary frowned, but except for a hiccup here and there, she remained silent.

Lila hung her head, wrung out from her confession.

"Aren't you the deputy who was kidnapped a while back?" Hillary whispered.

A nod sufficed. People in Eckardt County still talked about the incident. How could they not? When an outsider brought a notorious serial killer in their midst, it was front-page news for weeks. Even made national headlines. Ambiguity was no longer a factor.

This floor was hard.

"Mrs. Peterson, we should meet up with Dr. Remington-Thorpe."

Hillary shook her head and curled into herself. "I don't want to see her that way." She squeezed her eyes shut. "I want to remember her how she was ... before she was killed."

"I understand." Lila rose, dusting off her rear. "Will you be okay here? I do need to go to the ... see Dr. Remington-Thorpe."

Hillary stared up at Lila. "It's okay. I've been here before." She wrapped her arms around her knees and drew them closer to her chest.

After a second's hesitation to make sure the woman would truly be fine, Lila moved to leave.

"Deputy Dayne."

She shifted.

"Find my daughter's killer. Please. Make them pay." Hillary's voice dipped into something feral.

Lila recognized the wildness. The mother bear coming

forefront. She had felt the same savage urge when she ended the life of her baby's murderer.

She gave a nod. Words were not necessary nor should they be spoken. The person responsible for the death of Kerri Peterson would not go without punishment.

A COOL, DAMP nose nudged Elizabeth's cheek. She dragged open one eyelid, blinked until her vision cleared. Bentley chuffed low in her throat.

"What, girl?"

Buzzing from the nightstand echoed in Elizabeth's fogged mind. Groaning, she gingerly rolled onto her back and reached over. She slapped her hand about until her fingers grazed a corner of her phone. After a few failed attempts, she clawed the lip of the Otterbox and drew the phone into her hand. The buzzing continued.

"I'm going to sue the person bothering me," she muttered as she stabbed at the incoming call icon. "What," she snarled.

"Sheriff Benoit?"

"If you need police assistance, call the department. I'm out on leave. Goodbye." She began to pull the phone away.

"Sheriff, please!" The female screech on the other end gave Elizabeth pause.

She pressed the phone to her ear once more and draped her other hand over her eyes. "Whoever this is, I'm really not in a good place to be answering calls."

"I know and I'm sorry to bother you, Sheriff. If it wasn't

important, I wouldn't be calling you."

Elizabeth tried to comb through her drug-addled brain to place a name with the voice—it was familiar, but she couldn't grasp who it was calling her. "I have a whole department of competent deputies and an undersheriff—"

"Sheriff, this is Erin O'Ryan. Something has happened with my daughter Andrea."

Elizabeth brought her arm down to her side and stared at the darkened bedroom ceiling. Bentley shifted on the bed, crawling under Elizabeth's arm and settling her muzzle on her owner's thigh. Elizabeth tangled her fingers in the collie's silky hair. "What do you mean by something has happened?"

"I knew something was wrong. She'd been keeping things from me, hiding stuff. Now this."

"Erin, I have no idea what you're talking about."

"Elizabeth, it's starting all over again."

A chill lanced her body. The fog in her head cleared. Elizabeth struggled upright, pushed Bentley off her leg, and leaned on her elbow.

"What is starting all over again?"

"Andrea was involved in something just like Denise. Like Brendette."

Two incidents in her life could stop Elizabeth in her tracks. Rehashing the events of 9-11. And the mention of her two closest friends in the same breath. Her mental cogs froze.

Then Elizabeth's woozy mind clicked into gear once more, and she was hurtled back in time to a night in an apartment off base from where Joel was training. She remembered every detail, from the *Fifth Element* Leeloo costume she wore, how crazy she was acting at that adults-only Halloween party, to the number one song in the country playing on continuous loop on the CD player. Elizabeth had been startled awake by a phone call from a boy on the cusp of adulthood telling her that his eldest sister, her best friend whom she'd been closer to than her own sister, was dead. Kyle's heart-shattering news was followed up with the report that Bre hadn't been the only one to die. Denise Russell had been killed in an accident.

Teeth gritted against the pain—both physical and emotional—Elizabeth kicked free from the bedding. "Where are you?"

"I'm at the hospital trying to get to my daughter, and your damn deputy won't let me anywhere near her."

"Erin, you and Rick do as my deputy tells you. I'm on my way."

"Elizabeth, it's my daughter."

"Who is considered an adult in the law's eyes. She has the option to allow you access or not. I warn you to obey the orders. Don't make me further ruin your night, understand?"

Silence met Elizabeth's orders. She swung her legs over the side of the bed, her bare feet settling on the thick rug. "Erin."

"Yes, fine, we understand. Please hurry. I don't know how much longer Rick will wait. Especially with that ... *deputy*." Erin sighed.

Elizabeth wasn't sure which deputy was on security detail, but the tone Erin took made Elizabeth suspect it was Deputy Young. Damn it, she didn't need a racially charged situation on top of what was already going down.

"I'm coming. I'd be there faster if I wasn't on the

phone."

"Sorry, I'll let you go." The connection went silent.

Elizabeth dropped her phone on the bed and scrubbed her face two-handed. Bentley nudged her elbow and earned a pet. "How am I going to get to the hospital?" she asked her dog.

The bedroom door came open, letting in a slash of light from the hallway. Rafe stepped into the open doorway.

"I knew someone would call you. This blows Dayne's order to hell."

"What orders?"

"To keep you out of it." He shook his head. "It was never going to go like she hoped. Not when the parents found out."

"Rafe, what is the intel?"

He cupped the back of his neck. "Shit, Ellie, you shouldn't be a part of this."

"It's too late for that. Out with it."

Sighing, he came into the room and sat on the bed next to her. "We have one DB and one injured."

"Who is the DB? Erin O'Ryan confirmed her daughter, Andrea, is the injured one."

He looped his arm around her waist and tugged her flush to his side. "It was Kerri Peterson."

Elizabeth squeezed her eyes shut and leaned into Rafe. "Erin told me her daughter was involved in something like Bre. Was she right?"

"I don't know. Lila knows something, I don't know how, but she does. It's why she ordered you off this."

"I'm pulling rank."

"She's got a point, Ellie. You're in no condition to handle this, and you're on potent pain drugs. Any defense lawyer would have a heyday with your involvement."

She slowly drew in a deep breath, wincing when she extended her battered muscles too far. She lifted her head from his shoulder and looked him in the eye. "When I accepted the nomination to run for sheriff, I did it with the promise to clean up this county. We all know there's a stronger motive than to set right what is wrong. I will not let a minor setback like surgery keep me from my end goal."

Rafe kissed her forehead. "I figured as much, but the warnings need to be stated."

"Lila can't handle this alone. She's still holding on to her pain from her losses a year ago." Elizabeth braced her hand on his thigh and leveraged herself upright with assistance from Rafe. "My sabbatical is over."

"Get dressed. I'll take you to the hospital."

CHAPTER FIVE

A FTER A BRIEF visit with Olivia, where she learned nothing new, as the ME hadn't started her exam, Lila returned to the ER, concerned when she didn't see Hillary Peterson in the hallway where she'd left the woman moments before. Then Lila shrugged it off for more pressing matters. The constant stream of radio chatter chased her steps, which quickened when she heard Kyle's voice break over the waves. He was headed back to the department. She had to finish here at the hospital before he heard about tonight's incident.

"Deputy Dayne?"

She grasped the radio and removed it from her shoulder. "Yeah, Young?"

"Doc says he's releasing Ms. O'Ryan. She doesn't want her parents to know."

"I'm heading back, be there in a sec."

"Dayne, the sheriff is here."

Color me unsurprised.

Lila rounded the last wall and entered the corridor taking her to the ER. She could see Young blocking the doorway to Andrea O'Ryan's room. Dominic was next to Young, his back to Lila, facing the waiting room. He shifted his weight from his left leg to his right, and Lila glimpsed Fontaine's profile in the waiting room entrance.

Young returned her radio mic to her shoulder strap as Lila approached. "Sheriff's keeping them busy," she said in a lowered voice.

Dominic glanced over his shoulder. "Lila, get in there and talk with her."

"Young, pull your unit around to the door and I'll escort her out. Dr. Thorpe, if you wouldn't mind, hang here a few."

Dominic acquiesced with a curt nod. Young took off to do as ordered. Right as Lila moved to enter the exam room, she caught Fontaine's eye. From that simple glance, Lila sensed the urgency. She pushed into the room.

Andrea O'Ryan gasped. Clothed in an oversized green sweatshirt and baggy jeans to replace the Vampira costume, the young woman appeared ready to jump out of her skin. She clutched the extra folds of the sweatshirt. "Are you the deputy—"

"Yes." Lila cut her off. "Deputy Young informed me you do not want to leave with your parents."

Andrea nodded so hard Lila was concerned her head would pop off her neck.

"Okay, that's fine. You're old enough to make that decision. Where do you want to go? Do you have a place separate from them?"

The young woman's features wavered, tears pooled.

"Andrea, we don't have time for a breakdown. The sheriff is keeping your parents preoccupied, but it's not going to last for long."

"Just get me out of here without them seeing me. Please."

Lila held out her hand and the girl came to her. "Deputy Young is bringing her car around."

"I'm outside," Young broke over the radio.

"Our cue." Lila wrapped her arm around Andrea's shoulders and ushered her out of the room.

Dominic walked ahead of them as they rushed down the hall. When Lila peeled off to the exit, he kept on toward the waiting room. The voices coming from there were getting louder. Lila peeked over just as Fontaine backed away and Erin O'Ryan stepped out.

"Andrea!"

Andrea yelped and curled her body into Lila.

Ignoring the angry barrage behind her, Lila hurried Andrea outside and bundled her into the back of Young's unit.

"Take her wherever she tells you," she ordered Young from the open passenger side door.

"Don't leave me." Andrea grabbed the back of the front seat.

"I'll follow in my car," Lila promised.

"No," Andrea cried, reaching over the seat to grab at Lila's hand. "Don't leave me."

"We've got company coming," Young said.

Lila spotted the O'Ryans making a beeline for them. Snarling, she flung herself inside Young's car, slamming the door behind her. "Drive."

The tires barked against the pavement as the car lurched forward. Sheriff Benoit appeared in the ER doors; Lila tilted her head.

Once on the street, Young pointed the car in the direction of Juniper's business district.

"Where are we going, Andrea?" Lila asked, twisting in her seat to face the younger woman in the backseat.

Andrea shrank into the leather seat, hugging her body. "Kerri ... We had an apartment on Apple Avenue."

"I know where it is," Young said.

"I can't stay there." Andrea's voice cracked. "They'll find me." She bit a knuckle and stared out the window.

Lila and Young looked at each other. Young shrugged and returned her focus to driving. Lila shifted to face forward again.

"If you don't want to stay there, why are we going?" Lila asked.

Andrea remained silent.

Patience wearing thin, Lila grabbed her radio. "Alexis, patch me through to Deputy Lundquist."

"He's here," came the response.

"Lila, what is going on?" Kyle demanded.

She was going to have renege on her demand to keep him out of the investigation. No way was she going to search that apartment alone. No better time to break the news to him than right before an evidence search of a victim's dwelling. "I'll explain later. First, call me."

Once his call came through, she clicked off her radio. No way was she about to blast out where they were headed over the radio.

"I need you to meet me at the apartment complex on Apple Avenue," Lila said by way of greeting.

Her phone began buzzing against her cheek. Gritting her teeth, she pulled it away. Fontaine was calling her. Too bad. She wasn't talking to him.

"What's at the apartment complex?" Kyle was asking.

"Once again, I'll explain. Hurry up. Over and out." She disconnected her call with Kyle.

Her phone buzzed again. Fontaine again. She slid the icon to ignore.

"He's going to keep calling you until you answer," Young commented.

"I'll keep on ignoring him."

"What if it's the sheriff?"

Lila shook her head and focused on the headlights illuminating the road.

"She didn't keep anything in our apartment," Andrea said in a small voice.

"Why do you say that?" Lila asked.

"It's why you're having Deputy Lundquist come." Andrea pushed herself up, then wound the right sleeve of the sweatshirt between her hands. "They wouldn't let us keep anything in our homes."

"They who?"

Andrea bowed her head. "Don't leave me there."

Frustration pounded like a kick drum inside Lila's head. "Andrea, I can't help you if you won't be straight with me. Who are you talking about?"

The young woman lifted her gaze to Lila. "I can't tell you."

Biting down on her lip was the smartest move.

"We're here," Young said as she pulled into a small parking lot fronting the apartment complex.

Fontaine was incessant. Lila chucked her phone onto the dashboard.

"What the hell am I supposed to do with her?" she snapped.

Young turned off the engine. "Think it would be okay if she stayed with me?"

"I don't think that's—"

"Please?" Andrea begged.

"At least for tonight," Young said.

"They won't look for me if I'm with her," Andrea added.

Lila really wanted to know who "they" were that Andrea kept referring to. Her detective side was fully convinced she was talking about Kerri's killer or killers. Rational side was saying she couldn't be 100 percent certain it wasn't the O'Ryans Andrea didn't want finding her either.

It could be both.

"For tonight. Tomorrow, we discuss a better option." Lila looked pointedly at Andrea. "You will give me a full statement and explain yourself tomorrow. We'll go in and she can grab some things."

"Are you going to wait for Lundquist?" Young asked.

Lila nodded. "I'll have him take me back to the hospital for my unit." She exited the car.

She paused before closing the door, then reached in and grabbed her phone. Turning off the vibration was going to cause a bigger dustup with Fontaine. Not that she cared. Instead, she clicked her radio on, leaving it at a low volume. She shoved her phone back into her uniform breast pocket. A thorough scan of the parking lot and the street assured her they hadn't been followed or were being watched. If anyone wanted to assault them, they wouldn't do it here.

She followed Young and Andrea to a center doorway in

the first apartment building. They climbed two flights of steps and went two hundred yards down the hall to apartment 234. Andrea knocked on the door with the side of her fist.

"Where are your keys?" Lila asked.

"They took them."

The infamous *they* again.

"I thought it was just you and Kerri," Young said.

The locks rattled and the door cracked open, revealing a third young woman with dark black skin and tight black braids.

"Andrea," she shrieked and reached for her roommate.

The two women hugged.

Young didn't hide her cringe. Lila practically read her mind. If Andrea's parents had racist leanings and they didn't know about this roommate, was it any wonder that Andrea didn't want them to find her here?

The roommate dragged Andrea into the apartment, allowing Young and Lila to trail behind.

"What happened?" the roommate asked.

Andrea shook her head and pulled from her friend's grasp. "I can't stay here tonight. You should probably find somewhere else to stay for a while."

The roommate frowned. "Kerri?"

Holding up her hand to cut off her friend, Andrea walked away. Lila waved for Young to follow her as she strode after Andrea.

Lila held out her hand. "Deputy Dayne."

The roommate blinked in confusion, then took her offered hand. "Allegra King." Her grip moist, she made short work of shaking Lila's hand and then snatched hers back to wring her hands. "What happened to Kerri?"

"I can't answer that." Lila's radio hummed with incoming information. "You should do what Andrea suggested. Pack up a few days' worth of clothing and stay with someone where no one would expect you to go."

Allegra pressed a fist to her lips.

Lila nodded to the back rooms in the apartment. "Hurry up."

The young woman spun on a heel, her long braids flying, and rushed off.

Alone, Lila studied the small apartment. It was nice. Too nice for three college-aged girls to be able to afford on their own. Considering the current housing market in Eckardt County, that was saying much.

Lila stood in the main entryway. To her left was a small kitchen with a tiny, circular table and two chairs. Dominating the center of the apartment was a seating area with a single futon and two recliners angled to face a large flat-screen TV hanging on the wall. Directly to her right was an open door, and from where she stood, she spotted a desk. It might be Kerri's room.

Young lingered in the hall beside an open door where light spilled out. Andrea darted across the hall into another room.

A familiar voice came over the radio. Lila turned it up and pulled it from its secured position.

"Are you here?"

"Outside. Which building?" Kyle asked.

"Building one, and we're on the second floor. Apartment

234."

"On my way up."

Lila secured her radio and motioned for Young to join her.

"Do not let her out of your sight all night."

"I'm supposed to be on duty all night."

"We'll adjust." Lila rubbed her nose. "I'm probably going to have a sit-down with the sheriff after this."

"Ya think." Young didn't ask a question—it was a blunt statement. "Andrea, we need to go. Now."

Lila stopped them before Young led the frightened woman out of the apartment. "We need to search Kerri's room and both yours and Allegra's. Is that okay?"

"Do whatever you need to. I don't know what you think you'll find."

"You'd be surprised."

Allegra emerged from her room with a stuffed duffel bag draped over her shoulder. "I'm not so sure I want you poking around in my room without me here."

"You're free to stay and observe me and my fellow deputy."

Fear flashed through the woman's dark eyes.

"Maybe she should stay at the Thorpes'," Young suggested.

"Who's that?" Allegra asked.

Lila shook her head. "Neither one of them will be home. Allegra, do you have somewhere to stay where you'll be safe?"

"I can stay with my dad. He lives in Burlington."

"Then get there."

Allegra stared at Andrea, indecision playing havoc on her

face.

Lila dug out a business card and thrust it at the young woman. "We won't go in your room if you aren't okay with that. If you change your mind, call that number."

Allegra took it and palmed the card. She didn't say another word and exited the apartment with Young and Andrea. Once the trio was out, Kyle entered.

"What's going on? Why's everyone acting like they have some big secret to keep from me? And what is Young doing with the O'Ryan girl? Out with it. You told me you'd explain."

Sighing, she placed a hand on his chest. The rough fabric of his uniform rasped against her fingers. Beneath the layers of polyester, Kevlar, and cotton, his breath see-sawed in and out. When she first met him, she'd nicknamed him Viking due to his stature, his fair hair, and even his deep gravelly voice. Now that they were a couple, she realized how much he embodied the moniker. After she told him the truth, he was going to need to lean on his Viking persona.

"Lila?" Her name came out choked with emotion. Such an out-of-place reaction from him.

She gnawed on her lips, staring into his blue-green eyes. God, why was it so damn hard to tell him that his older sister's death might have a connection to tonight's homicide? This was as difficult for her as doing a death notice. Why did he have to be here for this? Certainly, there was some training Ellie could send him to somewhere to spare him the agony of this investigation.

Kyle grasped her hand and clutched it. "Tell me."

Grinding her molars, she pulled her hand from his and

stepped around him, heading for the bedroom she suspected was Kerri's. He grabbed hold of her upper arm and hauled her to a stop.

"What the hell? Lila …"

"We had a young woman murdered tonight. We need to search her bedroom for clues as to who would have done it. Or why."

He scowled at her blunt retort. "Who?"

Lila reached across her body, and pulled his hand from her arm, keeping hold of him. Their tenuous connection vibrated with anxious energy. Give her a homicide scene and the work of processing it or reading a murderer's mind over this emotional upheaval any day.

"Kerri Peterson." She forced the name past her lips.

Kyle's arm slackened, his fingers slipping an inch along her palm. "Hillary Peterson's daughter?"

She nodded.

"Andrea O'Ryan is connected?"

"She found me and took me to … Kerri's body."

"Why couldn't you just tell me that in the first place?" He pulled away. "How does her death constitute keeping me away from processing the scene?"

"You had a car accident to deal with."

"Anyone could have handled that. I should have been there. Damn it, Lila, what aren't you telling me?"

She released a shuddering breath. What was she going to do when he broke?

He stared at her, his piercing gaze boring holes into her.

Lila closed her eyes. "There appears to be a connection to … to your sister's death."

A strangled noise, then Kyle stumbled back a few steps and squatted in the middle of the apartment entryway. Head bowed, he buried his fingers in his hair, and breathed deeply.

Once more, Lila was left in a frozen state as another person was left to cope with their grief and emotions. But Kyle was different than Hillary Peterson. Lila knew him, intimately. This should not be a problem.

Ungluing her feet from the floor, she squatted in front of him. "Kyle, look at me."

He lifted distraught eyes to her. Stress etched his features. He dropped his arms, resting them on his thighs. "No one could have warned me?"

Lila reached up and cradled his face. "I didn't want anyone else telling you."

He shook his head, freeing himself from her caress. "How are you so sure it's connected?"

"There are too many concerning variables. Key among them are items that were at both scenes."

"How do you even know about my sister's death? It's not like I told you. And I know Ellie would have never told you."

Lila fidgeted with the seam of her uniform pants. "I've learned about it."

Kyle bolted upright. "How?"

"I'm a detective, Kyle, how do you think?" She joined him, crossing her arms. "Ellie left a box in her office."

He sniffed. "With her out of the office, you took it upon yourself to confiscate it and poke your nose where it didn't belong."

"Oh. My. God! Are you seriously going there? I'm the

investigator in this department. It's my job to be read in on all cases. Even the cold ones."

"It's not a cold case. Didn't you figure that out? It's been closed. By Sheehan's predecessor."

"Denise Russell's is not."

This stymied him. He blinked at her, his mouth gaping.

"Listen. Whatever happened twenty-five years ago is circling back around. The anniversary was obviously on Ellie's mind if she had that box in her office."

"My sister's death tore my family apart at the seams, Lila. It killed my parents and turned my baby sister into a ghost who jumps at her own shadow. I won't allow you to dredge up old wounds."

"You don't have a choice in the matter." Lila flung her arms to her sides. Why did she expect him to react any differently than he was? Fontaine, the others, they had warned her.

"Whoever killed Denise and caused your sister's death has struck again. I can't stand here arguing with you about it. We need to go through this apartment." She removed gloves from the kit he'd brought with him and put them on. "I'm going through Kerri's room."

She left him standing in the foyer and entered the bedroom. Lila headed straight for the dresser and opened the top drawer. Behind her she heard the distinct snap of a glove being put on. She glanced back through the door and saw him walk to the hall.

Drawing in a cleansing breath, she turned back to her search. The hardest part over, she could focus on the task at hand, knowing that Kyle always put the job first.

They would hash this out later. Lila was about to find out just how far she could push him past his comfort zone.

Herself, as well.

CHAPTER SIX

Day 2: Friday, one a.m., the twenty-fifth anniversary of the deaths of Denise Russell and Brendette Lundquist

"SHE WON'T ANSWER."

Elizabeth eased back into her office chair and managed to prop her tennis shoes on the makeshift footrest of a loaded cardboard box. Tilting the seat helped relieve the pressure on her abdomen. If only she had the energy to maintain the position. For the love of Pete, she felt like a newborn babe. How could one little surgery wipe her out like this?

If she hadn't overdone it by going to the hospital, over-exerted herself arguing with the O'Ryans, and pushed her healing body past the brink trying to chase after Lila, she wouldn't be in this mess. No. She'd be in her bed, sleeping off the next round of pain meds, letting her body mend itself.

"You shouldn't have done this. I could have handled it," Rafe said as he took a seat on the corner of her desk.

The chair creaked, inch by inch, into its upright position. Elizabeth gritted her teeth against the searing heat rippling through her stomach muscles.

They had come to the sheriff's department, hoping someone was here who knew what the hell was going on and could update her on the situation. They struck out on all fronts. Rafe had discovered all the deputies were still out of office and on radio silence. The night dispatcher, Alexis Zachery, had been left completely in the dark—or was refusing to answer, thanks to Lila's misguided orders.

All of this was sending Elizabeth into an uncharacteristic bout of temper.

"There was no way Erin would ever deal with you and you know it." She gently rubbed her belly right above the incision area. "Besides, she was already worked up from Lila's intervention."

"Of all the people something like this could have happened to, it just had to be Rick and Erin." Rafe pinched the bridge of his nose. "My headache is turning into a migraine."

"We need to find Hillary."

"I asked Fitzgerald to look for her." Rafe frowned. "You should take another pain med."

"I should, but I'm not going to."

"There's no reason to *man up* with that type of pain, El-lie."

She gave him her best deadpan glare—*best* being an operative word, because, well, she hurt. "I'll choose pain over feeling like a deadweight."

"You setting yourself back days of healing isn't smart either."

"Not interested in your opinion, Dr. Raphael."

"If Olivia weren't in the middle of an autopsy and Dominic tied up in the ER, I'd sic them both on you."

Elizabeth grunted. Let Rafe grump at her. Better than sitting here in the silence while her mind played games.

Better yet, she could review Bre and Denise's cases to compare with what happened to Kerri. After a bit of a struggle, Elizabeth slid her feet off the box. She inched the chair around.

"Time to go," Rafe said as he stood.

"No. I want that ..." She gaped at the empty spot beside the bookshelf that towered over her desk. "Where is my case box for Bre and Denise?"

Rafe muttered something that sounded an awful lot like *that's how she knew.*

Elizabeth glared at him. He wore a distinctly sheepish expression.

"Raphael Fontaine, what the Sam Hill is going on?"

"Elizabeth ..."

She gave him her ex-husband's favorite hand gesture, the one Joel referred to as the knife hand. "Don't you Elizabeth me. First, the orders to keep me out of the loop. Second, my deputy detective's disappearing act. Now I see that personal property of mine is missing. Are you in on this?"

"That box was not personal property. It was department evidence."

"Yes, it was, in as much as it was sitting in my office."

"Which still belongs to the county."

Damn it, he would have to be obstinately literal. "Besides the point. You're stalling. Where is it?"

A knock on the doorframe saved Rafe from answering.

Olivia, still wearing scrubs, her features a mask of weariness and sorrow, entered. "I'm going to take a wild guess and say that box is with the woman it should be with right now. Lila needs all the information she can get."

"She could have asked for it. Not snuck off with it while I'm down for the count," Elizabeth grumped.

"Would you have allowed it?" Rafe pressed.

She scowled at him.

"He has a point." Olivia slumped into the only other chair in the office that didn't belong to Bentley. "When it comes to Brendette Lundquist, we all know your penchant for holding on with a tight fist."

Sufficiently put in her place, Elizabeth let her head flop against the head rest. "Liv, why are you here?"

"Dominic told me what transpired at the hospital." She released a shuddering sigh and scrubbed at her face, wiping away the emotions. "I reached a point in Kerri's autopsy where I had to stop. I was hoping to talk with Lila, but I can't seem to reach her."

"We're not sure where Lila is or why she isn't answering any summons at the moment," Elizabeth said.

"I'll have to wait then."

Rafe resumed his seat on the edge of the desk. "Do you have a manner of death?"

Elizabeth could see the pain in the ME's stare. Like Elizabeth, Olivia would take this case personally. It was one thing to stay impartial when it was someone you didn't know. It was another thing when it was someone you did know. This case cut too close to the skin for Elizabeth and on the anniversary of her best friend's death no less.

"Kerri's killer strangled her. Her hyoid bone was crushed. Bruising on her neck indicates manual strangulation. I found tissue under her nails; maybe she tried to fight off her killer." Her smooth, dark skin paled.

"What?" Elizabeth croaked.

"Sex was involved. I can't pinpoint actual timing, whether it happened before or at the time of death. My instincts are screaming at me that this might have been erotic asphyxiation gone horribly wrong."

"Are you sure this wasn't rape?" Rafe asked.

Olivia shook her head. "I can't completely rule it out, but I'm just not seeing the signs." She closed her eyes, then bowed her head.

The steady tick of the clock over Elizabeth's head echoed in the silent room. Each second, each minute that expired gave the murderer a chance to slip away.

When Lila had gone missing and the whole department had been looking for her, the stress had not overwhelmed Elizabeth. Now she carried a sense of urgency she hadn't yet felt since taking this job. Kerri's death carried a crushing history, one Elizabeth had borne the weight of for more than two decades. And the guilt. If she'd been here …

"What was Kerri wearing?" she asked.

Olivia raised her head. Her solemn stare roused a fearfulness Elizabeth had not known before.

"Both Kerri and Andrea were wearing costumes. Kerri's was a black and red pirate."

If she had to hazard a guess, Elizabeth was dead certain it probably resembled the one Bre had worn the night she died.

"What else?"

"Lila also took a pair of chokers made of black velvet ribbon with a clear stone pendant into evidence," Olivia said.

"In the center of the pendant is an odd-shaped diamond in red ink?"

Olivia glanced at Rafe. "Yes."

Elizabeth shifted her attention to her undersheriff. "That's why Lila ordered me kept out of this?"

"She showed me the chokers as proof of the connection to Bre and Denise."

"Which gave you reason to let her railroad you?" Try as she might, Elizabeth couldn't keep the irritation out of her voice.

"Ellie," Olivia interjected. "All of you are too close to this. Lila is the outsider, unbiased."

"I am the sheriff."

"Who is recovering from surgery. Lila's doing the job you hired her for. This is what she does. Step back. Let her do it as she sees fit."

"She hasn't completely banned me from helping," Rafe added.

"No, just sicced you on me to keep me in line," Elizabeth snapped.

"Because she guessed how you would react. You're proving her right."

The statement burned.

"Ellie, how many times did you ask Lila to trust you?" Olivia asked.

Elizabeth gnawed on her lips. The ache in her abdomen had grown into a sharp, stabbing pain. Her tenacious nature was losing the battle on all fronts. "She didn't actually put all of her trust in me."

"Maybe it didn't appear that way, but she's still here. She's been through hell and she hasn't abandoned ship. I believe that testifies more to your leadership skills than you think."

"I think you're giving me more credit than is due. Her relationship with Kyle might have more to do with her staying than me." *Kyle! Oh, God.* She didn't have the brainpower or gumption to deal with his reaction. "Does Kyle know about any of this?"

Olivia and Rafe looked at each other.

"Well?" Elizabeth demanded.

"Lila said she would be the one to tell him," Rafe said.

"Do you know if she has?"

He shrugged.

"Sheriff?"

All three directed their attentions to the doorway. Alexis boldly stepped inside.

"I know where deputies Dayne and Lundquist are. By now he knows."

"They're together?" Elizabeth asked.

"Yes. At the apartment complex on Apple Avenue. It's where Andrea O'Ryan lives. Where Kerri lived." Alexis nodded and backed out of the office to return to her post.

"They're doing their jobs," Rafe said softly.

Which meant Elizabeth needed to be there to oversee the evidence collection. Or run interference if the O'Ryans showed up there. Elizabeth grabbed the edge of her desk and managed to pull herself upright. "Let's go."

"Where do you think you're going?" Rafe demanded.

"To the apartment complex. We need to be there."

"No," he barked, coming to stand in front of her.

"Not arguing with you about this. If they find something crucial, I want to be there." She tried to circle him, but he blocked her.

"I wouldn't," Olivia said, she, too, coming to her feet. "You need to go home. You look like you're about to collapse."

"I'm fine."

"You're not. As a doctor and your friend, take my advisement and go home. If you're not careful you will rip those stitches and suffer Dominic's exasperation."

Elizabeth snarled.

"Need I remind you, this is why you hired Lundquist and Dayne in the first place," Rafe said. "You're going home."

She opened her mouth, but he cut her off.

"I'm pulling rank." He took her arm gently. "I'm taking you home."

Olivia closed the door leading to the bullpen and followed them out the second door to Elizabeth's office. "I'm going back to my autopsy. I'll touch base with Lila tomorrow ... well, later this morning."

"I want to know the results," Elizabeth wheezed. Damn, she hurt.

"Rafe or Lila will tell you in due time. You sleep."

After what felt like eternity, Rafe helped Elizabeth into his Charger. The second he closed the car door, she laid the seat back, not bothering with the seat belt. Wincing, she gritted her teeth against the aching.

"I don't know what the hell I was thinking letting you do this," Rafe groused as he drove out of the parking lot.

"Better you than someone else," she panted.

"Elizabeth, when are you going to accept you have limitations?"

She peered at him out of the corner of her eyes. "The answer to that would be never."

CHAPTER SEVEN

A s ANDREA HAD predicted, Lila was coming up short on all fronts in finding anything that would lead her to Kerri's killer. Or her extracurricular activities. The closet, dresser, desk, and an array of plastic totes stored in the room produced nothing more than the usual trappings of a twenty-year-old woman.

Kneeling beside the bed, Lila scrounged under it. She drew out a few shoe boxes and sorted through them. One held a pair of strappy, formal heels; another contained a pair of ankle-high boots. Otherwise, the boxes didn't reveal anything out of the ordinary. There was a larger package she slid out to inspect. The outline of the footwear on the side of the carton indicated a pair of knee-high boots. Lila flipped the top aside.

Empty.

Still, Lila rifled through packaging, then paused. Nestled among the discarded tissue paper and cardboard pieces was a crumpled white gum wrapper. She picked out the small wad, setting her flashlight aside.

The gum brand's red lettering was distorted by bold, black markings. Lila carefully peeled open the sides of the wrapper, stirring the fragrant scent of cinnamon. The smell hit her, tickling a thought. Where had she come across this before? She rotated the wrapper. Numbers. A phone number.

She pawed out her phone. She had a slew of missed calls from Fontaine, dispatch, and Fitzgerald. Oh well.

Lila tapped in the number and placed the call, hitting the speaker button. The other line rang three times then went straight to voicemail with an automated message telling her the owner was not receiving calls and the mailbox was full. Lila scrambled to her feet.

"Kyle?"

He emerged from the bathroom next to Andrea's room. "What?"

Lila held up the wrapper. "Look."

He squinted at the small piece, then moved closer. "A phone number."

"I called it, went to voicemail, mailbox is full."

He took the wrapper, his nose wrinkling. "Cinnamon gum."

"Do we know someone who chews that type of gum?"

"Lots of people chew this gum."

"I know that, but I'm talking about someone who we come into contact with on a continual basis."

Kyle gave her a look that screamed *really*.

Grunting at his nonverbal sarcasm, she turned to head back to Kerri's room. "Guess I'll just keep trying the phone until the owner answers. If it isn't a burner."

"Wait."

She huffed, then gestured for him to hurry up.

"Don't you find it weird that three college-aged girls have nothing suspicious in this place?" Kyle waved a hand at the rooms. "There is no alcohol in the apartment. What free-wheeling, underage person doesn't have some stashed?"

"You checked the kitchen?"

"Quickly. Nothing." He eyed the small room to his right. "Even in the navy, some of those guys had ways of getting it. They usually got caught, but it didn't stop them from trying again."

"I'll look. They could have it disguised. If they aren't keeping it here, maybe they have a secret hideout. Would explain why Andrea and Kerri were out in the middle of nowhere tonight. Dressed up for a secret Halloween kegger."

Kyle's eyes narrowed. "You didn't tell me they were in costumes."

"You were too busy getting pissed at me for not telling you in the first place." Lila crossed her arms. "Then pitching a fit because I knew about your sister. Where in all of that would I have had time to tell you about the costumes?"

Kyle's phone rang. "Evidence, Lila. If they were at a party, what happened to the other people who were there?" He dragged his phone out and looked at the ID. "It's Dr. Remington-Thorpe." He answered the call, listened, then lowered the phone and tapped the speaker icon. "You're on speaker, Doc."

"Lila, I wanted you to hear this," Olivia said, her voice echoing in the background. She was in her morgue. "I'm finished with my preliminary exam. I'll do a thorough autopsy midday."

"What did you find?" Lila asked.

"The coyotes did a number on her body. I can't pinpoint a time of death. You'll have to create a timeline so we can narrow it down."

"If you had to hazard a guess?" Lila pressed.

"I don't even know where to start. My preliminary manner of death suggests strangulation." Olivia sighed, the weight of her job coming through the line and settling on Lila's shoulders. "There are strong indicators of sexual activity."

Kyle's features hardened. Lila inched closer to him. Should she touch him? Would he even accept her comfort?

"There's no sign she used drugs, but the tox panel will find it if she did."

Kyle jerked, his hand holding the cell began to tremble. That had been the "official" ruling for his sister's death: drug overdose leading to hypothermia. Lila grabbed his phone from him and he about-faced like the well-drilled seaman he once was and walked down the hall.

Lila took the phone off speaker. "Olivia, have you sent in for the blood and tox panel?"

"Not yet. Kyle reacted badly, didn't he?"

"Yes. Did you happen to find a phone on Kerri's body?" The young woman's generation had grown up with smartphones, and they wouldn't be caught dead without one.

"No. She might have lost it or her killer took it. Something of interest I found—she had bruising on the inside part of her calves that looks like a zipper. You know, like the kind from boots."

Lila frowned. Those boots might be the ones missing from the box in Kerri's room. They weren't on her body when she was discovered. "I need to get back out to the scene and scour it."

Olivia cleared her throat. "Heads-up, I spoke with Elizabeth earlier. She's going to be on a tear when she's rested. I'm fairly certain Rafe will be right along with her."

"Warning noted. Go home. I'll meet you later."

"Lila, you should get some rest, too."

"Can't, Liv, I'm on duty." She ended the call.

No sounds came from the back bedrooms. Curious, Lila headed there. The bathroom was empty. Andrea's room as well. She found Kyle standing in the center of Allegra's room, staring at the ceiling.

"We don't have permission to search her room," Lila said softly.

He glanced at her, then pointed at the ceiling. "What do you see?"

Scowling, she entered the room. "Kyle, we can't …" She looked up where he pointed. "What the hell?"

Vinyl tile panels made up the ceiling, and one tile gaped at a corner. Had Kyle not walked in past the glass light fixture, it wouldn't have been noticed.

"Want me to move it?" he asked.

"Anything we find in there will be useless for our investigation because she didn't give us permission to search it."

His eyes flashed. "Probably because Allegra is hiding something."

Kyle was the right height. All he had to do was reach up and shift the tile aside. Lila stared at him. Had he done it? Had he poked around to see if something would give him an excuse to search Allegra's possessions? Her niggling little friend raised her ugly voice in the back of Lila's head. She should have never let him become involved in this.

"Now or never, Lila. If she gets wind, whatever is up there will disappear."

"If she didn't already take it with her."

She shook her head. This was ten shades of wrong. She was a better investigator than this. They needed to walk right out of here and ignore what they found.

"How are you going to see what is in there?" Did she just ask that?

"Not like I haven't picked you up before."

Growling, she waved at him to go ahead. What was she thinking? *Lila, you're an idiot!*

He shifted the tile until it came out, setting it on the bed.

Lila stood in front of him. "For the record, I don't approve of this."

He grunted as he squatted. Arms wrapped around her thighs, he hoisted her up like she was nothing more than a fifty-pound bag of feed. Lila shot up over his head and stopped centimeters from smacking her head into the tiles. She flicked on her flashlight.

"A little to the left," she directed.

She was eye level with the edge of the tile and able to just see inside, but it was too dark. She took his phone, activated the flashlight app and video, then stuck it inside the gap. Lila watched the video feed as she rotated the phone.

"Something was up here, but it's gone now. The dust has been wiped away in places." A small, white object caught the edge of the light. "I see something."

"What?"

She reached in, though the angle was awkward, and was

able to finger the object and roll it closer to take it in hand. As her fingers passed over the roughened tile, they hit on something slick yet tacky. She dragged that into her grasp as well. Kyle lowered her to the floor, taking his phone back when she was out of his arms. Lila unfisted her hand. Nestled in the folds of her palm was an identical wad of gum wrapper and a patch of some sort.

Lila sniffed the wrapper. "Cinnamon." She met Kyle's gaze. "What do you bet it has the same phone number as the one I found in Kerri's room."

"Find out."

She pried the corners apart and smoothed out the wrapper. Sure enough, the same exact phone number was scrawled across the gum's brand name. Along with the number was a tiny, white, unmarked pill.

"Well, looks like we found what she was hiding up there."

"Don't touch it," Kyle said. He was all business as he prepped an evidence bag for the pill, yet a few minutes ago he was a shuddering mess at hearing that their recent homicide victim could have drugs in her system.

"Do you think it's ..." Lila dared not finish her thought. If she voiced it, would it make it true? Would it drive him to the edge again?

Kyle tipped the gum wrapper and the pill fell inside the bag. "Wash your hands to be safe." He took the patch and the wrapper to seal them in their own evidence bags.

"These girls have some explaining to do." She scrubbed her hands three times to be safe. "But we can't say a damn thing to Allegra."

"We can claim we found it in Andrea's room."

Choking on her shock, Lila glared at him. "Are you seriously going there?"

Determination turned his features to stone. This was not the man she'd spent her off-duty hours with. Kyle Lundquist was as straitlaced and clean-nosed as they came, and that was certainly admirable in her eyes since she cut her LEO teeth on the streets of Chicago working in one of the most backsliding police departments in the country.

"And when a lawyer learns that we lied about where we found this, because Andrea points the finger at Allegra to save her own skin, then what?"

He remained stone silent.

"I think we're done here." She jerked the evidence bags from his hand. "Take me back to the hospital so I can get my car." She turned for the door.

"Lila ..."

She spun on her heel and jabbed a finger at him. "No. We are not having this conversation. I went against my better judgment and allowed you access. I was wrong. From here on out, Fitzgerald will be helping me. You're out."

"That's not fair."

"No, it's beyond fair. A defense lawyer would have a field day with this the moment it was revealed you have a personal stake in this investigation. Whoever killed Kerri will walk. And if they had anything to do with Denise Russell's death and your sister's, you will have set a killer free to kill again."

"You don't have the authority to order this."

"I don't, but I can damn well twist the arm of the one who does. Don't push me."

They stared each other down. Lila felt the fury pulsating off him, and she didn't care. If he wanted a fight, he was about to get one. She was primed for it. Hadn't been in one since the night, over a year ago, when she killed her attacker after he tried to finish what he attempted to do years before.

Kyle wouldn't push for a fight. Not when he knew what was at stake. They were still weathering the trauma of her kidnapping and assault at the hands of her kidnappers and Kyle's injuries by a serial killer. Lila's demons continued to wage a war on her, and at times she'd lash out, Kyle being the unlucky recipient of her suffering. Yet he remained, easing her through the fear despite his own anxiety. Their relationship kept them sane.

But it was beginning to bleed into their working relationship. This was why fellow deputies should not sleep together. Especially when one outranked the other.

His features relaxed. "Fine." He huffed, sliding his phone in the breast pocket.

"Put the panel back," she said and turned for the door. "We're done here."

Hopefully, they were done with this conversation. As she strode down the hall, Lila got the sense their headbutting on this investigation was far from over. Lest she forget, there was Elizabeth to contend with in this matter as well.

Oh goody.

HE WAS WAITING for them, perched on Elizabeth's porch steps, skating the pool of light coming from the bulb above the door.

Elizabeth hadn't encountered Kelley Sheehan in a handful of months. Mostly in part because he hadn't spent a whole lot of time at The Watering Hole, and Elizabeth's schedule kept her busy between administrative and sheriff duties. Sheehan visits weren't a priority for her as of late.

"Shouldn't you be ruling your serfdom?" Rafe asked him.

Sheehan cocked his head and regarded the undersheriff while rotating his cell phone between his hands.

"Deputy Fontaine, I need to have a private word with the sheriff."

"I don't think—"

"We'll have it in my living room," she interrupted Rafe.

Rising from his spot on the steps, Sheehan towered over her. For a brief moment, Elizabeth felt as she had the day she'd gone toe-to-toe with him, arguing about the real reason Bre had died. He'd shrugged, said what was done was done, and there was nothing a hysterical girl like her could change about it. She'd felt helpless, powerless. Useless. Even Deputy Sheehan had taken her for granted, telling her in essence to shove off. Was he about to steer this new conversation in the same direction?

He backed up the last few steps and stepped aside. When she reached the porch, Elizabeth looked Sheehan in the eye. She'd allowed his callous remarks and misogynistic behavior all those years ago to rule her life from that moment forward.

And yet, in the years after she'd won the election and ousted him from the sheriff position, he'd done everything opposite of the man she'd painted him to be in her mind. Still, with the revelation that Bre's death had potentially been repeated today, Elizabeth was of the mindset to consider Kelley Sheehan suspect.

Steeling her backbone, because there was no way in hell she'd ever walk into her home hunched over and showing signs of pain, Elizabeth opened the door and gestured for Sheehan to join her.

The ugly expression on Rafe's face barely registered for her. He could be pissed all he wanted. She was still the sheriff. With a tilt of her head, she gave him his marching orders. After all, he was still on duty.

Rafe pointed at her, then himself—his silent gesture they would have a talk about this later. Then he left the porch and slipped into the dark.

Sheehan had made himself comfortable in a large, leather armchair, still rotating his phone against his knee. Across the room, sitting where she had direct eye contact with him, Bentley stared. Here was the sole person Elizabeth's canine companion didn't trust.

Despite the pain and her fatigue, Elizabeth moved to stand beside her dog. She wanted to sit—really, she wanted to lie down—but in this scenario she held the higher ground, and keep it she would.

"Spit it out, Kelley. Got a long day ahead of me."

He ceased his repetitive motions and pocketed his phone in that ever-present denim jacket. In a leisurely manner, he placed his right snake-skinned boot on his left knee and drummed dexterous fingers against his jean-clad leg. "I got an interesting phone call from Randall Abbott tonight."

"Isn't he one of your bosom buddies? Calls between the two of you are probably a dime a dozen."

"Elizabeth, sit down before you collapse."

"I'm fine."

He sighed. "You're not. But you're stubborn." He drummed out a quick beat, then uncrossed his leg and stood. "You take every bit of that mulish nature and use it to your advantage." He headed for the door.

"What the hell? This is all I get after you stake out my porch to demand an audience with me, running off my undersheriff? Not gonna fly."

Sheehan paused and looked back at her. "I would tell you to sit this one out. Let your detective handle it so you can heal from your surgery. But I see that anything I say will fall on deaf ears."

"Sit what out?"

With a snake-like smile, he tapped the side of his head, then out the door he went.

"We're not through, Kelley," she called out.

Through the open window she heard his chuckle. "Oh, I'm well aware of that. Go to bed, Elizabeth."

Once the smack of his boots against the porch faded, Elizabeth stumbled to the couch and sank into its plush arms. Bentley scuttled over to her and butted her snout under Elizabeth's elbow.

"I know, girl." She hooked her arm around the dog's neck and hugged her close. "I wish he wouldn't be so damn ridiculous with his riddles."

Bentley nuzzled her cheek, giving her a kiss.

If Elizabeth had to hazard a guess as to why Sheehan told her about the call—and it was a wild guess—Mayor Randall Abbott would be making an unannounced visit in the near future. Let that be a problem she'd deal with later.

Right now, she wanted to sleep.

CHAPTER EIGHT

Day 2: Friday, 7:32 a.m.

LILA LEANED BACK in her chair at the department and watched the first vestiges of dawn peek through the windows behind the dispatcher's desk. With a yawn, she stretched, letting her head rest on the headrest, and closed her eyes. For the remainder of her shift, she had stayed at the department, typing up her report on the Kerri Peterson murder and subsequent fallout, and then studying and memorizing the Russell/Lundquist cases.

For the last four hours, she'd done a damnable job of trying to forget what Kyle had pulled at the girl's apartment. Four hours of kicking her own ass for reneging on her own orders to keep him out of this. Finding that pill and the patch, those gum wrappers with the phone number, and anything else was jeopardized because he refused to toe the line with protocol. Maybe, just maybe, Lila could salvage this thing by talking with Allegra and getting her to agree to at least give some statement. Andrea would be the key to convincing the other woman.

Lila rubbed her eyes. Gawd, they hurt from the lack of sleep. An hour ago, she'd checked in with Deputy Young, filling in the only other out-of-towner in the department on what happened twenty-five years ago and how it pertained to last night's murder.

Everything about those two cases, separate in certain ways and yet not, was giving Lila a headache. Things were missing like the reports, witness statements, a thorough autopsy on both women. It smacked of a massive cover-up. Something the sheriff made note of herself in a small notebook left among the case files. While the sheriff at that time had passed away, there was one man who'd had a front row seat to the events twenty-five years prior.

Disgraced ex-sheriff Kelley Sheehan.

Elizabeth pointed accusing fingers at him for having some hand in the cover-up, but she never came out and said it. Her claim—and justifiable—was she didn't have any evidence. Lila was going to have to do something Elizabeth simply refused to do herself. Sit down and have a nice long chat with the former sheriff.

Oh, that would go over as well as a bee sting on a hot day.

"Morning, Deputy Dayne."

She peeled one eyelid open to spot the day dispatcher, Georgia Schmidt, passing her chair. "You're in early." Lila rocked her chair forward and rotated it to face the dispatcher's desk.

"This is my normal time." Georgia stashed her purse in a drawer. "Alexis updated me on last night's events."

"You're aware of its connections to a twenty-five-year-old cold case?"

"I am." Georgia glanced at the sheriff's office then headed for the coffeemaker. "What are you going to tell her?"

A fresh mug of coffee would taste good right about now,

except Lila made plans to meet at Young's and was hoping to crack Andrea's cocoon. Then Lila intended to head home to catch a few zz's before she moved onto her next step in this investigation.

"I'm pretty certain she knows something about it. More than she should. Frankly, she needs to stay out of it."

Georgia slid a fresh filter in the basket then dosed out the grounds. "You know that's not going to fly."

The echo of boot heels barking against the polished cement hallway alerted of a new arrival. By the purposeful strides, Lila had a good idea who was coming at them.

"All too aware of that." She stood and gathered the evidence and reports scattered across her desk, tucking them back in the box.

"Morning, Rafe."

"Georgia."

Bracing herself, Lila shoved the rest of the files in the evidence box and slapped on the lid. She peeked over her shoulder. Fontaine had cut through Elizabeth's office and was making a beeline toward Lila. She took the box in hand and swung it around to face him.

He halted feet from her barrier. "Mind telling me why you broke protocol and ignored my phone calls? All night."

She thrust her shoulders back and glared at him. "You promised me you'd keep the sheriff away from this. I explicitly requested that you make sure she was kept out of the loop."

"Elizabeth is the sheriff. She was going to be dragged into this one way or another. It still doesn't give you the right to circumvent authority. I am the undersheriff and act on her behalf. You answer to me, and that means answering your damn phone when I call."

Oh, so not the right thing to say at this juncture. This attitude. His *I've got the big dick and I'm going to swing it around*, mentality was why they did not mesh. How the hell did Elizabeth stand his ego? Wasn't the ego trip the exact reason she divorced his older brother?

Elizabeth, even as sheriff, would have never pulled the I-outrank-you card. Ever.

"Know what, Fontaine? You want to run this investigation, go right ahead." Lila let the box drop at his feet. "You can start from ground zero and take it from there." She turned on her heel. "Good luck getting anyone to cooperate. Including your lone witness."

"Lila," Georgia called after her.

Nope. Not even.

"Damn it, Rafe."

Deputy Brent Meyer bumped into her in the hallway. The rookie with dark blonde hair was usually paired shift-wise with Lila. Since Elizabeth's unexpected surgery, they had been separated to allow Lila, a more seasoned law officer, to run nights. She had been molding him into an investigator, helping to further drive a wedge between him and his father, Pratt Meyer, a man of influence in Eckardt County with a shady side. Despite the revelations that came about when Lila first moved to Juniper, Brent and his father hadn't fully mended fences.

"Hey ..." He glanced into the bullpen. "What's going on?"

Lila lobbed a sneer back at the undersheriff, who was

starting to come her way. "Ask the Great Ape. I'm going home." She slipped around Meyer and made tracks for the exit.

"Dayne!"

"Go to hell, Fontaine!"

"Damn it, Lila! Wait!"

She hesitated. Had she heard the hallow echo of contrition in his bellow? Lila ground her molars. Should she even grant him grace and turn back? The old-school Lila, the one who grew up on the rough streets of Chicago, the one who had forged her way through life despite her wino mother's every move to thwart her, that Lila reared her head, yelling at her to flip Fontaine the bird and walk out the door. Oh, how she wanted to give into those urges.

A hand on her shoulder made her jaw clench. She didn't allow a whole lot of people to touch her, but reflection in the glass doors told her it was one of those few given permission. With the way her emotions were rocketing all over the place, it wasn't a good idea for him to even stand next to her.

"Meyer, I'm not in the mood."

"None of us are."

She craned her head to the side, the kinks in her vertebrae popping, easing the tension built up in her neck. Meyer seemed to sense her unease at him touching her and dropped his hand, hooking it on his duty belt instead. Lila about-faced, twitching at Fontaine's close proximity to her as he stood feet behind Meyer.

Meyer stepped aside, angling himself to face both her and Fontaine. "You two talk. We can't lose face or ground with this investigation." When had the rookie become the mediator?

Lila eyed the young deputy. "Do you even know what this is about?"

"I'm up to date on the whole situation. Fitzgerald saw fit to read me in."

"Saves me the trouble," she muttered. She glared at Fontaine. "If he wants to play Lord Fontaine, he can go right ahead."

He had the good grace to cringe at her biting words. "I lord nothing over anyone."

Lila snorted. "Have I got a deal for you on an ocean-front view on Lake Shore Drive."

Slowly and altogether deliberately, Fontaine crossed his beefy arms then closed his eyes. Lila could just hear his brain screaming as he counted backward, a maneuver she was sure he'd adopted when dealing with her until he got his temper under control. She itched to poke the beast, that urge to fight still brewing inside her. She needed to get to the gym and beat the hell out of a punching bag or a sparring partner. Too bad her typical sparring partner, Meyer, was going on shift.

Fontaine's features relaxed, and he opened his eyes. "Where is Andrea?"

"Safe."

"Not what I asked."

"That's the answer you're going to get."

"Her parents—"

"Can suck a rotten egg for all I care." Lila took a step closer to Fontaine. "Andrea knows things, and she's too damn scared to tell anyone anything. You go near her and she's going to bolt."

Fontaine dropped the beast act. "She has nowhere to go."

"So you think. Kerri's killer probably has a good idea Andrea suspects them, and they'll go after her next. You want that on your conscience?"

Meyer eased in between them. "She's got a point."

"It doesn't change the fact that you're overstepping your authority. I need to know what's going on so when the sheriff or I are thrown under the bus like last night, at least we're prepared."

Lila made a noise low in her throat. "The O'Ryans are bottom-feeders."

Meyer's mouth gaped and he took a step back.

"Excuse me?" Fontaine barked.

"You heard me. Their own daughter wants nothing to do with them, and last night was proof enough for me to understand why. I warned you to keep Elizabeth away. Pretty certain Erin O'Ryan was the one who dragged her into this, and you went along with it." Lila slapped her hand on the push bar. "If you want this investigation done right, I'm your only chance."

She shoved the door open and stepped outside. "Continue to walk all over me waving that big shiny badge in my face you're on your own." She let the door glide shut behind her as she went down the stairs.

F-bombs floated down behind her. She grinned. *He'll never learn.*

Halfway to her vehicle, her phone buzzed inside her pants pocket. She removed it as she unlocked the car, not bothering to look at the caller ID. "Dayne."

"It's Young. Are you on your way?"

Lila slid into the seat. "I'll be there shortly—just leaving the department."

"She woke up screaming again."

The engine purred to life. "You get a why out of her?"

"Not that I could understand. She turned into a bawling, blubbering mess until she passed out. She's still sleeping."

Lila flipped the phone to Bluetooth. "Try to get her up before I get there. I can't hang around forever waiting for her to wake." She drove out of the parking lot.

"I'll see what I can do." Young cleared her throat. "If it sounds like I'm being nosy, I'm not."

"When someone prefaces with something like that, they're doing the exact thing they're claiming they're not."

The woman chuckled. "Fine. I'm being nosy. How'd it go with Lundquist?"

"Not great. Now I've got Fontaine riding my ass." Lila checked her rearview mirror. "I need you to pull a lot of weight on this case. A lot of people in this department are too close to this and will not think with clear heads."

"What about Meyer and Fitzgerald? They're from the community."

"Meyer was too young, and everyone overlooks Fitzgerald enough that people actually say stuff in front of him without realizing who he is. If Fontaine and Lundquist continue to meddle, we're going to get nowhere."

Lila pulled into a local coffee shop and parked near the front door.

"You're the *načá*. Just tell me what to do and I'll do it," Young said.

"N-what?"

Young made a clicking sound with her tongue. "Your Chicagoan is getting in the way of your tongue. *Načá* is chief."

Every now and again, Young would slip into her native Sioux language. Lila knew Spanish and Portuguese. She recognized a few Italian phrases. She had even picked up a bit of Haitian Creole because she'd grown up on the same floor as a family from Haiti. Hopefully, her success at learning a new language would catch up as Young used more of her native Sioux.

They'd started out wary of each other, circling like two territorial lionesses. Over the year since Young joined the department there had been tiny shifts in their interactions. Lila was working on letting her guard down with people, something Kyle and Elizabeth were gently prodding her to do. Corey Young was the right person to force her into that change.

"You still like dark roast?" Lila asked.

"Uh, yeah. Why?"

"You've got fifteen extra minutes to rouse the girl. Over."

Lila ended the call and pocketed her cell as she exited the car.

Freya Lundquist, Kyle's baby sister, owned and operated Kaffe Korner. A woman with a terrible case of social anxiety but a talented barista and baker. Freya—Kyle's parents had a thing for naming their daughters after the Nordic ancestry, but, funny enough, not their son—when not working away at her ovens in her café was usually sequestered, alone, in her childhood home. Kyle was the only living soul she allowed to touch her or be in the house with her. It was the single-most reason Lila had never stayed with him—he overnighted at her place all the time.

A tiny bell above the door jingled. The tall, lanky blonde, her icy-blue eyes framed with bright red glasses, stood behind a glass display counter, half loaded with the day's baked goods. Freya, looking like she'd teleported here from the 1950s with her hair pulled back in a poofed ponytail and wearing a form-fitting black top over a rust-orange skirt, topped off with a floral printed apron, brandished an empty baking sheet.

"Good Friday morning to you, Deputy Dayne."

Put some muscle weight on her, paint on a perpetual scowl, and shade her eyes a hair more gray than blue, and Freya would be the female equivalent to Kyle.

"Just you today?" Lila asked as she approached the counter.

A flicker of distress passed through the woman's eyes. Lila took caution. She had no need to cause Freya to have a panic attack.

"For a few moments. Samantha is running a bit behind, and the kids will be in soon."

Samantha being Freya's business partner who manned the cash register and day-to-day to allow Freya her solitude in the kitchen. The "kids" she referred to were a trio of college-aged young adults she employed to run the customer-service side of her business. Freya was always careful to employ only girls, but one young man had swayed her to hire him to manage her new drive-thru window. Kyle suspected Freya relented on her firm no-male workers stance because the young man was gay and struggling with his identity.

"Mind if I get some coffees to go and a half dozen Danishes, if you have some made up?"

Freya's smile felt genuine this time. It usually looked pained and forced. Maybe Lila was growing on Kyle's sister.

"What flavor would you like? I've got blackberry, apple, lemon/blueberry, and plain."

Lila didn't know what Andrea preferred, but she'd caught Young downing a tray of blackberries one morning while she sat in her squad car outside the elementary as she patrolled the kids heading inside. Lila rattled off her order and wandered over to the window.

"Kyle didn't look right when he came home this morning," Freya said over the rattle of tissue paper.

Lila shifted, putting her back to the brown, red, and orange gingham curtained window, a little shocked Freya made small talk.

"Is everything all right?" she asked, setting the box of Danishes on the cash register counter.

Oh man, how was she going to talk her way out of this one? Kyle would have never told his sister what he learned last night, not if it meant sending her into a catatonic state. Lila didn't know the full extent of Freya's situation but knew enough to not talk cop shop. Especially about the murder of a young woman.

"It was a rough one last night. Nothing to worry about." Man, that lie burned.

Freya's forced smile returned, and her frosty eyes were locked onto Lila, holding her captive by sheer will. Somewhere beneath the layers of fragility was a ribbon of steel. Was Freya harboring a secret strength she wanted no one to exploit?

Freya spun from the counter, her crinoline skirt flaring out, and she went about filling the biodegradable travel cups with the coffee roasts.

Lila shivered. She moved away from the window and wandered closer to the counter to pay.

The bell tinkled. Lila glanced over her shoulder and smiled. A woman with Cruella de Vil hair entered the café looking like she'd just arrived from a party in Zombieland. Marnie Benoit's Goth style rubbed a lot of people in Juniper raw, but she was the sheriff's sister and folks kept their comments to themselves. Lila suspected it had more to do with a regular patron to Marnie's bar, The Watering Hole.

"Deputy Dayne." She nodded.

Out of the corner of her eye, Lila caught Freya jerk at the sound of Marnie's voice. The travel cup Freya had been putting a lid on splashed to the floor. She whipped around, her face pale, making the subdued pink lipstick she wore stand out.

"You," she wheezed.

Lila froze from the sudden shift in the atmosphere. Gone was the cheery, relaxed Freya. Before them stood a woman on the verge of a panic attack. Freya, her chest rising and falling with each rapid breath, clutched at the coffee counter. She looked like she was about to crawl over the top of it and scramble through the serving window.

Marnie, in turn, gaped at the other woman. At a loss for what she was seeing, Lila kept her mouth shut.

From the back of the café, a door slapped shut, making all three women twitch.

"Freya, I'm here!"

Lila eased closer to the cash register. "Samantha, we're out here."

The full-figured brunette emerged from the kitchen. "Uh, Freya, let me take care of this." She reached for her business partner.

Freya swatted away Samantha's hand and ran into the kitchen. The crack of the door hitting against something punctuated Freya's escape.

"Crap," Samantha muttered.

"I'm sorry, Sam. I should have waited another hour," Marnie said.

Samantha took stock of the situation. "Deputy Dayne, let me finish this up for you." She circumvented the puddle of coffee and refilled another cup.

"Is she going to be all right?" Marnie asked as she came to stand beside Lila.

"I don't know," Samantha answered and turned back to the counter.

Lila held up the cash. "Keep the change." She gathered the drink carrier and the Danish box. Time to exit stage left.

Marnie caught Lila's eye as she turned to leave. The flash of hurt in the light hazel eyes lined in kohl threw Lila. Ducking her head, she left the café. Whatever was between Freya and Marnie was not something Lila wanted to be in the middle of. Was Kyle aware of the fracture in his sister's psyche in regard to Marnie?

Lila shook away the questions. She didn't have time to figure this out. She needed to get to Young's and grill Andrea about last night's events and her ramblings.

CHAPTER NINE

ELIZABETH STARED AT her living room wall, only hearing the morning news headlines playing out on the TV screen as she stroked Bentley. Her canine protector's head nestled in her lap, tongue hanging out, the rest of her body contorted in odd ways as she laid on the sofa beside Elizabeth. Border collies were such goofy dogs.

Today she felt stronger. Less tired, despite her excursion in the middle of the night. Some of her rapid recovery might be due to the simple change in what she took for pain relief. She was through with taking the prescribed narcotic. Better to have a dull ache than to feel like she was high as a kite. Elizabeth needed her wits.

In her few moments of sleep, she dreamed of Brendette. She dreamed of her death, except she, Elizabeth, was the one dying at the hands of Brendette's shadowy killer. Elizabeth woke in a panic, gasping for air, pawing at her throat where the killer's hands had squeezed. Her raspy shrieks had startled Rafe, who had returned a half hour after Sheehan had left. Through waves of blinding pain, she allowed him to cradle her in his arms. An hour later, she kicked him out of her house.

Bentley shifted, nudging Elizabeth's stilled hand. She reached out and tickled the dog's belly. A contented chuff escaped the collie's snout as she resettled.

The news switched to a fluff piece, the bright HD colors catching Elizabeth's attention. She watched happy kids parading about in their Halloween costumes. The headline at the bottom of the screen was anything but fluff, declaring in bold white lettering the suspicious death of a young woman. Elizabeth narrowed her eyes as she read her town's name under the headline.

"So it begins," she muttered.

A rapid-fire knock on the screen door jolted her. Bentley scrabbled onto her feet, barely missing clawing Elizabeth's tender abdomen, and barked.

"It's me."

Elizabeth relaxed into the cushions. Bentley, too, relaxed, shaking the tension from her body.

"It's open."

Marnie traipsed inside carrying a drink carrier loaded with four large travel cups with a pastry box dangling by a finger. Elizabeth smiled at her sister's getup. She looked like a macabre version of Alice in Wonderland.

"What is this?" She waved her hand up and down.

"Our usual Friday morning tête-à-tête."

"Not what I meant. Your outfit."

Marnie set her wares down on the coffee table, then looked at herself. "What? Tomorrow is Halloween. You know I dress up every day leading up to it. I'm Alice from Zombieland."

"You're going to scare the kids."

Her sister snorted as she handed Elizabeth a hot cup. "They love it. Kids these days are into this kind of stuff.

Besides, I never see the littles—it's the older ones. Good morning, Bentley-boo." She graced the collie with a good amount of love.

"Did you see Seraphina last night?"

"She stopped by the bar right as the last of the kids were leaving. You should have called me with a heads-up."

"I'm a bit absentminded these days, what with all the drugs I'm on. Why was it such a big deal for her to see you?"

Marnie's left eyebrow wrinkled as she eyed Elizabeth. "You know who was there. There's always been bad blood between Seraphina's family and Kelley."

"Seems to be the general reaction of all well-rounded citizens when it comes to the ex-sheriff." Elizabeth sipped the coffee surprised at the wildly different flavors. "What is this?"

"Samantha's calling it Witch's Brew." Marnie began emptying the pastry box, laying out a variety of autumn-inspired baked goods. "I figured you weren't eating a whole lot but craving carbs." She held out an enormous muffin. "This baby is flavored with maple and pear. You'll love it." She kissed her fingers. "It's divine."

Elizabeth scowled at the overly large muffin. "I won't be able to eat all of that."

Marnie headed for the kitchen. "I'll cut it in half."

"What else did you bring?" Elizabeth asked, eying the other items sitting on the coffee table.

Bentley sniffed at the goodies but kept her distance, too well-trained to swipe human food.

"There's salted caramel apple fritters, pumpkin and chocolate muffins, and apple cider donuts," Marnie said from the kitchen.

"Are you trying to give me diabetes?"

Her sister cackled as she emerged, carrying two dessert plates with the halved muffin. "I made sure I got the ones made with coconut sugar. You're safe from diabetes for the time being." She handed the plate to Elizabeth and sat next to her. "Did something happen last night?"

"If it did, it's a police matter. Why?"

"I saw Rafe drive by with you going somewhere in the middle of the night. It had to be pretty dang important for you to leave while you're recovering."

Elizabeth wasn't shocked Marnie had seen her. The Watering Hole was a few doors down from her house, and they had to drive past it to go to the hospital. "It's nothing for you to worry about."

"Ellie, when it concerns you, I always worry."

"Well, don't. I've got a good team backing me and keeping things in line. Believe me, Rafe would never let anything happen to me." She took a bite of the muffin. The flavors of maple and pear made her taste buds sing. She moaned. "This is good. Freya is a genius."

Marnie didn't remark. Elizabeth glanced at her and frowned at the far-off look from her sister.

"Marnie?"

She bowed her head, the darker half of her hair curtaining her face, hiding it from Elizabeth. From an early age, when Marnie was old enough to realize how in tune her eldest sister was to her emotions, she'd pour her heart out and together they'd resolve the conflicts. That all changed the day Elizabeth ran off and married Joel Fontaine. The bond the sisters shared had been severed. It was ruined further when Brendette died and Elizabeth discovered Marnie's carefree personality had darkened. It was a place Elizabeth couldn't reach, and when she was frank with herself, it wasn't something she wanted to touch.

For a few years, the regret of not being there for Marnie and Bre nearly ate Elizabeth alive. She had to face her own shortcomings after Joel, a Delta Force operator, returned home from a mission that had gone horribly wrong. When she learned how close she came to losing him, it rattled her hard. Elizabeth reached out to Marnie from halfway across the world. Over the ensuing years, the sisters mended their bridges, but there remained a little black cloud hanging over them. Since her return to Juniper, Elizabeth had tried to root out the cause, but no matter how hard she dug, Marnie locked up tighter.

"Ellie." Marnie lifted her head, tilting it to look past her hair. "I want you to promise me one thing."

Frowning, Elizabeth reached for her sister's hand, surprised when Marnie grasped hers instead and intertwined their fingers. She was not the touchy-feely type.

"Anything."

"Whatever happens"—Marnie's gaze lifted from their joined hands to meet Elizabeth's—"whatever you discover, don't stop loving me."

Why would her sister even suggest that? Elizabeth was speechless. She tried to pull a rebuttal from her throat, but Marnie's features morphed quickly from solemnly depressed to perky. She gave Elizabeth's hand a squeeze, released it, and grabbed up another travel cup.

"Now, tell me what you really think of that muffin." She

brought the cup to her lips, staring at Elizabeth over the rim.

Oh, that was not going to fly. Elizabeth set her plate and cup on the coffee table, wincing at the compression on her surgical sites, then flopped back against the sofa.

"Nope. You're going to tell me right now what that was all about."

"What was what all about?" The innocent look fell flat on Marnie's pale features and dark painted lips. She looked more like the crazed Queen of Hearts than childish Alice. What Marnie tried hard to hide was waving a red flag in her eyes. Fear. Abject fear.

"You're spooked. I can see it. Why?"

Marnie turned away, drinking more of her Witch's Brew.

"You do realize I was married to the king of secrets and I work with two people who are great at the art of not saying. I'll eventually get to the truth."

"This is not a battle you want to wage with me, Ellie. Some things are best left in the past."

"The past has a way of rearing its ugly head and exposing everything you try to hide."

Marnie placed her cup and plate on the coffee table and shifted to face Elizabeth. "You're the clever one. You don't need me to tell you what you're going to find out on your own."

"If I'm so clever, then why has twenty-five-plus years gone by and I still don't know what made you into the woman you are now?"

"Why am I such an enigma to you? It's not that difficult. You're just too damn stubborn to look past the forest for the tree."

"What is that supposed to mean?"

Marnie stood. "I need to get to the bar." She gathered up her travel cup and the extra one from the carrier.

"You're not getting off that easy with me, Marnie."

"Today, yes, I am." She headed for the door. "Enjoy the goodies. Do it before the world caves in on you." She was out the door before Elizabeth could protest her leaving.

Trying to get up quickly proved futile. Elizabeth slapped the sofa cushions. "Damn it." This surgery was going to hinder her for weeks at this rate. She couldn't let that happen. She ground her teeth and scooted her rear to the edge of the sofa.

Boots clopped against the porch floor. Bentley trotted over to the door and chuffed at the new visitor. Elizabeth eased back into the sofa cushions and peered over her shoulder. There was no way to chase down her sister now.

Looming in the screen door, still wearing his uniform, Kyle looked as peeved as she felt. He didn't bother to ask, he just entered the house. Bentley escorted him into the living room then trotted herself into the kitchen, her bushy red and white tail wagging behind her.

Kyle didn't sit. He stood next to the coffee table, staring at the array of pastries laid out on the top. "Freya had an episode this morning."

"What? Why?"

He picked up the extra coffee cup and tested the roast, then set it down. "She saw Marnie."

Elizabeth closed her eyes and sighed. That partially explained Marnie's odd behavior.

Since Bre's death, Freya had suffered from unexplainable

anxiety attacks and an uncontrollable need to isolate. She refused all attempts for professional help, never giving a coherent reason why. And something about Marnie caused Freya to spiral. Nothing and no one could help her through it. There was no getting out of either woman why Freya reacted as she did. Elizabeth suspected it stemmed back to whatever happened to Bre.

Elizabeth met Kyle's icy stare. "How bad is it?"

"Samantha is running the café, alone. Good thing Freya had all her baking done." He slumped onto the chair behind him. "I can't stay at home. She's hysterical and tearing through the house like a madwoman. I think she twisted her ankle wearing those ridiculous heels, but she won't let me check her over." He clasped his hands together, dropping his gaze to them. "Lila's mad at me."

"What did you do, Kyle?"

Red infused his cheeks. Elizabeth's shoulders sagged. She knew him all too well to spot when he'd done something wrong and was embarrassed about it. He tilted his face away from her.

"Why would she have a reason to be mad at you?"

"Because I'm an idiot." He slapped his hands against his knees. "She gave me a chance to help her with this new murder investigation." He met Elizabeth's steady gaze. "I blew it, Ellie." He ran his left hand over his bowed head, a gesture his father had been notorious for doing when agitated. "I blew it so bad."

Their gazes met once more, and Elizabeth saw the agony churning inside Kyle.

"It can't be that bad. This is Lila we're talking about."

"Yes, Lila. The woman who is heading an investigation into the death of a young woman that closely resembles the death of my sister, your best friend. The same woman who warned me that if I screwed up, it would ruin every chance at catching this killer. After I already screwed up."

Elizabeth drew herself upright, easing the ache on her abdominal muscles. "Kyle." She gave him her sternest look, the one she had when she had babysat him as a young boy and he'd made Freya cry. "What did you do?"

He withered before her. "Nothing bad, just stupid. I broke the cardinal rule of a trained investigator—do nothing a lawyer can get thrown out of court. I gave her the excuse to kick me to the curb."

Bentley returned to the living room, hopping up on the sofa next to Elizabeth.

"It's not right," Kyle muttered.

Elizabeth was certain she knew what he referred to, and she couldn't disagree with him. "She's keeping me and Rafe out of this as well."

"We can't let her do this. I have a right to help find my sister's killer."

"I agree with your sentiment. However, I must admit, in the law's eyes, Lila's right. By inserting ourselves into the investigation and making it personal jeopardizes anything she does to solve it."

Kyle narrowed his eyes. "I hear a *but* in what you're saying."

"Lila told Rafe she'd keep us in the loop. We must abide by her rules."

"You don't sound like you believe what you're saying."

She looked down at Bentley and stroked the collie's silky ears. "I, like you, need to practice restraint in this matter. Lila is a capable detective. She's an outsider, someone with no ties and no bias. If anyone can finally bring closure to this decades-long question, Lila can."

"Keep beating around the bush. You might convince yourself of what you're preaching."

Elizabeth couldn't hold back her smile. She ordered Bentley off her lap and held out her hand. "Deputy Lundquist, would you assist me to my feet? We're going to the office."

He stood and grasped her hand, slowly easing her to her feet. "Then what, Sheriff?"

"I'm putting this investigation at risk by inserting myself into the proceedings."

CHAPTER TEN

LILA PARKED ALONGSIDE Young's department-issued unit in the gravel drive of the single-story rental. Pastry box and drink carrier in hand, Lila headed for the home's side entrance. Young got lucky finding this little Craftsman-style house for rent at the edge of Juniper's city limits. The property was backed by farmland maintained by the owner and, off in the distance, a line of trees marked the beginning of some of the richest hunting ground touted around here.

Lila was all too familiar with those deep woods. Not far from this place, she'd been held prisoner and escaped to face her demons. Out of the four people who had entered those desolate woods, only she had walked out of there alive. Her stride faltered. She stopped and stared through the trees bracketing a utility shed.

She had tried to bring Cecil out alive. Swore to him she wouldn't leave him. But his killer saw to it she would never hear Cecil's voice again, just as the killer had managed to end all natural chances of Lila ever being a mother.

The squeal of hinges followed by a sharp clap jerked Lila back to the present. The old aluminum screen door swung in the breeze. Unease set Lila on edge. Young wouldn't have left her house unsecured. Paranoia being what it was with a woman who had been snatched in the night and nearly killed in her own home, Lila wasn't taking any chances.

She backtracked and set the box and carrier on a tree stump. After drawing her sidearm, she pulled out her phone and dialed the last number to call her. While she waited for Young to answer, Lila scanned the area. Beside the small utility shed, a pot of purple mums lay on its side, potting soil scattered over the limestone rocks.

Young didn't answer. Lila shoved her phone back into her pocket.

She crept closer to the swinging door. "Corey! Are you here?"

A crow caw answered her holler. Lila shivered. God, that sound was unnerving. She inched around the corner of the house to the backyard.

Chaos greeted her. The metal patio furniture had been upended; the table and chairs lay in disarray, the bright red cushions flung hither, and the glass tabletop shattered across the cement pad. Lila's grip on her pistol tightened. Broken pieces of black and white ceramic mingled with the carnage. Lila crouched down and picked up a piece, a mug handle, by a jagged edge. A bloody smear ran the length of the handle. Lila paid better attention to the cement pad under her feet and found more spots of blood on the glass shards and the gray concrete.

She dropped the broken pottery and clawed at her radio. "Dispatch, I've got signs of a disturbance at Deputy Young's residence. Send backup. Now."

"I'm nearly there," Fitzgerald responded. Why was he already coming this way?

"Responding," Meyer said. Good.

"Deputy Fontaine is aware," Georgia piped in.

Which meant he'd be racing here like a bat out of hell in his Charger. Another confrontation with him was in order.

Lila rose to her feet. Glock gripped between both hands, she rotated, studying the ground. "Corey?"

The backyard was large, dotted by a smattering of old oaks and red maples. A fallow field of what had been soybeans stretched past the edge of the grassy lawn. Lila, alert and nerves firing her senses, walked through the yard, heading for the field.

A car on the gravel brought her to a halt. She turned, hearing a car door slam.

"Dayne?"

Fitzgerald.

"Behind the house!"

He came barreling around the corner of the house and, like her, pulled up short at the sight of the destruction on the patio. Fitzgerald drew his service weapon and strode toward Lila.

"Have you checked the house?"

"No. I wasn't going in there alone." She pointed at the shed. "Check back there."

He did as she ordered, and she moved in the opposite direction. She kept looking to the field. Her gut telling her that was the direction she should go.

"Clear," Fitzgerald called out.

Lila came to the far-left side of the yard where it butted up to a hayfield. Beyond the grassy acre was another gravel road leading back to the trees and more crop ground. If she recalled correctly, there was another homestead along that road.

"Clear," she yelled.

Dust clouds rose in the distance. Another vehicle coming along the gravel road. Hopefully, it was Meyer. Lila turned her back to the hayfield and returned to the edge of the patio, joining Fitzgerald.

"What do you think happened?" he asked, holstering his pistol.

"Someone came for Andrea."

He scowled. "Andrea was here?"

"We thought it was the safest place for her. Damn it, how'd they figure it out?"

"They who?"

"I don't know." Lila pushed past him and restudied the chaos. "Young must have brought her out here to have coffee. Waiting for me."

"Then these elusive *they* showed up," he offered.

"Maybe surprised them. Young would have put up a fight." Which would explain the blood. "Check the house."

They rounded the corner as Meyer parked his unit behind Fitzgerald's. He was out of the car and up the sidewalk, meeting them at the side entrance.

"What happened?"

"I don't know. We need to clear the house. Young and Andrea are missing."

His eyes widened. "Andrea was here?"

"Slick, Rookie," Fitzgerald muttered.

"Shut your trap," Lila snapped. "Weapons drawn. I don't know what we're walking into."

When both men were set, she led the way into the house.

The floor plan was simple. They entered through a small mudroom with a door to the basement to the left and the main entrance into the kitchen. Meyer headed for the basement, and Fitzgerald followed Lila into the kitchen.

Nothing seemed out of order. She pressed on into the joined dining and living rooms. Undisturbed as well. Lila hung a right into a tiny hall leading to the single bedroom and bathroom, Fitzgerald peeled off to check the bathroom, and Lila entered the bedroom. The bed looked as if someone had a power struggle with the bedding, the blanket piled on the floor, the sheets pulled from the mattress and a tangled mess. Andrea must have slept here.

"Clear," Fitzgerald said.

"Clear!" Meyer called from the basement.

Lila holstered her Glock. "Whatever happened occurred outside." *Shit!*

She and Fitzgerald returned to the living room. A pillow and folded blanket sat on the edge of the leather sofa. Young would have slept out here to protect Andrea and to give the young woman her privacy.

Meyer emerged from the kitchen. "Now what?"

"Do either of you see Young's service weapon?"

A distinct piercing siren cut through the quiet morning. That would be Fontaine.

"I think she has it with her," Meyer said.

"Or *they* took it," Fitzgerald remarked.

They! Damn it, who were they? Lila had planned to press Andrea this morning on who were these *they* she kept referring to last night.

"Meyer, go intercept Fontaine," she ordered and turned

to the end table situated between the sofa and the wall.

Lila spotted a small, black flip phone tucked between a stack of *Guns and Ammo* magazines and a thick book on police procedure. She slipped the phone out of its hiding spot. It was a cheap burner, one anyone could pick up at their local Walmart. Flipping it open activated the home screen, no password. Not smart. She pulled up the call history and choked.

"What?" Fitzgerald asked.

Where had she shoved those gum wrappers? Lila searched her pants pockets and found one of the wads. With the wrapper smoothed out, she compared the numbers.

"What is that?" Fitzgerald pressed.

Outside the sirens died. The slap of a car door echoed across the yard. *Here comes trouble.*

Lila hit redial on the last time the number was called at two thirty this morning. She pressed the phone to her ear and waited. Fitzgerald opened his mouth to say something, and she halted him with a raised finger. Two more rings went through before the call was abruptly ended.

Closing the phone, she held a finger to her lips. His features screwed up in a scowl, Fitzgerald nodded. Fontaine's agitated voice at the back of the house put her into stealth mode. Lila managed to hide the phone and wrapper in her pockets before Fontaine entered the main area of the house, Meyer a few steps behind him. The younger deputy planted himself in the kitchen doorway and stayed there.

"You had Young protecting Andrea?" Fontaine fumed. "Alone."

Lila, with an unamused smile on her lips, shook her

head. "I'm not getting into it with you." She took a step to walk past him.

Fontaine shifted to block her way. "You're done, Dayne."

A quiet calm washed through her. She tilted her chin up and met his steely gaze. It seemed their earlier confrontation was far from over.

Crashing doors made everyone flinch. Fontaine stepped aside, giving Lila full sight of the kitchen. Meyer had turned around as Young barreled into her home, cursing in her native language.

"Deputy Young!" Fontaine barked.

She jerked upright and glared at the undersheriff. Her sidearm dangled from her hand, blood dripping from a long gash on her palm. Young's brown hair was barely contained by the hairband, and her face was streaked with dirt and blood. Her once-white T-shirt was blackened and red, her jeans ripped and filthy.

Lila shoved past Fontaine. "Corey, what happened?"

Young, fury and pain etched into her features, lifted her uninjured hand to her face and shoved back her wild hair. "Some assholes came out of nowhere and grabbed Andrea. She managed to get free and ran across the field. I had to fight off the other one. When they couldn't catch her, they took off in a mud-caked piece of shit and chased after her. I ran after her, but she was too far ahead of me. I lost her in the woods on the other side of the field." She recoiled as she switched her Sig to her good hand and held the bleeding appendage aloft. "This eventually drove me back here."

How had they known where Andrea was? Had Kerri's

killer tracked them last night when they went to the apartment and then followed Young home? Then why not act last night? Had they gone after Allegra? Who were *they*? Lila wanted to scream. There was no time for that.

Lila pointed at Fitzgerald and Meyer. "You two go. See if you can pick up Andrea's trail."

The two men were gone in a hurry.

"I think they found her." Young leaned against Lila. "They drove that direction along the road. Real easy for them to cut her off when she tried to make it into the trees. I was far enough behind I wouldn't have seen it."

"Did you get a good look at them?" Fontaine asked.

"Hell no. The assholes were wearing Halloween masks. I didn't even recognize their voices. I know for a fact they're men, and one of them will be nursing tender balls." Her features hardened. "And no, before you ask, I didn't see the plates, if it even had any. The truck was completely covered in mud; I couldn't tell what color it was. It looked like one of those old-school Toyotas with a roll bar." She balled the hem of her dirty shirt in her wounded hand. "Damn, that hurts."

"Fontaine, take her to the hospital," Lila said.

"I don't think so," he growled.

"We don't have time to argue." She passed Young off onto the man. "I'm going out there to see if I can find her."

"Damn it, Dayne. This stops now."

"You can stand there and piss on the rug all you want. We're running out of time." She headed for the door.

"Lila!"

"If you threaten to fire me, Fontaine, you and the sheriff will be having a nice long chat." She paused at the doorway and looked back at him. "Andrea's life is in danger, and we have no clue from whom."

She ran to her car and jumped into the driver's seat. The tires threw gravel as she whipped her car around and headed for the road Young said the abductors had taken. The questions of how they found Andrea raging in her head, Lila raced to catch up with Fitzgerald and Meyer.

She shook free of the unanswerable. All that mattered right now was finding Andrea and hoping that she'd managed to elude her would-be kidnappers.

The last thing Lila wanted on her mind was the potential for another murdered young woman.

God help them all if that came to fruition.

CHAPTER ELEVEN

E LIZABETH WAS GREETED by an empty department and a stone-faced Georgia. Even Bentley's chirp of joy at seeing the dispatcher wasn't enough to lighten up Georgia.

"What are you doing here?"

Elizabeth sat in the chair at Kyle's desk, and he ducked out of the bullpen. Smart man.

"Not obeying my doctor's orders. For that matter, anyone else's orders." Elizabeth held up a hand to halt Georgia's oncoming tirade. "Save your breath. It won't do you any good. Where is Rafe?"

"Rushed to Deputy Young's house. Andrea O'Ryan is missing."

"What?" Kyle barked upon returning.

"What he said," Elizabeth followed up.

"Lila saw fit to protect the girl by having her stay with Young," Georgia said. "Apparently, someone else figured that out and came after her this morning. Young has been injured and Rafe is taking her to the hospital. Lila, Ben, and Brent are looking for Andrea and the men who are after her."

"I'm going out there," Kyle said, heading for the exit.

"You stay right there," Georgia ordered. "We are down and out all of our deputies, and you're the only one left standing." Her wildly curly hair was coming free of the clip.

It was a bad sign when Georgia's normally stoic and calm personality was on the fritz. "Mayor Abbott is demanding a meeting. I don't know how, but he heard about last night."

Yes, Elizabeth was certain he had, thus leading to his mysterious phone call with Sheehan. It appeared her suspicions about Sheehan's impromptu visit were right on the nose.

"That prick can stew in his own juices," Kyle remarked.

"While I agree," Elizabeth said, "he won't be so easily put off. Has he stirred up the other mayors?"

Georgia's features scrunched. "Didn't sound like it. But this is Randall. If he can make a scene with witnesses, he will."

Elizabeth hissed between clenched teeth. While she loathed Kelley Sheehan and grudgingly admitted he had been useful in the past, she really did hate Randall Abbott. Elizabeth was a woman who prided herself on not being a spiteful person, but something about that man made her want to claw out his eyeballs. Maybe it was because he was part of a group of individuals who had long run a ring of corruption she was trying to boot out of positions of authority in Eckardt County. Slippery snake that he was, Randall managed to polish his reputation and con the voters into believing he wasn't associated with any of them. Like Sheehan, Randall managed to keep his dirty deeds hidden.

If she was honest with herself—and boy, was she ever honest—she would never put Lila in the line of fire with Randall Abbott. That would be a confrontation ending in blood, his blood. When it came to men like Abbott, Lila did not have the patience. Elizabeth felt certain it stemmed back to her disastrous relationship with a man who turned out to be a killer.

"Georgia, put him off as long as you can. Use my sabbatical as an excuse." Elizabeth headed for her office. "I need to meet with Olivia to get an update."

"When do you plan to do that?" Georgia asked.

"Five, ten minutes." Elizabeth breeched the doorway and pulled up short at the sight of another figure standing in the second doorway leading from the hall.

"Seraphina, what are you doing here?"

The woman smiled. "Well, I thought I'd come see …"

Kyle came into Elizabeth's peripheral.

Seraphina's smile faded. She blinked and placed a hand against her chest, a move that seemed too old-fashioned for a woman like Sera. "My, Kyle Lundquist, you certainly grew up."

"I did," he said solemnly.

Sera's smile returned. "How many times have I come back to check on Mom and not once seen you? Where have you been? And you a deputy. Working for Elizabeth."

Elizabeth noticed the tense lines forming in Kyle's neck. He wasn't much on talking about himself. A point of contention between him and Lila, who was a secret hoarder herself. Elizabeth was privy to most of his life due to her longstanding relationship with his family and because she was his boss. Thanks to a secret Bre let slip, Elizabeth knew that when Kyle was a kid, he'd had a crush on Sera. Typical, embarrassing preteen interest in the older teenage girls.

"Good to see you, Seraphina," he said gruffly, then turned to Elizabeth. "I'm going to contact Deputy Fontaine and the others and get updates."

"Sounds good."

He closed the door behind him.

Seraphina stepped farther into Elizabeth's domain and closed the side entrance door. "Did I say something wrong?"

Elizabeth shook her head. "Don't take offense. That's just who Kyle is." Sometime during their small exchange, Bentley had slipped into the room, too, and was occupying her piece of furniture, an old sagging armchair Elizabeth couldn't seem to part with.

She gestured at the chair across from her desk. "You were going to tell me why you stopped by?"

"Oh." Sera waved off the offer. "I stopped by your house to see if you needed anything with you laid up, but you weren't home. Figured this was where you'd come. You always were a workaholic."

"Not true." Elizabeth gingerly eased down into her chair, sighing as the plush leather cradled her body.

"Is something going on?"

"This is a sheriff's department. There's always something going on."

Seraphina nodded, hemming, looking like she didn't get the answer she wanted to hear.

"Everything good with your mom?" Elizabeth asked.

"Yeah. Still being stubborn about leaving here and moving closer to me. I'll wear her down."

"It's always hard to go someplace new when all you've ever known and loved is out of reach."

Seraphina seemed to consider what Elizabeth said and shrugged. "Maybe. Well, if you're busy, I should probably let you be. Think I'll go catch up with Marnie."

Thank God Seraphina was bailing quickly. She moved as if to stand.

"Oh, don't get up on my account. You take it easy." Seraphina grabbed the door handle. "When you get back home, let me know, and I'll bring you something decent to eat."

"I appreciate it."

Once the side door clicked shut, the opposite door opened, and Georgia stuck her head in, her features red and tight. "You have a guest."

Elizabeth frowned her dispatcher's warning. "Who?"

Georgia stepped inside, opening the portal to hell, and allowed Erin O'Ryan entry. Oh, the joy! Georgia closed the door with a clap.

Erin stalked up to Elizabeth's desk. "Where is my daughter?"

Head tilted to the side, Elizabeth eyed the angry woman before her. "That's a good question."

CHAPTER TWELVE

IT TOOK ELIZABETH a good fifteen minutes to free herself of Erin's unwanted presence. Somehow, she managed to buy her deputies time to locate Andrea without giving Erin any heads-up her daughter could have potentially been kidnapped. She was fairly certain Erin wouldn't stay away from the department for long. Just as demanding and self-absorbed as she'd been in school.

Elizabeth commandeered Kyle again to chauffer her to the hospital. Bypassing the front parking lot for the small employees-only one at the back gave them quicker access to the morgue.

"Are you sure you want to do this?" Kyle asked as they headed to Olivia's domain.

"Better that question to be directed at yourself. Bre was my closest friend, but she was your sister."

"I learned my lesson last night."

Elizabeth paused. He did the same.

"Did you?" she asked.

She couldn't miss the tic in his jaw.

Studying the man before her, Elizabeth still saw the distraught, angry young man who had yelled at her for letting his sister down. He had grown up, had moved his life toward helping families like his find closure, far removing himself from that emotionally raging teen. Yet deep down, he, just like Elizabeth, hadn't shaken the trauma of Bre's death and the fallout.

"On the one hand, I see why Lila wanted us to stay out of this," he said, resuming his walk to the morgue. "I did learn my lesson. I can't think and act like an untrained individual. This is my duty."

"I agree."

With that, they rounded the corner.

Olivia rotated her chair as they entered the autopsy room. "Ellie, you should be at home."

"I should be doing a lot of things, Liv. One of them is not at home recouping from surgery when I have the unexplained death of a young woman on my mind and now the abduction of another."

Olivia's eyes widened. "Who was abducted?"

"Andrea O'Ryan." Elizabeth shook her head. "Just what I don't need right now. Have you completed Kerri's autopsy?"

"I have." The ME stood, picking up a folder. "I think you should read the report versus seeing her."

"Olivia—"

"Elizabeth, take my advice and read the report."

She placed a hand over her mouth to prevent her from saying what she really wanted to. Thankfully, Kyle stayed out of it. Giving her lips a soothing rub, Elizabeth regained her temper and scrutinized her friend.

Deep lines kinked the corners of Olivia's eyes. If Elizabeth weren't mistaken, Olivia appeared to be wearing the same scrubs from the day before. Had she bothered to go home at all? In the last year, she'd picked up vibes with

Olivia and Dominic, but Elizabeth was so busy with her own life, she couldn't put a finger on what it was between the two. If it was bad, Elizabeth figured Olivia would say something to her. At least, she hoped her friend would.

"Olivia, I know you're looking out for my mental state— and Kyle's as well—but I can't do a thorough job with this homicide investigation with only a report. Please. Trust me."

Olivia gnawed on her lips. Sighing, she dropped the file on her desk. "Fine." She moved to the cooler unit.

Elizabeth and Kyle followed. In the middle of the cooler sat a single gurney, the body draped with a privacy sheet. Olivia stood beside Kerri's gurney, waiting for Elizabeth and Kyle to join her.

Over the last two years, Elizabeth had stood next to a handful of gurneys draped in such a manner. None of those homicide victims had given her the aching need for revenge that was slithering through her body. Had the men in charge twenty-five years ago done a better job, hadn't covered up whatever took place that snowy night, Elizabeth wouldn't be standing now beside the body of a woman who had fallen victim to a repeat offender.

She met Olivia's worried gaze and nodded.

Olivia drew back the privacy sheet and laid it, folded, just under Kerri's shoulders, hiding the tops of the Y-shaped incisions. To give Kerri dignity, Olivia had sewn her eyelids shut, but the terror-filled expression still lingered, the rigor mortis having not left the body yet. So young, her life having just begun.

The bruises on Kerri's neck stood out against the ghostly white skin. Elizabeth mapped every inch of the discoloration;

the size and depth left no doubt this had been the work of a man. The idea he had done this to Kerri fueled a rage deep inside of Elizabeth.

"Were you able to get a window on her time of death?" she asked Olivia.

"The onset of rigor while she was on my autopsy table led me to believe she had been dead at least an hour before Andrea and Lila found her. Coyotes are opportunity scavengers, and she was left in their territory."

"Are you saying she didn't die where she was found?"

"That, I can't verify for certain. Lila and Kyle will have to determine if my findings are correct. But, if I were to hazard a guess, I'm ninety-five percent certain she was killed somewhere else and her body left where she was found."

Elizabeth clenched her fist. She would not succumb to the urge to smack something. "Did you learn anything else?" she asked.

"I'm waiting on the blood tests and toxicology. Lila was adamant on testing for drugs."

Any investigator would do the same, but Elizabeth knew her deputy detective was trying to rule out the similarities between Kerri and Bre. Even Denise's death, ruled accidental because she had inadvertently run out in front of a truck, had been decided was caused by drugs. Another lie, another cover-up, because those were not the friends Elizabeth knew. They didn't do drugs.

"Were there any signs that would make Lila insist?"

Kyle stiffened. He avoided meeting her gaze. Something about her line of questioning stemmed back to last night's stupid mistake he had mentioned. Would he come clean with her? Would Lila?

"Not on my end, but something tells me she suspects," Olivia answered.

Elizabeth touched Kerri's forehead, smoothing back the wispy curls of her dark brown hair. She cupped the side of the young woman's head, rubbing the pad of her thumb against the chilled cheek.

"Kerri, what did you get involved with?" Elizabeth whispered.

"I probed further on the strangulation marks," Olivia said. "As bad as the bruising and how crushed her hyoid bone is, this suggests rage, not passion. I'm rethinking the erotic asphyxiation."

"She had sex before she was killed?" Elizabeth asked, stepping back from the gurney.

"Yes, sometime before. If it was with her killer or not, I can't determine. There was no semen, which means the male subject was wearing a condom or couldn't ejaculate. I couldn't find any chemical traces to prove if there was a condom, but it could have been some newer type that is free of lubricants and spermicide."

"There would still be some kind of DNA?" Elizabeth pressed.

"Yes, and I've taken as many samples as I can to differentiate between Kerri and the male subject or subjects."

"Would Hillary know if Kerri had a boyfriend?" Kyle asked.

"It would be a question to ask her when we pay her a visit."

Olivia cleared her throat. "Speaking of Hillary, she still

hasn't come to ID the body." She drew the sheet back in position.

"A good reason to go see her."

They left the cooler. Elizabeth waited for Olivia to close the unit door, her gaze fixed on Kerri's body under that sheet.

He won't get away with this again. I swear it.

In the silence of the morgue, Elizabeth felt the power of her vow take hold. Unlike the deaths of her two friends, Kerri's murderer would not go unpunished. He didn't have the lackeys and cronies able to cover up and hide his sins this time. Justice would be meted out.

A sound behind her made Elizabeth jerk about.

"Hillary?"

The red-eyed woman gaped at their motley trio. "Sheriff Benoit. Dr. Remington-Thorpe. I'm sorry."

Composure regained, Elizabeth settled her hand on her hip. "No need." She glanced at the door. How long had Hillary been standing there?

"Is she …" She pointed at the cooler.

"Do you want to see her?" Olivia asked.

Hillary chewed on her already swollen lips. Most probably a nervous habit the poor woman had been inflicting on herself all night. She glanced from the cooler to Olivia, and then back at the exit, doing her best to avoid looking at Elizabeth and Kyle.

"This was a mistake. I shouldn't have come." Hillary moved to leave.

"Hillary, wait." Olivia circled around the grieving mother, blocking her chance to escape. "Please give yourself a moment." She moved to her chair and patted the backrest.

Elizabeth remained in her spot, letting Olivia be the compassionate doctor.

After a few agonizing seconds, Hillary stumbled over to the seat and sank into it. Her body sagged, looking as if she'd melt to the floor. Grief did that to a human. Once the weight of their sorrow was spent, the body, having been held upright by invisible wires, collapsed, leaving the human in a pile like a puppet cut from their strings.

Elizabeth knew the feeling all too well.

Olivia placed a hand on Hillary's shoulder. "Have you eaten or drank anything?"

"I can't ... eat." Hillary pressed the heel of her hand against her forehead. "I don't ..."

"It's okay. It's to be expected." Olivia left Hillary to fill a paper cup from the water cooler.

Elizabeth gestured for Kyle to vacate the autopsy room. With a curt nod, he did as ordered, then Elizabeth inched closer to the distraught mother, who blinked at her.

Olivia returned to Hillary's side, holding out a cup to the woman.

Hillary stared at the blue-and-white waxed-coated paper she cradled in both hands, then took a hesitant sip. Her hands trembled as she lowered the cup, placing it firmly on her lap. Hillary kept her head bowed.

Seated on the corner of her desk, Olivia tilted her head at the grieving woman, a sign that she was giving Elizabeth the floor.

"I told myself I couldn't see her like that." Hillary's shoulders slumped. "That I wouldn't remember her as she died, only how she lived." The water in the cup rose, hovering near the lip. "It was how I dealt with my husband's death. I can't do that again." The paper cup crumpled in her grasp and the water sprayed her pants.

Elizabeth moved to her side and reached out, taking hold of the sobbing woman's wet hand, and held it as Hillary worked through her grief. Times like this, it was always best to let the wounded get their bearings before speaking with them.

After Hillary had control over her crying, she gave a shaky sigh and wiped the water from her hands onto her damp pants. "Sorry."

"There is nothing to be sorry about," Elizabeth assured.

Drinking down the last of the water gave Hillary a few more seconds of borrowed time. She crushed the cup in her hand and fidgeted with the pointed edges.

"I realized I didn't know my daughter anymore."

Elizabeth schooled herself. "How do you mean?"

Hillary pressed on the edge sticking out until it caved. She tilted her thumb to look at it, an angry red mark in the center of the pad then tucked her thumb inside her clenched fist. Hillary bolted upright, startling Elizabeth.

"I want to see her."

Olivia came to her feet, shifting around to put herself between the cooler unit and Hillary. "Are you certain?"

"Yes."

Wild eyes, red-rimmed and dry, stared at the cooler unit door. The speed with which Hillary's emotions were changing gave Elizabeth whiplash. Best to give the grief-stricken mother room, so Elizabeth backed away. Her movements caught Hillary's attention, and she focused that strange, glassy-eyed stare on her.

Elizabeth didn't know much about Hillary. She was Marnie's age but hadn't moved in the same circles as Marnie or Seraphina. What Elizabeth did know of the woman, she'd fallen in love with a man from south central Iowa who had joined the Marine Corps, while she was in college. He had been KIA in Afghanistan, and she moved herself and her baby daughter back to Juniper. Cut-and-dried, nothing more to add to her knowledge of the woman. But the expression on her face worried a knot in Elizabeth's gut that had nothing to do with her missing appendix.

Olivia opened the cooler door and stepped aside. Elizabeth did the same, giving herself a visual line of sight inside the room. Hillary, having lost a bit of her fortitude, entered the cooler with tentative steps and went straight to the gurney. Olivia joined her, waited for Hillary's tiny nod to pull back the shroud, then drew it back only far enough for Hillary to see her daughter's face.

There was a split second where the air seemed to be sucked from the room. Hillary's features crumpled and she sobbed her daughter's name, draping herself over Kerri's still form. For a brief moment, Elizabeth wanted to do the same.

Olivia backed from the gurney and silently slipped out of the cooler. She gripped Elizabeth's elbow and escorted her away from the door.

Propped against the counter on the opposite side of the room, they both waited. What did Hillary mean by saying she realized she didn't know who her daughter was anymore?

A heartbeat later, Hillary flew from the cooler and ran

out of the morgue. Olivia rushed to the door, calling after her, but the mother was halfway down the hall and heading for her escape. Better to let her go.

While Olivia remained in the hallway, Elizabeth returned to the cooler and hesitated. Hillary had thrown the privacy sheet to the floor and exposed her daughter's body. The sight of the autopsy incisions and the damage inflicted by the coyotes after her death had laid bare to her mother's grief-stricken eyes.

Groaning, Elizabeth picked up the sheet. She shouldn't have left her alone.

As she was laying the sheet out over Kerri's body, a flash of silver caught her attention. Piled on the gurney, nestled between her neck and shoulder, was a silver locket. Elizabeth picked it up and pried open the oval. Inside was a tiny picture of a man in uniform holding a baby. Kerri and her father. Elizabeth shut the locket and gripped the necklace.

Father and daughter were together again. Both ripped from this world in an act of violence.

Elizabeth settled the locket in the hollow of Kerri's neck and laid the sheet over her. She would be buried with the necklace.

God help them if Hillary chose to join her husband and daughter.

She needed to watch over Hillary in the event she did decide to do the unthinkable.

One death was one too many.

CHAPTER THIRTEEN

LILA, WEARING ONLY a tank and pants, threw her vest and sweat-drenched uniform top into her car, then slammed the passenger side door. If she wouldn't break her foot, she'd have kicked the tires too.

They'd lost Andrea. They hadn't found a track, a trace, anything to prove she'd run this way or that the abductors had gotten her.

"Now what?" Meyer asked.

Between the three of them, they'd spread out as far as comfortable and searched a two-mile radius. When the terrain got rough and dense, Fitzgerald convinced her it was futile to go any farther without ATVs or horses. Although reluctant to give up the search, Lila admitted he was right.

"We need to get a BOLO on the truck Young saw. Let's just hope someone, somewhere in this county has seen it or knows who owns it. Those bastards have her. It's not going to be good for her if we can't find her soon." She recognized the resignation in her voice. How she hated hearing it. "Andrea was our strongest link to finding out what happened to Kerri and what the hell is going on. Those infamous *they* knew it too. We're going to have to do this the hard way now."

"The sheriff has to be the one to approach the O'Ryans

about their missing daughter," Fitzgerald said.

Lila ground her molars.

"He's right, Lila. Time for you to relinquish authority. A storm is coming," Meyer said.

"It's already here. It's been here for decades," she snarled. "Damn it!" She circled the hood.

"What are we supposed to do?" Fitzgerald demanded.

She paused in opening the driver's side door. "You should get sleep. Meyer needs to get back on patrol."

Both men protested to her orders.

"I don't care!" Lila pressed her fingers to her forehead, took a deep breath, and let it out in a rush. "At this point, I don't care what either of you do. Technically, you're under Fontaine's supervision. Ask him what he wants." She yanked open the door. "I need to get back to the department and work."

The approaching Ford Interceptor put a halt to Lila's escape. Groaning, she went to meet the sheriff. Kyle exited the SUV first, but Elizabeth managed to get out before Kyle could round the hood of the Ford.

"Sheriff, why are you out here?" Lila asked.

"Doing the things the people of Eckardt County voted me in to do." Elizabeth rested against the SUV grille. "Deputy Detective, update me."

Lila glanced at Kyle, who avoided making eye contact with her, then back at the other two deputies. Sighing, she went to rub her face, stopping when she noticed the thick cover of grime on her hand, hooking it instead on her duty belt.

"Is this not a good time for you, Deputy?" the sheriff

pressed.

"Honestly, no, it isn't."

Lila and Elizabeth stared at each other. After a few blinks, Elizabeth broke eye contact.

"Fitzgerald, your shift is over. Go get some sleep. Meyer, head out. Deputy Fontaine is getting out a BOLO for the description of the truck and the men Young was able to provide. I need you patrolling. We will reconvene later today."

That she knew about the situation didn't surprise Lila. No. What surprised her was how fast Fitzgerald and Meyer moved to obey the sheriff's commands. Both men accepted their orders with "yes, ma'am," and left.

Lila finally caught Kyle's eye. The simmering ire in his gaze backed Lila to the cliff's edge. He could be irritated with her all he wanted.

"I appreciate what you've been attempting to do for the last twelve hours, Lila. We both can." Elizabeth shifted her stance, arching her back. "However, I can't in good conscience allow you to carry this burden alone."

"It's not a burden."

"After spending the better portion of my adult life trying to unravel the truth to my friend's death, I can safely say, yes, it is."

Kyle propped his hip against the SUV, hands hooked behind the shoulder straps of his tactical vest.

Elizabeth tilted her head toward him. "He, too, knows what it's like."

Lila pursed her lips. Oh, Kyle sure knew the burden. Which made him more likely to pull another stunt like he did last night. Bet he didn't say one word to Elizabeth about that.

Lila turned her attention to the sheriff. "May I be frank with you?"

Elizabeth nodded.

"I still firmly believe this is beyond a bad idea having either of you involved in the investigation. So bad I can only imagine how the lawyers will have a field day with the evidence and charges brought against whomever did this." Lila leaned toward Elizabeth. "It will ruin Kyle's career and get you voted out next election cycle—*if* the voters will wait that long."

"I hear a *but* in your statement," Elizabeth said.

"Yes, there is a *but*. You're right. I can't do this alone, even with Meyer and Fitzgerald. You're the lone person able to open the doors I want to kick in. But that's not a tact I'm willing to take. This isn't Chicago; it won't fly here."

Elizabeth hung her head for a moment, then lifted fiery eyes to Lila. "See, that's where you're wrong."

Lila frowned. "Come again?"

"I want Chicago-style tactics on this investigation. We're going up against a killer with a penchant for mob-like approaches to his or her dealings."

"We don't even know where to begin with this. How have you—None of your notes in the box gave any indication you had come to this conclusion," Lila sputtered.

Elizabeth gave her a motherly smile. "Because it was a theory rattling around in my head, I didn't dare write down for fear I'd be wrong."

Lila noticed the shift in Kyle's stance. A subtle air of arrogance he hadn't shown around her in a long while, not since they had first met when she joined the sheriff's department. If he wasn't careful, he would find himself knocked down several pegs.

"Go on," Lila prompted.

Elizabeth pushed off the SUV with a bit of effort and took a few settling breaths. "Let's take this back to the department where it's cooler and where I can get everyone on the same page." She turned to head for the passenger side. "Then the two of you are going home and hashing out your differences."

Lila's face heated. "Sheriff, I really don't—"

"Lila Dayne, if there's one thing I've learned in my forty-odd years on this planet, it's the ability to spot a tiff between lovers."

"More like he told you and you're interjecting to prevent a fallout," Lila remarked.

Elizabeth glanced back at Lila. "Take it from the woman with a failed marriage after twenty-two years: the silent types are the most emotional."

Lila lifted an eyebrow; Kyle gaped at Elizabeth with a furrowed brow, looking like a confused Herman Munster.

"Yeah, Viking, she means you."

Elizabeth pointed a finger at Lila. "You too. Get in your car. Let's go."

Leave it to the woman in charge to have the last word.

"YOU DIDN'T TELL her about Hillary. Or Erin's visit."

Elizabeth massaged her neck, regretting her decision to skip taking a powerful narcotic. The piddly amount of over-the-counter pain meds weren't cutting it.

"Ellie."

She slid her gaze over to the man driving her Interceptor. "Kyle."

"If Erin is still at the department and she sees Lila walk in, she's gonna have a cow."

Elizabeth smiled at the idiom. She was never sure where it had actually come from, but hearing Kyle fall back on it amused her. Transported her back in time to a moment when it was her driving and he riding, as she took him and Freya to get ice cream from the Baskin Robbins before it closed for the season.

It had been unseasonably warm that year, too. Brendette, also babysitting, promised to meet them at the ice cream shop with her young charges in tow. She and Elizabeth, seniors, were planning to attend a huge Halloween party later out in Soap Creek with their entire class. Elizabeth fondly remembered the costume she wore that night, she and Joel going as Morticia and Gomez Addams, two lovesick weirdos.

Kyle had been complaining about Freya getting into his things, and Freya had shot back telling him to not have a cow. The young girl's delivery had left Elizabeth in stitches and her brother unamused.

"Sheriff?"

She looked at the grown man next to her. God, how she wanted to go back to those days. Back when evil had been something only preachers railed about from the pulpit or images portrayed on the TV from a distant city or country. Before anger turned a boy into a world-weary man and left a young woman terrified of her own shadow. Back to a place where Elizabeth hadn't lost her best friend and her sister and hadn't set on a path to watching her marriage self-destruct.

"Are you okay?" Kyle asked.

Blinking away the moisture filling her eyes, she turned back to the window. "I'm as okay as one can be after having a tiny, infected organ removed from her body."

"Do you need to get something from your house?"

"No. I'll just raid the med kits at the department."

"What about Erin?"

Elizabeth propped her elbow on the edge of the window and cradled her head. "If she's there, I'll deal with it."

"We still have the issue of Mayor Abbott potentially coming in."

"I will have no compunction of siccing Lila on him."

Kyle snorted. "That I want to see."

"You watched her kill the man who tried to kill her twice. I don't think her putting an ass like Randall Abbott in his place will be all that thrilling."

"Better him receiving the double-edge blade of her tongue than me." He turned the SUV down the street heading for the department. "Thanks for throwing me under the bus. Really strokes the male ego when his boss has to run interference in his love life."

Elizabeth perked at the single word. "Do you love her?"

Panic ran rampant over his face. "I didn't say that." He gripped the steering wheel tight enough his knuckles turned white. "I swear to God, Ellie, if you tell Lila I said that …

You realize she'd run screaming for the hills."

"Well, do you?"

"I really don't think that's any business of yours."

She chuckled. "The harder you deflect, the more I want to believe it's true."

"True or not, Lila's not the kind of woman you just throw around that kind of a declaration. She still hasn't gotten over ... Besides, I can't even convince her I'm okay with not having kids."

Kyle turned the SUV into the sheriff's department lot and parked the Ford in her assigned spot. He cut the engine, but they didn't move.

"I know this is awkward, Kyle. Really awkward. But is she okay with not being able to have kids? The option was ripped away from her. She lost everything she loved and nearly lost her life, twice." Elizabeth gripped his arm, feeling the twitching muscles underneath. "I'm not with her during the off hours. I can only see what she wants me to see. What she wants her counselor to see. How is she doing?"

He shook his head, letting his hands fall away from the steering wheel and into his lap. Elizabeth released him, tucking her own hand against her abdomen.

"It's been over a year." He sighed. "Over three since the initial attack. She still wakes up screaming."

Elizabeth squeezed her eyes shut, flashing back to the night in a torrential downpour, when she put a bullet through the head of the man trying to kill her deputy. Joel warned her she'd have her own setbacks. He even talked her through some of her own episodes of regret for taking a human life, even if the bastard had deserved it. What Joel did make clear to Elizabeth was that while she had some demons to exorcise, Lila's trauma would go much deeper.

"What about you?"

Kyle had been injured. Had gone through hell when he thought he'd lost Lila. Yet he'd bounced back easier. Almost too easy.

He was spared from answering her when another car pulled into the lot and parked next to them. It was Lila.

"We better get this over with," he said, popping the door handle. "She's going to want to go home and clean up."

"I'm serious." Elizabeth's statement came out like a whip crack. She regretted nothing. "You two are going to work through whatever it was you did wrong. Make it right."

"With Lila, it's never that easy." He ended the conversation by exiting the car and shutting the door.

Elizabeth might not get the last word in on this conversation. Her gaze tracked to the woman exiting her own car. Lila, however, would.

CHAPTER FOURTEEN

RAISED VOICES ECHOED along the department hallway, reverberating in Lila's head. She had a headache from dehydration, no sleep, and the lack of caffeine, and if the voice she heard mingled among all the others was who she suspected, her headache was about to explode into a migraine.

"Why is Fontaine even bothering to argue with her?" she muttered.

Elizabeth, walking beside her, sighed. "Because Erin O'Ryan manages to drive people to madness."

"Was she the *popular* girl in school?"

Kyle snorted. "The head bitch."

Lila and Elizabeth eyed his stoic form.

"How did ..." Elizabeth shook her head. "Never mind. I know how."

"That makes Rick the star quarterback," Lila added.

"Nope. He was a baseball player," Elizabeth supplied, stopping by the side entrance to her office.

"Same thing."

The voices went silent. Lila tilted her head to see around Kyle's looming figure. No one was at the end of the hall, waiting for them. How long before someone realized they were here and pounced?

"You better get in there and gather yourself," Kyle told Elizabeth. "We'll waylay the mob."

"I'll need five minutes."

Down the hall a new conversation, this time not as heated or as loud, struck up. It would give Lila and Kyle some cover when they headed that way.

"You're getting more than five minutes, Ellie. You've already pushed yourself too far. Get in there, lock the doors, and let us handle it," Lila ordered.

Elizabeth pushed a fingernail into Lila's name tape. "Don't overstep your undersheriff. He's already chewed me up one side and down the other for your insubordination, after he explained to me the benefits of why I hired you in the first place."

Lila frowned. Fontaine did what? "Is he sick?" she asked softly.

Elizabeth smiled. "Not one bit."

A wicked thought hit Lila. "Maybe he's sexually frustrated?"

Kyle choked and moved a few steps to the side.

Elizabeth, cheeks turning a bright shade of pink, lost her smile and cleared her throat. "Okay, I think I'm exiting out of this conversation now." She slipped inside her office and peeked back at the two through a crack. "Behave." With that, she closed the door.

"Knew it," Lila whispered.

"You didn't have to voice it," Kyle said.

"Call it as I see it." She headed toward the bullpen.

He fell in step with her. "Better finish buttoning your top."

Lila glanced down at her hastily donned uniform top and her sweat-and-dirt-ringed tank. Didn't need to stir up the masses looking unprofessional, despite the fact she'd been barreling through fields and timber searching for a kidnapped woman. She slipped the last button home as they rounded the corner and entered the bullpen.

Fontaine, Georgia, and Meyer were there along with Young, her hand bandaged and held aloft. Standing in the center of the ring of desks and sheriff's deputies was Erin O'Ryan, her features pinched and bloodless. She stared daggers at Lila. But it was the white-haired man turned out in a spiffy pair of khaki slacks and a dark-purple polo with MAYOR embroidered on the left side that kept Lila's full attention. She'd had brief encounters with Juniper's mayor, Randall Abbott, and those encounters gave her the distinct impression she was in the presence of a sleazebag. Didn't matter how good-looking the man was, his type reminded her of the man who ruined Lila's future.

He stepped out of the shadowed corner near Fitzgerald's desk and flashed a straight-toothed smile. "Deputy Dayne and Lundquist, pleasure for you to join us. Where is Sheriff Benoit?"

"Sheriff says sic 'im," Kyle said under his breath.

Lila returned the smile, baring her canines. Oh, this was going to be fun. She met Fontaine's gaze. With a tilt of her head, she hoped he'd get the message that she was asking for permission to proceed without him running interference.

"That woman needs to leave," Erin O'Ryan spat out. "She's the reason my daughter is missing."

"Now, Erin, we all know that Deputy Dayne was not

there when it happened." Abbott's gaze shifted to Young. "Correct, Deputy Young?"

Young stared at the mayor, fury brightening her eyes. The look must have bothered the man, as he turned away.

Fontaine, his features twisted, took a step forward. Lila jerked up her hand, halting him in place. He blinked once and nodded.

Permission granted, Lila stalked forward. "Mayor Abbott, unless you have a legal reason to be here, you need to leave."

"Deputy, I believe you overstep—"

"You don't. That's what I thought. Goodbye."

"You listen here." He shook a finger at her.

"No, I don't listen here. We don't answer to you. Unless you have useful information that pertains to Andrea O'Ryan's abduction, you are not welcome in our office. If you refuse to leave, I will have Georgia contact the Juniper police and have them escort you out of the building."

He moved toward Lila, his hands balled at his sides. His movement forced her hand to her weapon, with all the male deputies in the room doing the same and closing in. The collective sound of men in protector mode and Erin O'Ryan gasping brought Abbott to a halt. Lila lifted her hand, easing her fellow deputies back. Abbott looked from her to Kyle, then back. His body relaxed and he tipped his chin up. Too bad it wasn't raining so the ass could drown when he walked outside.

"Deputy Fontaine, you allow this woman to speak for your office?"

"That would be the sheriff's decision," Fontaine said.

"Seems she's already given her edict through Dayne."

"Why should I expect anything less from an office run by a woman." Abbott sneered at Lila. "If Kelley were still here, things would be different."

"Because there wouldn't be any women running the place," Lila remarked.

He didn't grace her remark with an answer. Instead, he gestured for permission to leave. Lila stepped aside, making a lane between her and Kyle that the mayor had to pass between. Abbott glanced back at Erin then Lila watched him stride down the hall and out the door. Once he was outside, he put his phone to his ear and looked back through the glass. Oh, to be a fly on the brick wall and hear what he was saying to whomever he had called.

"What do you mean Andrea was abducted?" Erin croaked.

Lila put her back to the hallway. "You didn't tell her that?" she asked Fontaine.

"I didn't have an official ruling in that regard," he answered moving to the sheriff's office door as it opened.

Elizabeth stepped outside and leaned against the door-frame. "Erin, please come into my office."

The distraught mother stood there, gaping at the sheriff. Georgia moved out from behind her desk and escorted Erin into the sheriff's office.

Elizabeth nodded at the slew of deputies in the bullpen. "Deputy Dayne, you have the war room." With that, she returned to her domain, closing the door.

All eyes turned to Lila. A tremor rippled through her body at being put on the spot. Despite the years she'd been in this department and the times she led task forces, Lila still struggled with the leadership roles put on her. Once upon a time, she had been confident enough to lead hardened Chicago police officers, though it had been a blip in her life. Since her abduction and second fight for her life, Lila shrank from the responsibility even more. Except the sheriff refused to allow her to wriggle out of the duty. Right now, it made sense for Lila to lead so Elizabeth could deal with the troublesome public.

Give Lila one-on-one time with an arrogant bastard like Randall Abbott any day over telling a room full of her colleagues what to do and why they had to do it.

The brush of calloused fingers against her hand jolted her. She glanced to her left as Kyle walked over to his desk. His reassuring touch, even if they weren't on the best of terms at the moment, was enough to bully her out of her self-doubt. The affirmative nod from Fontaine bolstered her further.

Drawing in a deep breath then letting it out in a rush, Lila took center stage. "Where are we at on the BOLO?"

"All law enforcement agencies are notified and on alert," Fontaine said. "The statewide alert system has been activated, and all radio stations and social media outlets are reporting it. We're going to need more hands on deck when the phone calls start coming in."

"Young can help field calls," Lila said as she moved to the coffee station. "Georgia, call Alexis and have her come in early."

She sniffed the coffee in the pot. It smelled fresh. Lila filled the largest and widest mug full then poured a generous amount of sugar and cream in the coffee. Liquid energy.

She turned back to the group. "We still aren't sure that Andrea didn't escape capture. We're going to need better equipment than our two feet to get around in that timber to see if we can locate her."

"You're not going to get ATVs around back there. The terrain is rough and any paths that are there will be narrow because the trees are dense. You'll need horses for that," Young said.

Lila winced at the thought of getting on the back of a horse, something she had never done in her entire life. "Who's willing to do that?"

"Meyer and I will go," Fontaine said. "I've called in some local guys who have horses trained for search and rescue." He checked his watch. "They're planning to meet us at Young's."

The sheriff's office door opened, and the leading lady herself exited with her faithful companion at her side. "I've sent Erin home with strict instructions to stay there." Bentley plopped down in the center of the bullpen; Elizabeth headed for the coffee station and poured herself a cup. "We've got a few hours of reprieve."

"I don't know how long we can keep Abbott or any of the other busybodies out of our hair," Lila told her.

Elizabeth tipped her mug toward Lila. "Keep your hackles raised and your teeth bared and that should scare them away." She settled on a chair beside Georgia's desk.

"Let's piece this timeline together, starting with Kerri's discovery and go forward." Lila moved to the recently added dry-erase board. "Where's the sheriff's evidence box?"

"On your desk," Georgia said.

Fortifying herself with another gulp of her sugared caffeine, Lila faced the board with uncapped marker. "Have at it, people. We've got a girl to find and murderer to catch."

CHAPTER FIFTEEN

ELIZABETH WATCHED HER deputies ping-pong discoveries and ideas off each other. What a cohesive machine they had become in the last two years. Her hiring decisions had paid off in the extreme.

"Has anyone gotten the autopsy report from Dr. Remington-Thorpe?" Lila asked.

"We did." Elizabeth pointed to Kyle.

He produced the report, handing it over to Lila. While the deputy detective read through the findings, Elizabeth closed her eyes and leaned back in her chair.

She'd overdone it. No, she *was* overdoing it. If she didn't take a step back and rest, she was going to end up as everyone was warning, in a bad way, possibly with an infection, and laid up far longer than expected. She steeled herself. Elizabeth wouldn't be dragged down by something as trivial as fatigue or pain. Not when a life was at stake and another life had been snuffed out. He had killed before. Possibly twice. And Elizabeth was going to make damn sure he didn't get away to do it again.

Sensing his deep scrutiny, she met Rafe's gaze dead-on. The hard jawline and wrinkled corners of his eyes warned she would get a lecture the moment he had her alone. He could be pissed at her all he wanted. There was no way Rafe would argue Elizabeth out of continuing down this path. She focused on Lila.

"Dr. Remington-Thorpe is placing Kerri's death at least an hour prior to her discovery?" Lila closed the file. "That would put it happening at the same time I was in position. I didn't hear anything out there, and I was there for more than two hours before Andrea showed up."

"You were also setting up your blind and making sure your car wouldn't be spotted by our partygoers," Kyle pointed out. "There was enough distance and timber to soften any sounds."

"I still would have heard something. My window was down, and it was quiet enough for sound to carry. You said she fought back—I should have heard her cry out."

Elizabeth sensed where this was going. If Lila ever believed for one minute that she could have saved Kerri and didn't, the guilt would destroy her already traumatized mind.

"Deputy Dayne, she was being strangled. I doubt she could make any sound. The ME said the force of the strangulation crushed her hyoid bone. I saw the bruising."

Lila stood there, silent, blinking. Elizabeth practically read her mind and prepared herself for the next question.

"Was it rape?"

"No." Kyle butted in before Elizabeth answered. "She'd had sex, but it's still undetermined with who."

"Lila," Elizabeth said softly. "If it's any consolation, Olivia firmly believes Kerri was killed at a different location but left where her body was found. It could have been a mile or more away from where you were parked."

Lila's features took on the deep wrinkles and squinty eyes

she got when she was deep in thought, mulling over a puzzle.

"It could be where her boots were left. And maybe her phone. I need to get back out there and search."

"We're both going," Kyle piped up.

"I agree. You both head out there," Elizabeth stated. "Widen your search. Rafe and Deputy Meyer will handle the search efforts for Andrea."

"What about Hillary Peterson?" Lila asked.

"Hillary showed up while I was at the morgue. She's in no position to be answering anyone's questions," Elizabeth said.

"Not to mention she flew out of there and no one saw where she went," Kyle added.

"We're going to have to do what we can with what little we've got," Elizabeth said.

Lila frowned and then reached into her pants pocket to pull out her phone. Her frown deepened as she stared at the screen. "I think I need to take this." She flipped the dry-erase board over to protect the information on it from unwanted eyes and headed into the hallway.

Elizabeth turned to Kyle, but he shrugged, then followed Lila. Those two had their orders. They'd get to it soon.

Elizabeth lofted her now-empty coffee mug. "The rest of you have your assignments, too."

Rafe lingered next to her while Brent gathered a few things for his trek out to search for Andrea.

"Before you read me the riot act for disobeying doctor's orders, let me remind you, it's going in one ear and right out the other." Grinding her teeth to prevent any show of pain, she stood. "You and I both know in some way I'm going to pay for this. I'm willing to take the risk."

Sighing, Rafe lifted his hand toward her cheek, hesitated—probably rethinking his tender actions in mixed company—then lowered it. "Slow down. Rest when you can. Got it?"

"I can't make any promises, but I'll try."

The undersheriff and his deputy exited the bullpen, leaving Elizabeth with Georgia and Deputy Young.

"Corey, how's the hand?"

The dark-eyed woman lifted her bandaged hand. "Numb." She gave a one-shoulder shrug. "I've had worse."

Elizabeth smiled. "You get bored, you let me know."

"You're not exactly in any position to allow that," Georgia admonished.

"Yes, mother hen."

Georgia glowered at Elizabeth then her features lifted. "Marnie, what brings you here?"

What was her sister doing here in the middle of the day?

Marnie strode toward Elizabeth. "We need to talk." She took hold of Elizabeth's elbow and tugged her into her office.

"Excuse me? This morning, I got the distinct impression this is the exact opposite of what you wanted to do," Elizabeth said as her sister closed the door, then locked it.

Marnie released her hold and headed for the second door. "I can't afford to have unexpected visitors." She flipped the dead bolt, then turned to Elizabeth. "Sit down before you pass out."

Glaring at her baby sister, Elizabeth did as commanded, taking her chair behind the desk. "This better not be a chewing-out session because I'm here and not at home."

Waving her hand wildly, sending the plastic black, orange, and white bangles on her wrist into a clattering racket, she crossed the office floor in three strides. She gripped the armrests of Elizabeth's chair and bent down to meet her eye to eye. "What is going on?"

"I can't tell you what's going on. You know that."

"I had an unpleasant confrontation with Hillary an hour ago. She was screaming in hysterics. Sera had to slap her in the face to stop her and then took her home."

Elizabeth stilled. She studied her sister's features, seeing past the flashy makeup meant to disguise whatever secrets Marnie hid from her and the world, remembering the girl she used to be before Denise and Bre died.

"Why would Hillary need to confront you?"

Marnie pursed her bloodred lips then backed from the chair. "I have no idea. I couldn't make sense of what she was screeching about." She crossed her arms. "I'm just glad Kelley wasn't there."

"Because?"

Wonderland Alice in front of her did a fine imitation of the undead's inability to speak.

Elizabeth pushed out of her chair and shook a finger at her sister. "You come here to talk with me but refuse to talk. What the hell, Marnie?"

"You tell me what's going on. And I'll talk."

"This is an ongoing investigation with sensitive information. I. Can't. Talk. About. It."

Marnie snapped her arms at her sides. "I should have expected this from you." She shook her head, the black-and-white hair bobbing. "I should have never come." She about-faced and stomped to the hallway door.

"Marnie, really?"

"Yes, really, Elizabeth." She twisted the dead bolt. "Something horrible has happened, and I'm not about to be waylaid again." She threw herself through the doorway.

Elizabeth scrabbled out of her chair and hurried to the open door. "What do you mean again? Marnie!"

Her sister didn't so much as give her the bird as she marched outside and disappeared down the department steps.

"Damn it!" Elizabeth slapped the doorframe.

"Sheriff?"

Deputy Young poked her head around the corner at the end of the hallway. Shaking her head, Elizabeth waved off the deputy and returned to her office.

What the hell was Marnie talking about? Being waylaid again?

Elizabeth disengaged the lock on the main office door and swung it open. Georgia, standing at her post, frowned at Elizabeth.

"Ellie?"

"Don't bother, Georgia. I have no clue. Which seems par for the course on this whole situation."

Young held up a fresh mug of coffee. "Sisters. Am I right?"

Taking the mug from Young, Elizabeth managed a smile. "Right."

"DEPUTY DAYNE."

Lila watched Marnie hurry past as she made a beeline for the department steps. Kyle was coming down as Marnie went up.

"Deputy Dayne, you told me to call if anything came up," the voice on the other end of the connection said.

Lila couldn't place the voice. "I'm sorry. Who is this?"

"Allegra King. We met last night at my apartment."

"Allegra, I'm glad you called me. I need to—"

"Did someone kidnap Andrea?"

"Uh?" Lila bit her lip.

Kyle went to get into the driver's side, and she swatted him away. No way was his Viking ass getting into her seat and moving it back. With an eye roll, he moved to the opposite side of the car.

"Deputy Dayne, are you there?"

"Allegra, sorry. Where did you hear that about Andrea?"

Her question caught Kyle's attention, and he leaned on the car roof.

"Her mother called me."

This set Lila back on her heels. For someone who was a veiled racist, why was Erin O'Ryan calling Allegra? If Andrea was trying to protect her roommate from her parents, how did they even know about Allegra? Was Allegra lying about Erin calling her? The mysterious phone number Lila and Kyle had discovered in the girl's apartment came to mind. The owner of that number calling Allegra made more sense.

But how did that person know about Andrea?

"I'm confused," Lila muttered.

"Deputy, what is going on?" Allegra's panicked voice snapped Lila out of her wayward thoughts.

"It's a bit complicated. Can we meet up and speak in person?"

"I'm not coming back there. Not now. Not if they got Andrea."

"Allegra, please, you have to understand it from my position. I can't do my job to find Kerri's killer if I don't have one of the two people closest to her to speak with."

"I don't think you get it from my position. Kerri's dead. Andrea's been kidnapped. I'm next."

Kyle waved his hand, pointed behind her, and she turned.

Marnie was storming down the department steps and coming their way. Lila got inside the car, Kyle following suit.

"Why would you be next?" Lila pressed Allegra, watching Marnie rush to her car.

"Deputy, I shouldn't have called you. Sorry."

"Allegra, wait!" Her plea was met with dead air. "Damn it."

"Now what?" Kyle asked.

Lila stared at the number from her call history. "At least I have her phone number now. Doubt she'd answer if I called her back." She set her phone on the center console. "She claims Erin O'Ryan called her and told her about Andrea."

"You don't believe her," Kyle stated.

Marnie left the parking lot, heading back toward the center of town.

"Wonder what she was doing here?" Lila started the engine. "And, yes, I don't believe Allegra. I don't think Erin even knows that Allegra and Andrea are roommates."

"So, who would have told Allegra?"

"Good question."

CHAPTER SIXTEEN

L ILA WANTED A shower and a fresh uniform in the worst way. Time was of the essence. The clock was ticking, as they said. *They!* Who the hell were they?

Andrea, and now Allegra, kept referring to these infamous they, who scared the hell out of her. After Allegra's weird call, Lila highly doubted Andrea had been referencing her parents. As irritating as the two of them were, the O'Ryans didn't cross Lila as the type to elicit bone-rattling fear in a young woman who'd grown up under their thumb. No, those girls had been in with some not-so-great people. People who now had Andrea and doing God knew what to her.

Lila stopped the squad unit next to the crime scene tape strung between trees. Out here lurked key pieces of evidence that should lead them in the right direction. It just had to be out here.

"Do you still have the gum wrapper with the phone number?"

This was the first Kyle had spoken since they left the department parking lot. Lila had kept her own counsel as she drove, her mind spinning with more unanswered questions.

"Have I ever told you how much I hate Halloween?"

Kyle's gun holster squeaked against the leather seats.

"Once or twice."

"Worst night of the year if the weather was good. 'Course in Chicago, every night is the worse night, despite the weather." Lila canted her hips up and reached inside her pants pocket. She pulled out the untainted wrapper she'd kept, along with the phone she found at Young's, and held them aloft between her and Kyle. "Whatever those three girls are, were in to, is going to come from these finds. Between the number, this phone, and the drugs, something bad is going down or went down."

Kyle took the phone from her. "Where'd this come from?"

"I found it at Young's house. I think it's Andrea's. It had that number in the call history."

"Did you try calling it again?"

"Yes."

"If that's evidence, why are you carrying it around in your pocket? You're blowing our chance to nail someone to this." He cringed as his words hit him.

Lila decided to be the better woman in this case and let it slide. She took back the phone. "I'm getting a strong feeling this person isn't our killer."

"Doesn't matter. Whoever it is has connections to it and the criminal activity behind it." Kyle's eyes brightened. "I've narrowed down a few people I know for a fact chew cinnamon-flavored gum and prefer that particular brand."

"We'll circle back to it." She popped the center console and placed the items inside, then snapped the lid shut. "We've got work to do out here."

"Lila." The contrition in his voice made her pause exiting

the vehicle. "I am sorry."

She wanted to demand what he was sorry for. Stir him up. Keep the fight going. Why? She didn't know. This wasn't territory she'd ever tread before. People, especially men she slept with, didn't apologize to her. They didn't give a damn about her feelings. All her life, Lila was someone to be used and abused. The only person who'd ever done the exact opposite, made her feel like a voice to be heard and a woman to be respected, was dead.

Wrong—there was one other person. Sheriff Benoit. From day one, Elizabeth had shown Lila nothing but respect and care, despite Lila's attempts to sabotage her.

Staring at Kyle, she realized it was actually two people.

"Wow. Guess my word doesn't mean a damn thing." He went to leave the car.

Lila reached out and snagged his arm. "You're wrong."

He eased back, staring at her.

"It does mean something. Unfortunately, it's tacked onto another issue. We have to refrain from letting our relationship cross wires with the job. Our personal lives can't get in the way."

"You saying I shouldn't be here because of us and my sister?"

"No, I'm saying to box it up, Viking, and set it aside. Men are supposed to compartmentalize, so this should be easy for you."

"The experts don't know what they're talking about," he groused.

"Make it work. I need you at your best." She might regret these next words if they backfired. "Bre needs you at your best."

He blinked a few times, looked out the windshield, then back at her. His movements were quick as he reached up between them, cupped the back of her neck, and dragged her over the console to claim her mouth.

Lila didn't resist. She'd been craving this from him for the last eighteen hours. If she were honest, getting thoroughly kissed was a way better apology accepted method than uttering the words. Something could be said for the whole kiss and make up.

Kyle broke from the kiss first and pressed his forehead to hers. "We better get out there and work or I won't be held responsible for my actions if we stay here."

Lila smiled, shoving at his chest. "There's no room in this car with your hulking figure."

"Good thing you're tiny."

She snarled at him, biting his lip playfully. "I might be tiny, but I can still take you any day of the week. Let's go."

They geared up, donning bright orange vests and ball caps for hunters to spot them, doused themselves in an all-natural bug and tick repellent, then headed for the taped-off scene. It was still bow-hunting season in Iowa and neither Lila nor Kyle wanted an arrow shot at them. Though Fontaine had put out a warning to the local DNR to keep hunters away from this area, they never could be too safe. Some of the locals had a thing for not being told where they could and couldn't go during bow season, especially when it could mean losing that perfect deer.

Blood from the dead coyotes had attracted a horde of different species. Scavenging birds, some here to take advantage of the bug smorgasbord, took flight, settling in the tree limbs high above.

"How do you want to do this?" Kyle asked, adjusting the weight of his pack on his shoulder.

"We'll start at the point where her body was, walk out about ten paces, and work our way west. We've got to get past all the foot traffic from the techs."

"Looking for?"

"His exit point. After he killed her and brought her here, he went somewhere. It wasn't past me." Lila swatted away a fly buzzing her face. "Keep your eyes open for the unusual."

Giving each other about five yards of distance between them, they paced off from the yarn-strung stakes marking the area where Kerri had lain, keeping their backs to the point where they had entered the scene. Lila tugged her ball cap up to see better under the brim. She and Kyle carried cameras, primed and ready for photos.

Unlike earlier, when she was barreling through the woods near Young's house, Lila was taking her time. Examining the ground, the foliage, and the tree trunks for signs of passage. Most of the ground was covered in debris from the autumn shed. Dirt poked through the leaves and twigs in places. Occasionally, Lila would use the zoom function on the camera in certain spots.

She paused sixty paces from her starting point and looked back. She could just see the stakes. Far to her left, Kyle halted and squatted. He lifted his camera and took a photo.

"Do you have something?"

He studied the picture and shook his head, then rose to

his towering height. "Keep going." He checked his watch. "We should shift to the south in about twenty minutes, then work our way back to our starting point."

She gave him a thumbs-up and continued on. This part of the job was painstaking and tedious but necessary. Her success with past homicide investigations stemmed back to her tenacity at combing the crime scene for every detail. A fact, she'd noted, that had been sorely missing in the case files for Denise Russell and Brendette Lundquist. Either it came from piss-poor work ethic on the department's part or, as Elizabeth was bound to believe, a cover-up to benefit the killer or killers.

Leaves rustled. She glanced over at Kyle, noticing he, too, had stopped. Both reached for their side arms, drawing the weapons silently.

There was a slight breeze today, but this far into the woods one couldn't feel it. Lila peered at the treetops. They were still. She scanned the perimeter, her hyperaware senses and a deeply buried thread of panic kicking into overdrive.

She wasn't alone. Kyle was here. *Remember that.*

Closing her eyes, she drew in a long, deep breath, and let it out slowly. Her heart eased off its race to flee and her body lost some of its tension. When she checked on Kyle again, he was several feet ahead of her, walking cautiously forward into the higher weeds.

"Careful of poison ivy," she hissed.

He swiped at her and kept going, lifting his side arm higher. To hell with it. She followed, her own firearm lifted. It didn't take her long to catch up with him as they forged a path through the dry weeds.

A clank echoed through the trees, freezing them in place.

"Which way did that come from?" she whispered.

Kyle lowered his weapon and straightened. This was his territory. He was a hunter himself and in his element out here in the middle of nowhere. After waving her closer to him, he pointed in the direction they were going.

Lila stuck close, keeping her free hand on his back and checking their six as they crept between towering ash trees and low, dragging cedars. There was another clank. Kyle came to a halt.

"It sounded like it came from that direction," Lila whispered, pointing to their left.

"Everything echoes badly out here," he whispered. "Take a knee."

Settled on one knee, she glanced around. They were far from the taped-off area and the car. Beads of sweat slithered along her temples and between her breasts. Between the vest and the pack on her back, she was roasting.

"Now what?" she asked.

Kyle pressed a finger to his lips then cupped his ear.

Lila cupped her ear and strained to listen. After a moment, she finally heard what Kyle must have picked up on, the swish and slide of fabric and the tinny sounds of metal. Seconds later, another clank.

Without a word, he pointed to their left and motioned for her to follow. They were twenty paces from their resting point when she spotted it.

She tapped his shoulder and pointed at the large gash through the underbrush. A frown marring his handsome face, Kyle veered from his path. Lila exchanged her sidearm for her camera.

Here among the pines and cedars, a young woman had fallen, crushing the undergrowth beneath her body. The churned ground exposed the signs of a struggle. Bits of black and red gauzy fabric clung to stubbed weeds and twigs. As Lila snapped her photos, a glint in the still-standing weeds opposite her caught her eye.

"I see something," she whispered, then took a wide berth of the area.

Careful to avoid disturbing any more of the scene, she slinked through the weeds to the spot where the glint had come from. She parted the brittle yellowed foliage to expose a single, black knee-high boot.

"It's one of the missing boots." She took pictures, noting the zipper looked damaged.

"Do you see the other one?"

As she swept the grasses and weeds aside, another clank echoed through the trees.

"Found it," Kyle said, pointing a few feet to his left. "I think the boots were torn off her—the zipper is barely attached to this one."

"What do you bet the killer was looking for something she might have stuffed inside?"

"I'd say the probability of that is high, considering we can't find her phone."

Lila let him photograph the second boot while she removed a large evidence bag from her pack. With the boots safely ensconced in the bag and in her pack, she pulled out a roll of bright pink marking tape and attached several layers to the trees around the spot.

As they worked to document the spot, more clanks echoed through the trees.

"We need to find out what that it is," she hissed.

"Give me a second." He pulled out a map and some instrument. After a few moments of jotting something on the map, he shoved them back into his pack. "Let's go."

"What was that?" she asked as they once more drew their service pistols and headed toward the clanking sounds.

"Land nav. In case someone removes those markers and disturbs everything to erase the scene, I can get us back to this exact spot."

Lila peered back over her shoulder. "He must have been in an all-fired hurry to not clean up his mess."

"He had to get rid of the body." Kyle lowered his body, indicating for Lila to do the same. "Maybe because there were other people around."

"Andrea for one."

The clanking grew in frequency and louder. Kyle slowed their pace to a snail's crawl. By now, they both gave up worrying about slithering and crawling predators and vines that left behind a sticky, itchy payload. Movement between the trees and grasses pulled them up, and they both dropped to a knee. Lila landed on a rock and ground her molars to avoid crying out at the pain.

Before them was a large clearing, ringed by bare-limbed trees and trampled grass. In the center of the clearing was a burned patch, possibly a fire pit, with a wide swath of dirt circled by tree stumps and logs laying horizontally on stumps. Two men lumbered about the area, picking up metal poles and dropping them on a flatbed trailer. The trailer was loaded down with piles of canvas, wood planks, and more of the metal poles. One of the men, large and overweight, wearing dirty overalls and a disgusting ball cap, stopped to hock a snot wad.

Lila gagged and turned away. "Do you know them?" she whispered.

"It's Orville Patterson and Jim Thurnhall. Jim's the scrawny one. They're bottom feeders. Worse than the Kauffmann family ever was."

The two men grabbed the last of the poles and chucked them onto the trailer.

"Looks like they're breaking camp."

Kyle holstered his weapon and took up his camera, snapping pictures as fast as he could while Orville and Jim strapped down the contents of the flatbed.

Lila, keeping her sidearm in hand, checked their six. Assured they weren't being routed by an unknown assailant, she duck-waddled over to Kyle's right and jotted down the plate number of the trailer. She kept watch while Kyle continued to take photos.

Once the men were finished, they climbed into the large, silver Chevy Silverado. Jim drove the diesel truck out of the clearing and down a dirt track. The track had been well used, leaving a cutting path through the grass and timber.

Long after the sound of the diesel motor faded, she and Kyle moved from their hiding spot.

"How far do you think this is to the spot where Kerri was killed?" Lila asked as she wandered the perimeter of the clearing.

"I'm not sure. I'll have to measure." Kyle looked back the

way they came and froze. "Lila."

Her muscles seized at the timbre in his voice. She rotated to look where he was staring.

High above where they had hunched down, dangling by its neck in front of the boughs of two statuesque cedars was the effigy of a man dressed as a king. The thing looked like it had been set on fire before it was left there, scorch marks marring the once purple cloak and melting the plastic crown to the distorted head.

"Kyle, what does that mean?"

He lifted his camera and clicked a few shots. "I don't know."

CHAPTER SEVENTEEN

ELIZABETH HAD RUN out of drivers. So screw it. She would drive herself and Bentley to the scene Lila called in. Georgia had managed to rouse Alexis and get her in to help man the phones ringing off the hook, leaving Georgia to mother Young—whose hand bothered her enough that she was feeling ill, she didn't put up her normal tough-girl fuss. Georgia might be a decade older than Elizabeth, but that didn't slow Georgia down one bit.

Before she left—after much arguing from Georgia that it was a bad idea for her to drive—Elizabeth called Fitzgerald back to duty. She needed more manpower if things like this kept occurring, but there was no way she'd ever convince the county to part with more money to pay for more deputies. The powers that be had a huge fit when she pressed to hire Deputy Young more than a year ago. No amount of begging and pleading would gain her any favor. Elizabeth was lucky to get what she got.

Driving to the scene was a bit tricky with her still-tender abdomen. She took it easy and didn't make any sudden movements. Thankfully, she didn't have to turn herself in for driving under the influence, as the narcotics had long burned out of her system.

She slowed the Interceptor to a crawl as she passed the

waving yellow crime scene tape marking the area Kerri's body had been discovered. Rage burned hot in Elizabeth. She pointed the SUV away from the scene and continued along the gravel road.

Two and a half miles later the road would curve to the north and keep going toward the tiny, unincorporated town of Soap Creek. Elizabeth navigated the all-wheel drive vehicle off the gravel and on to a wheel-rutted path going back into the trees. This part of the county wasn't traveled much. No one lived back here. It was all timber and hay fields. Perfect place to do a lot of illicit activities where no one was the wiser. Or so those asshats thought.

She was all too familiar with this area. Had spent a lot of her free time during her teenage years back here partying and getting to know her boyfriend, Joel Fontaine, on an intimate level. This area had a history of teenage rebellion dating back to Elizabeth's grandparents' time. The ancient bar known as the Dew Drop Inn in Soap Creek had supplied the rebels with their bootlegged liquor then. Tradition hadn't stopped for the newer generation; they were just as apt or better with their technological upgrades to carry on the parties. No amount of change in the sheriff's department would deter them.

Elizabeth parked the SUV next to Lila's car at the edge of a wide clearing. Leaning into the steering wheel, she glared at the scene laid before her. She hadn't put two and two together. Hadn't paid close attention to the details when Lila and Rafe had relayed them. The rage she'd squelched moments earlier resurfaced.

This site of so many fun after-dark parties was stained in

blood.

Bentley scrabbled up on the console between the seats and laid her head on Elizabeth's shoulder, her warm nose nudging her owner's cheek. Elizabeth reached up and buried her hand in the dog's silky fur, tilting her head closer to her companion's.

"I'll be okay, Bentley." Elizabeth closed her eyes. "I'll be just fine."

She gave her collie one more good ear scratch, killed the engine, rolled down all of the windows, and slid out of the SUV. Bentley hopped the console and stood on the driver's seat, the front half of her body poking out of the open window. She wouldn't leave the car unless commanded to, but she certainly wanted to sniff out all the interesting smells wafting about back here deep in the woods.

So far, the only deputies on scene were Lila and Kyle. Neither one of them looked pleased that she was here.

"Did you seriously drive yourself here?" Lila demanded.

"How else was I going to get here? I'm not on anything more powerful than ibuprofen."

"Sheriff, we would have given you a detailed report on this," Kyle said.

"I don't give two shits about reports." She walked past them. "I need to see this for myself."

The two followed her down the slight incline into the heart of this hidden campground. Areas where the grass had been trampled underfoot were good indications of entry and exit points to shelters, probably some glorified tents if the canvas tarps and metal poles Lila and Kyle saw were anything to go by. The fire pit sat dead center of the trodden area, ringed by makeshift seating from tree stumps. Elizabeth could just see the outline of a circular object used to contain the fire among the ash.

"We found a spot between the trees we think was used as a potential outdoor bathroom," Kyle told her, pointing at the place. "The ground is drenched, likely from them dumping out the water used for a shower."

"Why break the camp down if this is all innocent?" Elizabeth muttered.

Lila touched her arm and guided her around. "Probably because of that." She pointed to the top of the trees.

The dangling dummy gave her heartburn. "Have you taken photos of it?"

"More than enough," Kyle answered.

"Cut it down. I want to see it."

The two glanced at each other before heading up to the tree line. While they worked to find the place where the rope was anchored, Elizabeth studied the campground with a more critical eye.

Her anger simmered as her mind took a wandering path of trying to make sense of what was before her. In twenty-five years, this place hadn't changed that much. With so few photos, and little to no evidence, she couldn't place Bre or Denise in this spot before. But now …

With a huff, she stomped back to the Interceptor. Bentley leaned forward as Elizabeth passed. She jerked open the back door, ignoring a twinge in her side, and grabbed out the evidence box she'd brought along, kicking the door shut before she walked back to the front of the SUV. She set the box on the ground and pulled out the files, her notes, and slapped them on the hood. As she rifled through them, she sensed a presence joining her.

"Sheriff?"

Elizabeth grabbed the photos she was digging for, rotated, and held them up in front of the campground. "Deputy Dayne, this is where my friend, Deputy Lundquist's sister, was found. Dead."

Lila took the photo from her and did her own study. The photo was taken with two inches of snow on the ground, but it was the exact spot. Even the trees on the edge of the frame were the same trees.

"I was certain of it when I pulled up." Elizabeth turned back to the hood and opened Denise's file. "About two miles farther is where Denise Russell was killed by a truck." She removed the single photo left in the folder and handed it to Lila. "If we were working on shaky ground before in connecting these twenty-five-year-old cases with your new one, it's gone now."

Lila shifted Elizabeth to the side and placed the photos back in the files, then picked up Bre's and read the reports.

Kyle, lugging the effigy, joined them. He laid the charred mannequin on the ground, then held up a crumpled sheet of paper. "This was pinned to the front. Couldn't read it from down here."

You're next.

"Who's next?" Elizabeth reached for the sheet.

Drawing it back, Kyle shook his head. "You don't have gloves on."

Right, preservation of evidence. She tucked her clenched fist under her arm. "Someone went to a lot of trouble to dress up a mannequin like a king, set it on fire until things melted and burned, then strung it up in the trees. Here. With a note that it's obvious the intended target did not read or cared to read, because it was still in the trees."

"Someone has a good idea who the killer is." Lila laid the file on the SUV hood. "Someone besides you suspects what really happened here twenty-five years ago and last night."

"And they didn't speak up last time. Probably couldn't have. This time, all bets are off," Kyle added. "They're going to expose the culprit."

"Sheehan," Elizabeth snarled.

"Don't jump to that conclusion, Sheriff," Lila snapped.

"It's the only conclusion."

"You get tunnel vision on this and you're going to make mistakes." Lila's light brown eyes turned steely. "This is why you shouldn't be involved in this investigation. It's why I didn't want you involved, because you will not think objectively, will let your emotions cloud your reasoning. If you run down that path, I will pull rank again."

Her deputy detective might have suffered at the hands of evil men, but she still maintained a will of iron. This fact alone was catalyst in Elizabeth hiring her. Why she had surrounded herself with her crew in the sheriff's office. They weren't afraid to question her authority. Two years into this position, Elizabeth was still a rookie when it came to procedure and investigation. Lila and Kyle were the seasoned veterans.

Their radios crackled to life. Georgia's voice broke through. "Deputy Lundquist, report."

Frowning, he grabbed his radio. "This is Lundquist.

What is it, Georgia?"

"Hon, I'm sorry to be the bearer of bad news, but you're needed at home. EMS is enroute. They said your sister has had an accident."

"Shit!"

Lila grabbed her radio. "Georgia, I'm sending the sheriff with him."

"I figured as much. I have Deputy Fitzgerald enroute to your last known location."

"Copy."

Elizabeth moved to gather the files.

Lila grabbed her hand and stopped her. "Leave them here. Get in." She shoved the files back in the box and dragged it away from the SUV. "Kyle, drive with caution—you don't need to get into an accident."

He blinked at her, then nodded.

Elizabeth, her fury having drained from her body leaving her exhausted and hurting, gaped at Lila. "Lila—"

"You don't need to apologize. I know exactly what's going through your head." She escorted Elizabeth to the passenger seat. "Go with him. Keep him calm."

Once Elizabeth was seated and buckled in, Kyle backed out of the area. Elizabeth watched Lila's figure shrink, then Kyle swung the Interceptor's big rear around and drove forward.

When the front tires touched gravel, he flipped on the sirens and lights. Elizabeth checked on Bentley, who had not been in the SUV when it was on the way to an emergency. Smart dog was hunched down on the floorboard, staring up at Elizabeth with soulful eyes.

"Kyle, don't go to that place in your head."

"I'm trying not to, Ellie. But this is Freya we're talking about." He never took his eyes off the road. "She's a ticking bomb."

A ticking bomb who had a setback earlier today. Had it culminated into tragic consequences?

THEY ARRIVED AT the Lundquist farmstead in record time. Kyle killed the sirens but left the lights flashing. Along with the ambulance, a black, two-door sedan sat in the gravel drive. Elizabeth leaned closer to the dash.

"What is Marnie doing here?"

Kyle muttered—she didn't catch what—as he parked the Interceptor in the yard, out of the way of the EMS vehicle. Before Elizabeth could release the buckle, he was out of the SUV. Bentley hopped the console and was out the open driver's side door. The passenger door swung open as Elizabeth tried to grab the handle. Kyle beckoned for her to exit.

While she appreciated the deeply ingrained training to be a gentleman from men like Kyle, there came a point where it irked her to be coddled.

"Get inside," she barked.

Giving her an exasperated huff, he turned and raced to the wraparound porch.

Elizabeth slid out of the seat and stretched her back. Bentley, having done her business, loped over and sat at her feet. Patting her collie's head with one hand, Elizabeth gently massaged her midsection with the other.

"Let's go."

Once she mounted the steps to the porch, the voices inside ratcheted up. Bentley remained on the porch, out of the way, leaving Elizabeth to enter the fray alone.

"What the hell did you expect was going to happen?" Kyle bellowed.

"I had no choice!" Marnie shot back.

"Both of you knock it off!" Elizabeth cut in.

The two were facing off in the living room, an area that once had been the receiving parlor in this turn-of-the-century farmhouse. Movement in the next room, the large dining room, caught Elizabeth's eye. Marnie wasn't the only unexpected visitor at the Lundquist home. Seraphina stood out of the way of the medics, watching the whole ordeal. She shrugged when she met Elizabeth's eye.

The medics hovered around a lucid-looking Freya. They must have sedated her—it was the only explanation for her not to be flying into a panic. Her hair was in disarray, her shirt ripped and bloodied, and her black skirt had tears, revealing the white frothy material beneath, speckled with dirt and blood.

"Marnie, why the hell are you here?" Elizabeth glared at her sister.

Marnie looked as if she herself had waded through a battlefield, scratched, bloodied, clothing shredded and dirty, and her once-immaculate makeup smeared and ruined. Of the three women here, Seraphina was the lone woman who didn't appear to be scuffed up and battle worn. Sighing, Marnie dropped onto a chair and stared at Elizabeth.

Seraphina tiptoed out of the dining room to stand beside Marnie. She leaned down and said something to Marnie, then ducking her head, she exited the house.

Elizabeth watched the other woman head for Marnie's car. Once she was tucked inside the vehicle, Elizabeth looked to her deputy. "Kyle, see to your sister."

He opened his mouth, but she shook her head. Shutting his mouth with a click of his teeth, he went into the dining room with the medics.

Elizabeth jabbed a finger at her sister and pointed out the door. Then out the door she went, Marnie's sullen figure following. They strode to the far end of the porch to a sturdy bench that looked out at the harvested fields and timber surrounding the Lundquist farm. Kyle rented the ground out to a high school mate who farmed the next property over so he didn't have to worry about it. Kyle wasn't the agricultural type.

Elizabeth took a seat on the bench. Marnie chose to sit on the porch railing, her back to the corner support beam, outside leg propped on the rail. She was the picture of the rebellious teen Elizabeth remembered.

Bentley invaded Elizabeth's space, hopping up on the bench and lying across her lap.

"I don't understand why you're here."

Her sister shook her black-and-white head, keeping her gaze directed at the wide expanse of grass.

"Marnie." Elizabeth's voice could have snapped metal.

Shivering, Marnie redirected her gaze to Elizabeth. "What?"

"I want answers."

"So would I."

The rebuttal threw Elizabeth. She pressed against the bench backrest. "Come again?"

The back of Marnie's head banged into the post; she stared at the slatted porch roof. "I didn't do a thing to Freya. I found her like that."

Elizabeth leaned forward, squishing Bentley's head into her tender abdomen. "You found her like that? Why were you even here?"

Once more, her sister clammed up.

"Damn it, Marnie! You and Freya have history of some kind to the point she goes into hysterics whenever you're around. You don't happen to drive out here to see her, knowing she wants nothing to do with you, just because. And with Seraphina of all people, too."

Marnie swung around to face Elizabeth and came off the railing. "Freya called me here!" She flung up her arms then jerked them back to her sides. "Sera and I met back up, when out of the blue, Freya calls me. She's begging me to get to the farm. Something is going to happen. I told her to call Kyle, and she screamed for me to come. The phone went dead, and I raced over here. I found her out back, clutching a knife and having a meltdown. She was covered in blood, but it wasn't hers."

"Then how did you get like this?"

"I had to wrestle the knife from her. After I managed to do that, she attacked me." Marnie sagged against the railing. "She kept screaming over and over that he was back to get her."

"Who was back?"

Marnie shook her head. She covered her face with her hand and rubbed, letting out a frustrated groan. Dropping her hands, she looked up, her makeup even more smudged, creating a creepy image of Satan's bride. "I don't know who *he* is she was going on about."

"You hit her?" a deep voice shouted.

Elizabeth startled. Red-faced, Kyle stomped up to Marnie and tried to grab her arm. Everything moved quickly. Marnie caught his arm, flung him forward, then swung him around, tripping him over her foot. As Kyle went down on his knees, Marnie released his arm, then shoved him face forward to the porch floor, ramming her knee into his back, pinning him.

"What the hell!" Kyle fumed.

Bentley scrabbled off Elizabeth as she bolted to her feet. "Marnie!"

"I only hit your sister to knock her out and cease her hysteria. It was either that or put her in a chokehold, and I was not about to let her relive that trauma." Marnie pushed off Kyle and stood, backing away to let him roll over.

"What do you mean *relive her trauma*? What does a chokehold have to do with that?" he demanded from his seated position on the porch.

Marnie glanced at Elizabeth, her face a mask of stone. With another hard shake of her head, she walked past Kyle and headed for the steps.

"Marnie," Elizabeth called after her.

Her sister stopped and about-faced. "I'm done here." With that, she hopped off the porch and fast-walked to her car.

Kyle climbed to his feet and alongside Elizabeth watched Marnie tear out of the driveway and speed for the road.

"Where did she learn to do that?" he asked.

"I didn't know she could." Elizabeth stepped past him, moving to the front door. "We need to talk with Freya."

"She passed out. I'm sending the medics back."

"Was Marnie right, the blood on Freya isn't hers?"

"Other than the rips and tears on her clothes and a few scraps, she has no wounds. The blood isn't hers. The moment I get those clothes off her, I'm taking them to my lab to test it."

"Marnie said Freya called her here. Said something was going to happen."

Kyle rocked back on his heels. "Why didn't she call me?"

"Marnie told her to, but Freya insisted she come." Elizabeth shook her fuzz-filled head. "What in the hell is going on?"

"That's what I'd like to know."

CHAPTER EIGHTEEN

LILA CLIMBED TO her feet, brushing the dirt and debris from her hands and knees. She arched her spine, hoping to ease the tight muscles screaming in agony in her lower back. Evidence bags, lined up in a neat row, filled a plastic tote next to her leg. Since Kyle had torn out of here with Elizabeth, Lila had worked to process as much of the scene as she could alone. She still hadn't found Kerri's phone. Given the way her boots had been damaged, Lila suspected Kerri had hidden her phone in one of them and the killer had taken it. Which meant there was something on the phone the killer didn't want anyone to see.

The department radio remained silent with no updates on the search for Andrea or what had gone down at the Lundquist place. No one had called her either. Lila checked her cell again for missed messages or calls. Zero.

Across from the roped-off area, Fitzgerald inched along the weedy parts, checking for more evidence. He'd shown up mere minutes after the other two left. Lila put him to work helping her with marking places and photographing.

"I think I've got everything I can find," she said. "I'll let DCI comb over it to see if there's anything else."

He turned to her. Dark patches under his eyes spoke of no sleep. He'd admitted as much when he arrived to help her. Instead of resting, Fitzgerald spent his time chasing rumors and looking for Andrea, gaining no new intel on either front.

"Got a theory on this whole thing?" he asked.

It wasn't what he asked but how he asked it that set off a red flag for her. "Do you know something about this area?"

"I know just as much as you do." He shrugged. "Maybe a bit more."

Lila crossed her arms and tilted her chin down. "Like, how much is a bit more?"

Her probing brought out his obstinate side. "Cripes, woman, I know what everyone else in this damn county knows. This is party central when it comes to illicit activity." He angled his body and pointed a hair more northwest of the campground. "Not too far up this road is a backwoods bar that usually supplies the alcohol."

"Is there now? Funny how the sheriff didn't mention this tidbit."

"Probably because she was hopping mad this place was tied to Kerri's death." Fitzgerald gave her a slick grin. Yah, he knew he had her on the hook. "I also know a certain two individuals who like to frequent said bar. Hide out there, in fact."

"Ben, I don't have time for your games. Spit it out."

"You said Orville Patterson and Jim Thurnhall were the ones cleaning up. Someone had to have paid them real good money to make either of them work that hard." He checked his watch. "This time of the day, they're blowing that wad on food and beer."

Lila checked her watch and grimaced. It was nearly five.

She'd gone all day with no food, no sleep, and one miserly cup of coffee. Her stomach let out a loud, rumbling growl. Fitzgerald's grin widened.

"Fine. Show me this place."

LILA EXITED HER car, slamming the door shut and gaped at the leaning building before her. "What kind of redneck hell is this?" Better question, how had she never known about this place?

Fitzgerald rounded his Crown Vic and paused. "The kind that caters to a mean class of backwoods residents. The likes of which wouldn't give you the time of day."

Following him, she glared at the back of his head, wishing she could burn a hole right through him. "Won't our uniforms stir up trouble?"

He glanced over his shoulder. "Only if you make trouble."

Lila sniffed. Right now, she was starving, tired, and running dangerously low on patience—there was no doubt she'd cause trouble. Making nice with the locals was Elizabeth's territory.

Problem was, there were no vehicles in the gravel lot. Not even a sign of the truck with the flatbed the two men had used to haul away the tents. Didn't look promising for Fitzgerald's theory the men were here drinking and eating.

A wooden sign hanging by the ancient door declared the establishment's name, hand carved deep into the warped and faded wood. DEW DROP INN EST. 1874. Certainly explained the tilt to the building. Through the sharp, crisp scent of deep autumn timber, Lila made out the warm aroma of aged wood and ancient bite of burned tobacco.

"Seriously, Fitzgerald, where are we? I've never been out here."

He peered through the opaque, probably lead, window to his right. "That's because Sheriff didn't see fit to allow you out this way. She sent me and Fontaine to cover it."

The revelation that Elizabeth had steered Lila away from patrol areas should have burned, but Lila found it relieving. Some parts of the county still haunted her.

"What is it?"

He craned his head in her direction; a lock of his blonde hair—long overdue for a trim—fell across his forehead, giving him a boyish look Lila hadn't seen in the man before. "This here is Soap Creek. One of the last unincorporated towns left in Eckardt County. Dew Drop Inn is its only functioning business, good and bad." He pointed at her. "Locals come here to hide from the likes of you."

Lila narrowed her gaze. "The likes of me meaning the outsider? Or cop?"

Fitzgerald gave her a lopsided grin carrying a hint of malice. "Take your pick." He gripped the old-fashioned handle and shoved the door inward.

Biting her tongue, Lila followed him inside. The aged building managed to transport her back in time to the days when sawdust covered the floor, patrons spit their tobacco juice in spittoons, and bartenders kept a sawed-off behind the bar. Except the bar itself had caught up with modern times by hosting three large HD TVs and kept their hardwood floors, while scuffed and scratched, clean and sawdust free. A half-enclosed staircase loomed to her left, probably leading to the owner's residence—Lila hoped that was what it was for and not other illegal matters. The main floor of the bar was open, broken up by random exposed support beams for the upper floor. Small tables and old high-back chairs scattered over the breadth of the establishment.

Lila caught a musky hint in the air. She drew in a breath, and the musk turned sharp, almost skunk-like. "They do realize joints are still illegal," she said under her breath.

"Do you see anyone smoking them?" Fitzgerald asked.

"I don't see a single person. It's after five p.m. and there's not a soul in here. For a place that supposedly serves food, where the hell is everyone?" Lila looked back at the door. "I don't like this."

The heavy clop of boots on wood jolted her. A pair of gleaming, pointed-toe boots emerged on the staircase, followed by the jean-clad legs of a man who had kept the entire sheriff's department on its heels. As he stepped down off the last plank, disgraced ex-sheriff Kelley Sheehan unwrapped a plastic-encased toothpick, flicked the wrapper away, and stuck the sliver of wood in his mouth.

"Deputy Fitzgerald. Deputy Dayne. Picture me completely surprised to find you darkening the doorstep of this fine establishment." He glared at her as he clamped down on the toothpick. "A place that isn't open. Now leave."

"Not in my nature to take orders from a man of questionable morals."

Sheehan chuffed, his head wobbling with his amusement. He shook a finger at Lila. "See, that right there is why

I like you, Deputy Dayne."

"Where's Leo?" Fitzgerald asked.

"Doing what every good bartender and owner does. I really don't know, and I really don't care."

"If this place isn't open, why are you here?" Lila crossed her arms. "This isn't your usual haunt."

Sheehan wandered behind the bar. "Correct, this isn't my normal evening ritual." He picked up a half-full bottle of Jack and a whiskey tumbler. "Would the two of you care for a slug?" He lofted the bottle.

"We're good," Lila answered, pointing at their uniforms. "We're on duty."

"By the looks of both of you, neither of you have gone off duty." After pouring himself two fingers, neat, Sheehan made himself at home where he stood. "Now, Deputy Dayne, to answer your question. I'm here because I have a stake in this here establishment."

"Yet you're rarely, if ever, here."

"Too far from the hubbub," Fitzgerald muttered.

Sheehan saluted the deputy with his glass. "Sheriff doesn't use you enough, Fitzgerald."

"He's used plenty." Lila closed the gap between her and the bar and leaned on the gleaming top. "What are you doing here, Sheehan?"

Enjoying his whiskey and staring at her over the brim of the tumbler was his response.

The crack of a door and the lumbering steps of two came from the back of the bar. Lila glanced at Sheehan and then pushed past Fitzgerald. Her fellow deputy grabbed her arm just as the two men she came to see waddled into the main area. The larger of the two pulled up short at the sight of Lila and Fitzgerald and slapped a beefy hand into his partner's chest, bringing him to a halt.

"Orville. Jim. I see you finished early," Sheehan said, swaggering over to the men.

The larger one, Orville, eyed Lila, a lecherous smile turning up the corners of his red, chafed mouth. "Sure did, Sheriff." His pig-eyed gaze drifted to Fitzgerald. "What's he doin' here?"

Sheehan stepped between Lila and the two roughnecks. "They came to discuss some things with me."

Fitzgerald flung Lila's arm away and he stalked up to Sheehan. "You're still keeping company with those two?"

"They have their uses." His gaze narrowed as he pulled the toothpick from his mouth and pointed it at Fitzgerald's nose. "Both are loyal to me. Something you fall short of."

"I don't side with no one except myself."

"As Elizabeth is learning all too harshly." Sheehan jabbed the toothpick into his mouth once more.

Orville stepped around Sheehan's side. Hooking his thumbs behind the filthy coveralls, Orville looked Lila up and down. "She don't look like your type, Benny-boy. Thought you were into the weirdos."

Fitzgerald's features hardened, his eyes darkened.

"Orville." Sheehan's voice was like the whack of a gavel. "I'd much appreciate it if you and Jim would hightail it on out of here while we three talk."

The fat man sneered, then slapped his partner's shoulder and the two of them started to turn.

"No, you're staying right here," Lila commanded. "I've

got questions for the two of you to answer."

Sheehan blinked at Lila. She suppressed the urge to flash a cunning grin at him. Oh, if she could read his mind. Bet those scheming cogs were spinning into overdrive, trying to figure out what she was up to.

Fitzgerald took a step to the side, a move meant to hem the men in. Say what you would about him, Fitzgerald certainly knew when his skills as an LEO were needed.

Jim, the slim one, glanced at Fitzgerald, then to Lila, then to his buddy. Caution reined this one in. Smart man.

Orville, on the other hand, decided to play a card that had never gone over well with Lila. Drawing in his sagging gut, he resumed his thumbs hooked behind the overalls and leered at her. "Just who do you think you are, li'l missy, to be ordering us around?"

"She'll be a big pain in your ass if you cross her," Fitzgerald remarked.

Orville's face flushed red, his pig eyes went mean as he took a step toward Fitzgerald. "Why, you little—"

Sheehan smacked a hand against Orville's arm. "Keep it to yourself." He tilted his head, studying Lila, then slowly shifted the toothpick to the opposite corner of his mouth. "This here is Deputy Detective Lila Dayne."

Something akin to recognition passed through Jim's eyes. "Wasn't she the gal that done killed a serial killer?"

"That would be her," Fitzgerald remarked.

Lila shot an unamused look his direction, but the ire fell flat on the man. He simply ignored her by keeping his eyes on the three men.

Orville sniffed. "There's no way this half-pint was able to

take down no grown man."

"Don't matter the size of the woman," Sheehan said. "It's about the size of the fight in her. You two boys need to take a seat. Let's hear what the good detective has to ask."

Jim didn't have to be asked twice. He planted himself on a barstool. Orville remained rooted where he stood, fingers stroking the wide denim straps, eyeing Lila.

"I asked nicely the first time, Orville. I won't repeat myself again."

The cold, dark tone in Sheehan's voice snapped the other man out of his stupor. Orville peered at the former sheriff then sheepishly waddled over to a stool beside Jim.

"Ask away, Deputy Dayne."

Lila met Fitzgerald's gaze. He sniffed, shaking his head, then stepped back toward the door to act as sentry.

"I think it best if you'd exit the bar, Mr. Sheehan."

The old man chuckled before he tossed back the rest of the whiskey. He slapped the tumbler on the bar top. "No need to stand on formalities." He nodded at the two men. "Might be best for me to stick around."

"So you can control what they can and cannot say to me? I think not."

"Sheriff stays," Orville asserted, crossing his arms.

"He's not the sheriff," Fitzgerald said from his spot by the door. "Hasn't been for a damn long time."

Orville opened his mouth, but Sheehan whacked his arm to shut him up.

"Look, Deputy Dayne, they can speak freely. Ask whatever questions it is you need to ask."

"You know what. No." She took a step toward Orville.

"We're going to do this at the department. Fitzgerald, escort Mr. Thurnhall to your car."

"I ain't goin' nowhere," Orville barked, scrabbling off the stool like a panicked raccoon.

"Deputy Dayne." Sheehan stepped between her and Orville, his hands up. "Lila. I would think after the assistance I've given you, I'd have garnered some kind of favor."

"I don't work on bribes and favors."

"That might be so, but had it not been for me, Sheriff Benoit would have never found you in time."

Lila clenched her jaw, grinding her molars at the unbidden memory. *Pouring rain beating against her body as she cradled the lifeless body of the man she'd thought of as a father, watching as a killer came at her with a knife.*

Lila jolted herself back to the present. "Any favors you've garnered are in debt to the sheriff." She glared at Sheehan. "Not me." She pointed at Orville and Jim. "Either they come with us to the department to discuss what it is I witnessed a few hours ago or you mosey on out that door and keep your nose out of official deputy business."

"What do you mean *you witnessed?*" Sheehan asked.

Lila crossed her arms.

Not getting the answer he wanted, Sheehan looked to the two men. "You know what she's talking about?"

The two looked at each other, then Sheehan, shaking their heads and shrugging. Apparently, that was not the answer Sheehan was looking for.

A dark, ugly expression came over him. "What did you two do?" he said in a low, lethal voice.

The men's faces went pale, their eyes widened. Orville's

throat bobbed. Unable to meet Sheehan's stare, he lowered his gaze.

Flummoxed by this shift in the ex-sheriff's demeanor, Lila took a step back. A male presence just to the right of her shoulder made her stiffen. Fitzgerald's hand clasped on her wrist. Of the two of them, Fitzgerald was the only one privy to Sheehan's mercurial moods.

"Know what, Deputy Dayne, you can have them." Sheehan bypassed her for the door. "Haul their sorry assess to the courthouse and read them the riot act. Whatever these lazy sacks of shit have done probably deserves a night in lockup. I wash my hands of them." With that, he quit the bar, slamming the ancient door in his wake.

Orville and Jim hopped off their stools, whining at the rattling door. Fitzgerald demanded they shut the hell up.

When Lila was able to find her tongue, she grabbed her fellow deputy's arm. "Follow him."

He blinked at her a few times, then his eyes lit up as he realized what she was ordering. "Keep your cell handy."

Left alone with the two men, Lila faced them, her hand settled on the butt of her sidearm. "What's it going to be? Here or lockup as Sheehan suggested?"

Their mouths opened and closed like drowning fish.

Lila's radio crackled to life. "All units be advised." Georgia's voice broke through the static. "Andrea O'Ryan has been located. Repeat. Andrea O'Ryan has been located. Report to headquarters."

Lila lowered the volume on her radio. "Hmm. Looks like department lockup it is."

CHAPTER NINETEEN

E LIZABETH DIDN'T WANT to leave Freya alone. Kyle didn't want to leave Freya alone. Once again, against doctor's orders, Elizabeth drove herself and Bentley back to the department. The darkening skies gave her ominous vibes.

She should be elated. Andrea had been found and by all accounts unscathed. What was off-kilter was how they found her. Rafe called Elizabeth after Georgia's all call. His single warning, "You're not going to like it," was enough to spin her wheels. For now, it wasn't mimicking the deaths of Denise and Brendette and the public relations nightmare those had become.

But how long before it did?

Elizabeth hadn't been here in the hours and days after their deaths, so she hadn't witnessed the initial investigations and the three-ring circus it turned into. She was living in North Carolina at the time while Joel, a freshly promoted army sergeant, was training for his next move up the regiment ladder. News of Bre's passing came two days later. It took another day for Elizabeth to gain the necessary leave since she worked on the base as a civilian contractor and get a plane ticket home. Joel wasn't allowed leave, and she firmly stood by her belief that if he'd been with her, things wouldn't have gone the way they did. She wouldn't have gone off the rails. Would have kept her cool.

The streetlamps flicked on when she pulled into the parking lot on the back side of the courthouse. Elizabeth eased the SUV into her spot then turned off the engine. Most of the deputies' units were here—Kyle's having been left at her house—save for one. Fitzgerald's was missing. Where was her wildcard deputy now?

Sitting here in her car, staring at the building's three-story brick and stone structure, she flashed back to the day she went toe-to-toe with the then sheriff. In her early twenties, ready to strangle the world into submission—little knowing how horrific the world would become a few short years later—Elizabeth wasn't about to let anyone, even a dirty, crooked man like the sheriff, get away with lying about something that was clearly a murder. In the background, standing a few feet away from his predecessor, Deputy Kelley Sheehan had watched her, never saying a word to back her up—to be frank, he never backed up the sheriff either—just stood there with that ever-present toothpick dangling from his smiling lips.

Elizabeth turned to Bentley as the dog propped her front paws on the dashboard. The red- and-white border collie tilted her head, staring at her owner under the glittering lamp light.

"Sheehan is involved in all of this. I can feel it in my bones." Elizabeth pressed a hand to her aching abdomen. "I just have to figure out how to get him to admit it."

When she pulled her hand away to open the door, she hesitated at the damp feeling on her fingertips. She lifted her hand into the light. Blood. Wincing, she lifted up her shirttail and peered at her stomach.

"Damn."

Spots of blood oozed from the sutures. She gently prodded the incisions, not able to tell if a stitch had ripped free, and managed to force more blood from the surgical area where they'd removed her appendix. Checking her shirt, she found bloodstains.

"Damn," she muttered again.

The moment she walked into that bullpen and Rafe saw the blood, there was going to be hell to pay. She glanced into the backseat and spied an Eckardt County Sheriff's jacket. That would help hide the tell-tale signs of her misdeeds.

Once she was out of the SUV, Bentley hopped down. The jacket zipped up high enough to hide the stains, Elizabeth, with Bentley at her side, hobbled to the department.

Raised voices were punctuated by shrill ringing phones. The noise echoed along the hall, battering Elizabeth's pounding head. Movement in the interview room stopped her in her tracks. While Bentley continued on to the bullpen, Elizabeth backpedaled and peeked inside the room.

Jim Thurnhall spotted her staring at him and, with a sheepish look, ducked his head.

"Jim, why are you in here?"

He tapped the tabletop with a dirty fingernail. "Uhh."

"Jim."

His head snapped up at her bark. "That Deputy Dayne dragged us in here."

"Us? Where's Orville?"

"He lipped off to her and she tossed his butt in a jail cell."

Shaking her head, muttering about stupid men and their stupid mouths, Elizabeth marched—despite her fatigue and pain—into the bullpen. All talk ceased, except for Georgia, who was speaking on the phone with Bentley sitting at her feet.

Elizabeth opened with, "Where's Deputy Fitzgerald?"

"Tailing Sheehan," Lila answered. She was kicked back in her chair, covered in grime, hair refusing to be contained by a hairband, fatigue dragging on her features while she plowed through a cheeseburger and fries. Lila swallowed, then swiped a ketchup blob from her mouth with a napkin. "I sent him on that mission."

"Why?"

"I'll explain later. You need to hear our illustrious under-sheriff's story first." She shoveled fries into her pie hole. "Where's Lundquist?" she asked around her food.

"Taking care of his sister." Seeing her deputy detective downing food made Elizabeth's belly ache. Except for the few bites of the goodies Marnie had brought her this morning, she hadn't eaten a lick.

As if reading her mind, and hearing her stomach, the nightshift dispatcher, Alexis, wandered over with a to-go carton from the sheriff department's favorite go-to restaurant, The Haven. "Here you go, Sheriff." She placed a plastic-covered fork on top of the biodegradable box. "Deputy Meyer stopped by your house and brought your meds." She held up a small grocery sack, the movement rattling the prescription bottles.

Sighing, Elizabeth took the items from the youngest member of her department. "Thanks." The tantalizing aroma of sweet tomatoes and pungent Romano cheese teased her nose and her stomach clenched in anticipation. This had to be The Haven's famous spaghetti and meatballs. Oh, how Elizabeth loved her crew. They knew her well.

"Sit down. Eat," Georgia ordered as she worked some miracle to quiet the phones. "They can talk to voicemail."

Brent wheeled over a chair and patted the backrest. The way these people were coddling her would normally have set Elizabeth on edge, but she was too exhausted and sore to care. She sank into the chair and placed the food container and bag of meds on the desk next to her. As she was about to ask for something to drink, a large, wet, cold bottle of water was set on the desk next to her food.

As she broke the seal on the bottle, Elizabeth checked the dry-erase board. More notes had been added to the timeline. Top among them a photo of the location of Kerri's possible murder and the discovery of Andrea. The timeline was starting to look better, but it was sorely lacking in vital information.

"Now that we have that all squared away, where is Andrea?" Elizabeth popped the lid on the to-go box.

"Down the hall, sleeping in the conference room on a cot," Rafe said.

"With the way ya'll were jabbering in here, I'm shocked she can even bother."

"After the day she's had, it's not surprising. We've got security measures in place to make sure we don't have a repeat of this morning's kidnapping. She's safe for now." Rafe settled on the edge of Georgia's desk, having full command of the room.

Elizabeth twirled sauce-drenched noodles on her fork. "Well?" She shoved the lot in her mouth.

As Rafe explained what he and Brent had done earlier that day searching for Andrea, Elizabeth destroyed the pasta and meatballs. She was far hungrier than she'd thought.

"We were loading the horses when Young called us." Rafe left the desk and went to the county map hanging on the wall. He pointed to a spot. "Andrea had been left here, with a burner phone, a bottle of water, and a note with instructions to get out of town."

Elizabeth squinted at the point above his finger. "She was left on Wailing Lady Lane?"

Wailing Lady Lane was an old road, part gravel but mostly dirt, and haunted. Story went that two farming families lived down the lane a quarter of a mile from each other, and miles from everywhere else. When the stock market crashed in '29 and the Depression really set in, hopelessness hit one of the men hard. Seeing no way out except his way, he poisoned his livestock and his family, killing all save his wife, who hadn't eaten the food he prepared, instead giving her portion to her three small children. The other man found her stumbling along the lane, wailing about her dead children. He took her in and reported the deaths to local authorities.

The next day, when his sister-in-law came to check on the family, she found an empty house. She called the sheriff. On a hunch, he went to the deceased farmer's homestead and found the missing couple and their small son. Dead. Poisoned just like the first family. No sign of the grieving widow. They never did find her, believing her to be the real killer of both families, and in her sorrow, she took her own poisonous concoction and died somewhere deep in the woods.

To this day, people swore up and down they heard her wailing on that road. No one lived back there now, the two farmsteads left to rot and fall in. Wildlife had reclaimed the properties. Only the stupid and the brave tried to venture back there, coming back with wild tales of strange sightings and sounds.

"Andrea was at the entrance to the road. Right where she could just get reception to use the phone." Rafe took root by the map, arms crossed and legs spread wide. "Young went out to get her."

"What did she tell you?" Elizabeth asked her other female deputy.

"Some wild tale about someone rescuing her from those two men," Young said. "She has no idea who it was, since the men had her blindfolded. Rescuer kept her that way until they dropped her off at the end of this Wailing Lady Lane."

"Did her kidnappers say anything?" Lila had polished off her meal and was nursing a cup of coffee.

"If they did, she's not saying," Young replied.

"Think she'll talk with you?" Elizabeth asked. "It appeared last night when you bolted out of the hospital that she'd created some trust with you."

"Doubt it." Lila rocked forward in her chair, planting her boots on the floor. "She wasn't all that forthcoming when I did have her attention. You'd probably have better luck with her. Somehow, we've got to keep it from her parents she's been found, or they'll be here harassing her and us."

"If the only people who know she's here are the people in this room that should be easy. I'll talk to her after she's gotten some sleep," Elizabeth said. "What about Orville and Jim?"

"Those two nimrods have yet to explain to me what they were doing at that campground." Lila gave Elizabeth a droll smile, her canines flashing. "Interesting fact—whatever or whoever sent them there to tear it down didn't involve Sheehan."

Elizabeth closed her food container. "Explain."

"I didn't come out and say I saw them tearing that camp down, but when I mentioned witnessing them doing something, this set Sheehan off. Those two weren't quick to explain themselves to him either. He got mad and left. I sent Fitzgerald to tail him. Hopefully, he hasn't been spotted."

Elizabeth sat back in her chair and scanned the faces in the room. Each one wore dog-tired, soul-weary expressions. They needed sleep. They needed refueling. Every single one of her deputies was overdue for some time off. Yet until this thing was solved and a murderer put behind bars, no one would take a respite.

A phone went off. All eyes drifted to Lila as she dug out her cell.

"It's Fitzgerald," she said before answering. "Yeah?" Her gaze met Elizabeth's. "I'm on my way." She ended the call and stashed her phone in her pocket as she stood. "Sheriff, I think it best you have a nice long con-fab with Tweedledee and Tweedledum. I'm off to The Watering Hole."

"To do what?" Elizabeth asked.

Lila headed for the hall. "To corner Sheehan," she called

back over her shoulder.

"Wait!" Elizabeth tried and failed to get up. Her body simply gave out. "I'm coming."

Lila stopped and about-faced. "Not right now. You handle Orville and Jim. Let me take care of Sheehan."

"Lila."

"Elizabeth, this is not the time to argue with me." Lila looked to Rafe. "She's bleeding, by the way." And with that, she disappeared down the hall.

All attention swung Elizabeth's way. Growling under her breath, Elizabeth lifted a hand and put a stop to the barrage that was sure to come.

"I'm fine. Deputy Meyer, bring Orville up here but put him in a different room than Jim. I want them apart when we grill 'em for answers."

While the younger man obeyed her order, Elizabeth managed to rise. Rafe was by her side in a flash, taking hold of her arm, and grabbing up her bag of pills. She had to bite her tongue lest she lash out at him. A stab of pain further curbed her temper.

"You're not up for a confrontation with Orville and Jim," Rafe said as he escorted her into her office.

"This isn't up for debate."

He closed the door. "I should take you home and cuff you to your bed."

Elizabeth snickered. "Don't tease me with a good time."

Rafe jerked then exasperation crept into his serious features. "I really despise the fact you learned all your innuendos from my brother and his army cohorts." He cupped her face, tilting it up to his own then pressed his forehead to hers. "You're going to end up in the hospital with a serious problem if you don't back off this case."

Closing her eyes, Elizabeth soaked in his presence, his strength. "I have to see this through. You are the only one who understands how important this is to me." She opened her eyes to meet his steady gaze. "Not only do I owe it to Bre and anyone else who was taken in such a manner, I owe it to myself."

"Why? You weren't even here when she died."

She gripped his bulging biceps, stepping closer to him. "I made things worse when I came back here for the funeral. I was the avenging angel, determined to find whoever killed my best friend and see them pay. All I did was prove to that prick Jones and all his cronies just how right they were when it came to their mindset about emotionally inept females."

Rafe wrapped his arms around her and tugged her flush to his body, kissing the top of her head before settling his chin there. "You're far from inept. You just have a hard time knowing your limitations."

Leaning in, she breathed in his scent. His normal balsam and cedar had faded behind the tang of leather, horse, and sweat. Call her crazy, but she did love the smell of an outdoors man. A girlish urge overwhelmed her, and she snuggled into his chest.

"Lila and Kyle should interrogate Orville and Jim. They're the ones who witnessed their activities," Rafe said, tightening his hold on her.

"Those two won't say peep with either one of those deputies." She wiggled her head out from under his chin and looked up at him. "Don't try to sway me out of it, Raphael

Fontaine. We can hit the weakest link."

One eyebrow lifted at her statement. "Jim?"

"As long as Orville is separated from him, Jim will talk."

Sighing, he closed his eyes. "Fine."

"Wow, that was a fast resignation."

He smiled. "Lila got me up to date before you showed up. She knew she wasn't going to get them to say anything and her plan with Fitzgerald was more important. I had hoped to talk you out of it and let me handle it. But ..."

"But I'm a stubborn mule."

"You said it, I didn't." He stepped back, putting a gap between them. "Take your meds."

She tightened her hold on him and drew him back. "When this is over, when I've finally laid Bre to rest, you and I are going to resolve this tension that has been hovering over us for years."

Rafe started to shake his head, but she gripped his chin and tipped it down.

"Don't argue with me. You want this just as much as I do. Screw the naysayers. This is the freaking twenty-first century—they can sit in the pot and stew. I'm done kowtowing to them."

"You're willing to lose the race for your next term before it even starts?"

"Who cares? Now kiss me."

With a chuckle, he drew her up and claimed her lips.

CHAPTER TWENTY

J IM WAS HUNCHED over, snoozing, when Elizabeth and Rafe entered the interview room. Next door, Orville was muttering and occasionally would bellow that he wanted to talk to Elizabeth. He could simmer.

Rafe shut the door with a clap. Jim jerked awake with a snort and a cough. He squinted at them, blinked a few times as he yawned.

"Sorry 'bout that, Jim," Elizabeth said, not one bit sorry as she settled onto the chair across from him. "Busy day?"

"Sum'in like that."

Rafe slapped the file of pictures on the table, then picked up the only other chair in the room and placed it near Jim, straddling the backrest as he stared at the other man.

Jim peered over at Rafe then sat up a little straighter. He pointed at the folder. "What's that?"

Elizabeth touched the folder, slid it closer to herself, and left her hand on top. "Nothing much. Just some photos."

"Of what?" Jim asked, his gaze bouncing back and forth between Elizabeth and Rafe.

"I think we'll get to those in a bit. Why don't you tell us what you've been up to today?"

Jim crossed his arms and tried to screw on a defiant face. It lacked effort. "I don't have to answer no questions about my day."

Elizabeth drummed her fingers on the folder. "No. No you don't have to answer any questions about your day. We know how loyal you are to Orville and Sheehan, and anyone else who calls themselves your friend. Right, Deputy Fontaine?"

Rafe rumbled his response as he settled his forearms on the top of the backrest.

"Ain't you s'psed to be on leave?" Jim asked.

"I should, but you see, Jim, someone decided to commit a murder last night. When that happens, it means I must return to my job."

"I heard 'bout that." Jim shook his head sadly. "Not right what happened to that gal."

"No, it wasn't. It's a sad, sad thing when someone thinks they have the right to end another person's life." Elizabeth scooted forward, resting her elbows on the table, pinning down the folder. "What makes it worse is it happened on the twenty-fifth anniversary of the death of Denise Russell. You remember that day, Jim?"

He stared at her, wide-eyed. "I do. I remember when the Lundquist girl was found dead the next day. It was a bad time for our town."

"Most certainly was. Now it's happened again. In almost the same way."

"But I thought that gal was murdered. She wasn't ran over by no truck. Or died by drugs."

"Murder can happen in any form or fashion, Jim." Elizabeth removed her elbow and slid the folder toward him. "What gets me is that whoever killed Kerri Peterson did it not too far from where Denise was struck by the truck. In fact, it was done in the same field where Brendette Lundquist was found dead." She opened the folder and exposed the top photo. "And for some reason they asked you and Orville to tear down this camp."

Jim gaped at the picture of him and Orville lugging poles to the flatbed trailer. "Where'd you get that?" He jabbed his finger at the image.

"This is what Deputies Dayne and Lundquist caught you two doing this afternoon." Elizabeth slid the top photo aside to reveal the one after it. "Loading up what looks like tents and poles and other equipment that would make for a nice cozy camp out there in the middle of nowhere. Except you forgot something." She slid out the next picture, the one of the charred and melted dummy king with the note pinned to its chest. "I could cite you for littering."

He snatched the photo from her and examined it. "We was told to leave it there."

"Who told you to leave it there?"

He shook the picture. "This ain't our responsibility."

"Jim, who told you to break down the camp?"

He tossed the photo at her. "I'm not gettin' no ticket for that."

"Jim, focus," Rafe snapped.

Under the deep tan, Jim's face washed out. "Sheriff, I don't know who told me and Orville to break camp. I don't know 'cause they didn't call us."

"How did you know to do it?" Rafe asked.

Next door, Orville let out a shout for someone to let him out. Jim slunk down in his chair.

"We got a text. From some number we ain't never seen

before. Said to get everything out of there today. We'd get paid to do it." Jim picked at a scab on his hand, scowling at his work. "Never said nuthin' about cops."

"Where'd they tell you to take the gear?" Rafe pressed.

Jim shrugged. "Didn't tell us. We parked the truck at our place."

"Do you have the phone this text came on?" Elizabeth asked.

"Orville's got it."

Elizabeth looked at Rafe. With a nod, he left the chair and headed next door. Elizabeth gathered the photos and closed the folder.

"Jim, you've been extremely helpful."

"I don't want no ticket, Sheriff."

She tapped the edge of the folder against the table. "Don't worry. We took care of the dummy. We'll let it slide this time." She stood and turned for the door.

"Sheriff? Do you wanna know who likes to go out to that camp?"

Her limbs stiffened. Slowly, she faced Jim. "You know who went out there?"

Jim gave her a slow nod. "I know 'cause Orville liked to spy on them. We'd go out and find a spot back behind and watch. We wasn't there last night on account Orville had a bad belly ache."

Elizabeth returned to her chair, pulling out a notepad and a pen. She handed it to Jim. "Write down everything and everyone you saw there."

As he wrote down each name and each event, Elizabeth's heart slammed against her chest. She had it. She finally had the Holy Grail of evidence.

CHAPTER TWENTY-ONE

L ILA MET FITZGERALD a block down from The Watering Hole. He'd parked in a way to keep an eye on Sheehan's vehicle. Fitzgerald exited his Crown Vic as she approached.

"He drove around a bit after leaving the Dew Drop," he reported as he closed the car door. "Stopped at the gas station, pumped gas, and bought some things inside. Drove out to Three Points to Mayor McKinnley's house and went inside the house."

"Why would he go to Jason McKinnley's home? I thought Jason didn't like him?"

Fitzgerald shook his head as he reached into the left breast pocket of his uniform. "Don't ask me. I'm just reporting what I saw." He withdrew a packet of gum and peeled out one for himself. As he unwrapped the slim stick, he glanced at her, then offered the pack. "Want one?"

Lila started to shake her head, but the brand and flavor gave her pause. Cinnamon. "Sure." She took a piece, opened it, and shoved the stick in her mouth while balling up the wax paper and stuffing it in her pocket.

The wrapper she'd found in the girls' apartment, along with what she believed to be Andrea's phone, was still stashed inside her squad car console. She wanted Kyle to turn in the pill and the patch they found in Allegra's room.

But how did she explain where it came from and how they knew about it without getting both of them in hot water?

Fitzgerald returned the packet to his pocket. "After he was done at McKinnley's, he drove straight here."

"How long was he with Mayor McKinnley?"

"Twenty minutes or so. If that was who he saw. Remember, Amy works from home now that she's expecting."

Lila frowned. "Why would Sheehan want to talk with Amy McKinnley? It barely makes sense for him to even talk with Jason. And how do you know she's pregnant?"

He sniffed. "Boy, you don't pay any attention to town gossip."

"I don't find other people's private business worth my time to speculate on unless it pertains to a police investigation."

Ignoring her comment, Fitzgerald jutted his chin at The Watering Hole. "He's probably perched on his throne by now. How do you want to play this?"

"Carefully." Lila hiked to the bar's front door with Fitzgerald on her six. "You hang back by the door. I'm going to act like I'm checking in with Marnie, then I'll head for his table. You make sure none of his cronies interrupt us."

"It's Friday night, day before Halloween. Gonna be loud in there."

"Perfect time to corner him, because people aren't going to be interested in eavesdropping. Too drunk to care."

"A lot harder for me to contain the situation if someone does decide to intervene."

Lila glanced over her shoulder. "I'm sure you'll find a way to make it work." With that, she pushed inside.

The theme song to *Ghostbusters* and jubilant voices blasted her. Seven thirty in the evening and everyone in the bar had strapped on a few to get the weekend started early. As Lila pushed her way through the press of bodies, she received a few hails from those who knew her and a few nasty remarks from those who didn't know better. She made it to the bar and wiggled in between a woman dressed like Lily Munster holding a martini glass and a guy dressed as some hairy concoction. Lily Munster moved on and Lila stole her spot, climbing up on the footrest.

The song rolled into the end, and the crowd kept shouting "Ghostbusters!" more loudly than the last time the singer asked that monotonous question. Lila cringed at the exuberant shouts banging against her eardrums.

Tonight's bartender, Deke, was passing out glasses filled to the brim with beer. Off to his left, Marnie's Cruella de Vil hair bobbed as she spoke with a light-haired woman at the end of the bar. Deke twisted to grab a bottle of rum from the back wall, but he paused when he spotted Lila's waving hand. She pointed to Marnie. He gave her a thumbs-up and tapped Marnie's shoulder.

The jukebox paused between songs, making the crash of human voices louder. Marnie turned to Deke, looked past him as he pointed at Lila. Michael Jackson's voice broke through the babble of voices, and the patrons let out a shout as "Thriller" began playing. Lila leaned up on the bar as Marnie made her way over. As she passed a cooler, Marnie grabbed a bottle of water infused with caffeine she'd began stocking for the deputies when they stopped by. She cracked the seal, tossed the cap in a recycle bin, and handed over the bottle.

"Deputy Dayne." She tilted her head just right under the orange and green glow of the pumpkin and ghoul lights, and Lila noticed a discoloration under the makeup on Marnie's right eye.

Lila tapped the spot under her own eye. "What happened?" She took a long gulp of the infused water.

"Long story. What brings you in tonight?"

Using her perch on the bar footrest, Lila raised her short body up and managed to just see over the top of the heads of those between her and the upraised spot where Sheehan was known to sit. He was there, his cell phone pressed to his ear.

"I came to see Sheehan."

Marnie looked to the doorway. "Are you and Ben working together?"

People parted, revealing Fitzgerald making his way to the bar.

"Guess we are," Lila replied as he made the hairy man next to Lila move out of the way.

Marnie met Lila's gaze. "I don't know what you're planning to do, Lila, but having Ben here and trying to talk to Kelley right now is not a good idea."

"He's just in a snit over what happened this afternoon," Fitzgerald remarked.

Marnie gave him a hard glare that made Lila tense. "Not remotely funny."

"No one said it was. It's the God's honest truth."

Lila scowled. Something about the way the two spoke to each other set off her Spidey sense. She shrugged it off, drinking more water.

"If you're going to bother him"—Marnie reached back, shifted some bottles around, and pulled out a bottle of Hennessy cognac. She thrust it out to Lila—"take this with you."

"I'm in uniform."

Groaning, Fitzgerald took the bottle from Marnie. "Good thing I don't give two shits what anyone thinks," he said. "Let's go."

Marnie gave Lila a raised eyebrow then shook her head before returning to her bartending duties. Overhead the jukebox switched to *The Addams Family* theme song.

Lila was bumped about as she tried to make a path to Sheehan's spot. Some guy in a Dracula costume managed to splash beer on her. His eyes widened when he was able to focus on her uniform. Took him a goodly time to get his eyes up off her breasts.

"So sorry, Deputy," he slurred. He grinned, then leaned forward. "Unless you don't care." He winked.

"Sir, if my badge won't deter you, I'm pretty certain a night in lockup will. Step back."

"Yes, ma'am."

Rolling her eyes, Lila navigated the rest of the way to the raised platform unscathed. Fitzgerald waited for her on the edge, eyeing Sheehan, who eyed him back.

"I don't want whatever it is you're peddling," Sheehan snapped as he placed his cell phone face down on the table. An empty whiskey tumbler sat next to a half-full bottle of Johnnie Walker.

Fitzgerald lofted the Hennessy. "Marnie said to bring this with us."

That bottle of expensive cognac made Sheehan's eyes narrow. "My statement remains the same. Take that bottle back to the bar and leave."

Lila grabbed a chair from a nearby table, swung it around, set it up against his table and sat, straddling the backrest. "Here's the thing. You and I are going to have a talk. It can be here with a bottle of cognac for you. Or it can be in the sheriff's office with her breathing fire down your neck and ready to claw your eyes out. Either way, this confab is happening. You choose."

Scowling, he beckoned Fitzgerald over. Once the bottle was within reach, he jerked it from the deputy's hand, popped the cork, and poured a god's portion in his whiskey tumbler, then slapped the cork home and set the bottle on the table beside the Johnnie Walker.

"What did those two numbskulls tell you?" he asked as he swirled the liquor in the glass.

"Nothing. Sheriff has them cornered."

"Whatever the hell they did, I had nothing to do with it." He sipped the cognac.

Fitzgerald took a seat next to Lila and kept his mouth shut.

"But they did do something for you. I recall you saying as much, and I quote, 'You finished early.' What did they finish early?"

Sheehan's whiskey-colored eyes bore holes into Lila. After a few moments of that, he threw back the rest of the liquor, set the tumbler on the table with a crack, and reached for the Hennessy. "When they trained you in Chicago, did you ever have a one-on-one with those Chicago-mafia types?"

"Most of those old-school types have gone by the wayside. It's gangs and cartels these days. And those guys are a helluva lot meaner than you and your old hick boys."

Sheehan chuckled as he poured himself another round. "You city folks. Really think you know the ways of the world." He exchanged the bottle for the tumbler. "Place one of your gangbangers here in the middle of nowhere, and betcha ten to one, they end up deader than a doorknob in less than an hour. Besides the hicks and the four-legged predators roaming these hills, they have to contend with the terrain and weather and trying to find shelter and food and water. Which won't come easy when everyone within a ten-mile radius owns a gun and ain't afraid to shoot first and never ask questions." He shook his head. "No, they might be meaner. But that don't make them smarter. Cartels, yeah, might stand a chance considering where they come from. Put one of our guys in a deer stand, and all bets are off. They'd pick off those sons of bitches like they were shooting fish in a barrel."

"Speak from experience?" Lila leaned forward.

He smirked, his grayed mustache twitching. "Nice try, missy." He took his time with the second glass. "Get on with what you came here to bother me about. I've got plans for later."

Lila returned his smirk with one of her own. "Nice try, you old coot. You can play magician with me all you want, but I'm getting an answer out of you. What did Orville and Jim do for you that didn't take so long?"

"Took out the trash."

She glanced at Fitzgerald. His tight lips and pinched features agreed with her. He didn't believe a word of what Sheehan said, either. Yet knowing Sheehan's compunction to twist the truth, he could be using a metaphor.

"What was this *thing* you witnessed those two numb-skulls doing?" Sheehan continued to swirl the cognac in the glass, his gaze trained on Lila.

"That pertains to an ongoing police investigation." She flashed her canines. "Can't say."

Chuckling, Sheehan sat forward, pointing his tumbler at her. "Now that right there is why I like you, Dayne. Your sheriff would get her panties all in a wad, allowing her female emotions to rule her judgment. You know the measure of things and how to keep it where it belongs."

"That's a blatantly sexist thing to say. I've known plenty of men who allowed their emotions to rule their judgment and they made piss-poor calls."

He sat back. "Then they weren't real men, now were they?"

Lila crossed her arms, laying them on the table. With her head tilted to the side, she regarded Sheehan. "Such anti-quated thinking. I hear a lot of that these days from a generation of bullies who never truly grew up."

Staring at her over the rim of his glass, Sheehan finished off the cognac, then set the glass down with a *thunk*. "I'm beginning to regret ever aiding the sheriff in locating you."

"I doubt regret is what you're feeling over that." Lila lowered her chin. "Tell me what really happened twenty-five years ago with the deaths of Denise Russell and Brendette Lundquist."

"Now we come to the actual reason you're here throwing a wet blanket on my peaceful night." He reached into an inside pocket of his jacket.

"How could sitting in a crowded bar during Halloween weekend be peaceful?" Fitzgerald snarked.

Lila tracked the ex-sheriff's movements as he withdrew a slim package from the pocket. A red, square box. Her heart beat a heavy staccato against her ribs. Sheehan removed a stick of gum from the packet, slid the box home, and then slowly unwrapped the piece. Lila dragged her gaze from the gum and met his steely-eyed one. A twitch in the corner of his eye was the lone reaction she received when he folded the gum into his mouth.

Within a span of less than thirty-some odd minutes, two men had produced a piece of the same brand and flavor of gum as the wrapper with phone number she had burning a hole in the console of her squad car.

"I find crowds soothing," Sheehan commented.

"More like it's easier to cover up your other activities with all the noise," Fitzgerald said.

"Just like your sheriff. Always looking for a snake under a rock."

"Where there's smoke and all that jazz."

Lila slapped the tabletop, making the bottles clink and the tumbler rattle. "I will not sit here and listen to the two of you have a pissing contest. I know you've got a thumb on the gossip in this county. You are well aware of the death of Kerri Peterson and how it closely resembles how Brendette Lundquist died. I also know you heard that Kerri's friend Andrea O'Ryan was kidnapped. Both women were wearing a pendant that was also found on the bodies of Denise Russell and Brendette. Now tell me the truth of what really happened to those two women twenty-five years ago."

Sheehan calmly chewed his gum. After a moment, he drew in a breath then sat forward once more to come nose to nose with Lila. "Elizabeth can do all she wants siccing her prized detective on me, but the answers will always remain the same. I had nothing to do with it. And the truth is in the files she's not-so-carefully absconded with."

"I've seen those files. There's exactly jack squat in them."

"That's everything. Denise was killed when she ran out in front of a truck on a snowy night. Brendette died from exposure after going on a grief-stricken binge. Simple as that. No ghosts to chase. Has nothing to do with that Peterson death." He leaned back in his chair. "Now. Shoo. You're bothering me, fly."

Lila sat there, staring him down. Eventually, Fitzgerald tapped her arm and he stood.

"We ain't getting anything else out of him, Dayne. Let's go."

Giving Sheehan another long stare, Lila pushed up from the chair. She kicked it aside. "This is far from over. How many more people have to die before you see the error of your ways?"

"The way I see it, Deputy, people die every day. When it's their time to go, it's time to go. No matter how it happens. Doesn't have a damn thing to do with me."

Leaving him with a parting scowl, Lila turned and headed off the platform. She and Fitzgerald pushed through the crowd back to the bar.

Marnie passed over the half-empty bottle of water Lila had left there. "Told you it wouldn't go over well."

Lila reclaimed the bottle and downed the last of the water.

"I'm gonna hit the head before we go," Fitzgerald said and pushed his way toward the restrooms.

"You okay, Lila?"

"Never better, Marnie."

With a perturbed look, Marnie wandered to the other end of the bar, back to the same light-haired woman she'd been talking with earlier. Lila stood there, stewing. Sheehan was an infuriating ass. How did he ever convince people to vote him in as sheriff for as long as he'd served?

Her vibrating phone knocked her out of her funk. She pulled it out of her pocket and checked the screen. A text from Kyle.

Meet me at my place.

She stared at the time on her phone. Almost eight. God, she needed sleep. She shivered at the thought of going to the Lundquist home. She'd only been there once, and that was when Freya wasn't there. How would his sister react to a stranger in her safe space?

Tapping her finger against the side of the phone, she froze. Sheehan was busy downing another glass of liquor. Lila checked to make sure her cell had the phone number in the call history, and brought the number up. She waited a second, then hit send, lowering her phone to her side.

"You ready?" Fitzgerald asked as he walked up. He made a face and slapped at one of his pockets.

Lila looked back at Sheehan. He was reaching for his

phone. But as she dragged her gaze back to Fitzgerald, she noticed that Marnie was also holding her phone, and she promptly tapped something on the screen. Fitzgerald took out his phone and stared at the screen. He touched it and then shrugged. Lila looked at Sheehan and caught him do the same thing, but this time shoving his phone in his jacket.

Something cold and slick went through Lila at what she witnessed. She ended the call and slipped her phone back in her pocket.

What just happened?

CHAPTER TWENTY-TWO

E LIZABETH HAD RAFE take the two men home and document the trailer and its contents when he got there.

She remained in the interview room long after Jim had left, reading each name on the list and matching it up with what she knew about the man. Her blood simmered with each one.

There was retired chief of police Joe Mitter, who damn well had backed her campaign to usurp Sheehan. The funeral director of the largest funeral home in Eckhardt County would be in the same jail cell with Father Tim, who herded the flock at the First Street Episcopal Church. Niles Murdock, who had hoped to trade in his cushy CPA for an RV and a trip across America, a pediatrician, even the middle school principal, all joining a bigger contingent of businessmen and professionals who hid behind the façade of upstanding family men.

A name not on this list—and one she found circumspect considering who had written the list—was Kelley Sheehan. Orville and Jim were diehard fans of Sheehan—why? No one knew for sure. They made it known far and wide they didn't consider her the sheriff, only him, so it shouldn't surprise her if Jim was still protecting Sheehan. Underhanded and deceitful though he was, Sheehan never crossed Elizabeth as perverted in nature. Yes, he took every opportunity to remind her that this job was not meant for a woman, but he always, *always*, treated young and old alike with an odd sense of respect, even while dropping in a few sexist remarks with those he could get away with doing it. But was it all for show? Was he really some kind of silent partner behind the encampment?

After all, his predecessor had been deeply involved, evidenced by his name at the top of this list. Why wouldn't the usurper do the same? Maybe that was Sheehan's motivation for keeping tabs on her with his sudden and unexpected help with a few cases in the last two years. He was watching her, making sure she couldn't place his name with those in this party camp.

Elizabeth stopped trying to slam the square peg that was Kelley Sheehan into the round hole of her expectations. It was making her head hurt.

Jim had left her with a second, more disturbing list. A longer list of all the young women who'd visited this out-of-the-way camp to entertain men who were old enough to be their fathers, uncles, hell, even their damn grandfathers.

Elizabeth grabbed the notepad and Orville's phone from the table and bolted out of the room. Storming down the hall, she spotted Deputy Meyer heading toward the bullpen.

"Brent."

He met her under the arched doorway. "Sheriff?"

She held out the phone. "See if you can work your magic and find who sent the texts to them to clear out the campsite."

He took the phone. "Is it password protected?"

"Nope."

"I don't make any promises. The person probably used a burner phone."

"I'm fully expecting it." She wagged the notepad with Jim's lists. "I have a strong suspicion we might match up someone on this list seen buying one."

Meyer shrugged. "Maybe." He turned to head back to the bullpen.

"Brent," she said softly.

His body stiffened. Slowly he turned to face her. "Sheriff?"

Elizabeth agonized over whether to tell him this or not, eventually resigning herself to the fact he deserved to know. "Your father is on this list."

Brent Meyer's family had a turbulent history. Pratt, his father, wasn't well-liked due to his money-grabbing and high-handed ways. His mother was serving prison time for her part in the illegal drug trade in Eckardt County. Brent's pinched, frustrated expression melted into one of calm. "It doesn't surprise me."

"His visits to this campsite aren't a recent development. He's been doing it as long as that encampment has been there. Take this information with a grain of salt considering the source."

"Do you want me to confront him?"

"No. It will either be me or Deputy Dayne. I don't want a new rift between the two of you if it turns out to be nothing but innocent visits or a lie on Jim's part."

Meyer forced a pained smile. "There will always be a rift between us. It'll never go away."

"Let's keep it from widening then." Elizabeth tapped the notepad against her thigh. "I also want you to take this list. Go over it, cross check each person with any connections with anyone else on here or in the county." She held out the notepad.

He took it. "Are you expecting something to lead back to Sheehan?"

"One can hope." She walked away, Bentley at her side, heading for the conference room.

She knocked softly. "Andrea, it's Sheriff Benoit. I'm coming in." She opened the door a crack and peeked in.

Andrea was sitting cross-legged on the cot. She had wrapped her arms around her in a clear attempt to protect and console herself. There were cuts and bruises on her face and arms. She had been allowed a shower and a change of clothes here in the department in the deputies' locker room. But a hot shower couldn't wash away the trauma and terror she'd faced in the last twelve-plus hours.

"Sherriff," she croaked.

Giving the girl her most reassuring smile, Elizabeth slinked inside. Bentley weaved past her legs before she shut the door and trotted over to the cot to sit in front of Andrea. The young woman reached out. The collie extended her snout and butted her nose into the girl's hand. Slowly, Andrea stroked the dog's silky head.

Elizabeth pulled out a chair and eased down onto it with a stifled groan. She was going to have to buckle and take one of her script painkillers. This day wasn't over for her, but her body had reached its limit.

"Been a trying day," she said.

Andrea continued to stroke Bentley, keeping her head down.

Sighing, Elizabeth braced her elbows on her knees and leaned forward. "I know I'm on your list of the last people on earth you'd want to talk with. I'm just letting you know that we plan to let you stay here as long as you need to. The sheriff's department is the safest place for you for the time being. And Bentley is a great emotional support dog." She moved to rise, wishing she didn't have to.

"Sheriff?"

Relief! She relaxed into the chair. "Yes?"

Andrea stared, her eyes glittering with a fire one would not associate with this young woman who'd grown up under the thumb of her bitter, backbiting parents. "Will you make the one who killed Kerri pay for what they did?"

The familiar vehemence of Andrea's tone resonated so deeply inside Elizabeth she wasn't sure what to say to the girl.

"Do you know who did it?" she finally asked.

Andrea shook her head. "Not specifically." She leaned closer to Bentley and buried both of her hands in the dog's fluffy ears. "But I know every person who was there. And why they were all there." A hardened expression erased the timid woman who'd sat before Elizabeth moments before. "I'm done being someone's pawn."

A zing of awareness brought Elizabeth's battered and exhausted body back to life. She sat up straighter. "What do you mean, Andrea?"

"When I was kidnapped and being dragged around by those two men, I swore that if I got out of it alive, I was going to expose the whole damn thing. After those others rescued me, I knew I was getting my chance."

"Deputy Young said you didn't hear any of them talk, kidnappers or rescuers. Is that true?"

"Sheriff, can we talk about this in your office? I'd feel more comfortable there."

Elizabeth glanced around the room and shrugged. Andrea was right. Her office was the safest place to avoid eavesdroppers or unexpected guests. She pushed herself upright and snapped her fingers. Bentley was at her side in a split second.

"Ms. O'Ryan, follow me. We're going to get down to the matter of this whole ordeal."

LILA PARKED HER car in the empty driveway. A single light peeked through a window on the first floor of the Lundquist family home. That she made it here safely was a miracle. Every inch of her body felt like hundreds of thousands of wasps were stinging her. She fumbled her way out of the vehicle and trudged to the side door where the light broke through the dark.

Kyle, barefooted and wearing a pair of low-riding jeans and a faded yellow Eckardt County Sheriff's T-shirt, pushed open the ancient screen door, holding it back to let her in.

"You look like death warmed over," he said, his low voice sounding more gravelly than usual.

"You sound like it, too," she countered as she passed him in the doorway.

The kitchen, stuck in a perpetual state of the nineties, was warm and smelled of pork roast, apples and onions, and the warm, yeasty scent of bread. Lila swayed to a halt and took in a deep breath. Her mouth watered at the heavenly aroma of a home-cooked meal. Though his sister was well-known for her baked goodies, Kyle was no slouch when it came to cooking.

"Hungry?" he asked as he moved to the oven.

Her stomach growled in response. "Apparently, I am. That burger and fries I ate a few hours ago is long gone."

He pulled out an oven-safe glass dish and removed the aluminum foil. Steam billowed up, parting to reveal the medium-sized pork loin covered in sliced apples and onions. "You didn't eat much today. After the day we've had, we need a solid meal." He removed another pan loaded with quartered sections of roasted potatoes and finally a cast iron skillet with a browned bread dome.

Lila wandered over to the stove. No matter how many times she'd personally witnessed his skills, it flabbergasted her. All of her young life, she'd never seen a man bother with things deemed woman's work. Oh, she'd seen her fair share of male cooks behind the wall in diners and restaurants. Some of the best places she'd gotten as close to a home-cooked meal were run by men of different ethnic backgrounds. But in the home, in front of the stove, Kyle was her first and only.

He paused while cutting into the bread and peered at her. "What?"

A tiny smile tugged up. "Nothing."

Shaking his head, he continued to make their plates.

"You sure you don't want me to shower first?" she asked as she took the plate he offered.

"This kitchen has seen its fair share of dirty work clothes." He set his plate down at a spot and slung his leg over the back of the wooden chair. "Freya will be in overdrive mode when she finally shakes the sedatives. She'll clean the entire house from top to bottom. Might as well give her something to make it worthwhile."

Lila dug into her food before broaching that topic. "What was the accident?"

Kyle scratched a spot above his right eyebrow with the end of his fork. "I don't know. When the sheriff and I got here, we found Marnie here."

"Wait, Marnie was here? After Freya's meltdown I saw this morning in the café because of Marnie, I didn't think they'd be anywhere near each other."

"You saw that?"

"Front and center."

He groaned. "Bad enough Marnie showed up with Freya working the counter, but you had to be there to witness it."

"Did Marnie tell you why she came?"

"Ellie found out that Freya called Marnie. Someone had come to the farmhouse, and by the way it looks, Freya attacked them. She wouldn't say who it was. Marnie didn't see anyone, but she found Freya bloody and frantic."

"She was hurt?"

"No." He reached over to the chair on his left side and picked up a rolled paper bag. "The blood on her was someone else's. I'm going to give over most of it to DCI, but I want to run my own tests." He set the bag down in its spot.

"Kyle, why would Freya attack someone?"

"I don't know. Marnie told Ellie she had to subdue Freya. By the time we got here, the medics had her doped up." He dropped his silverware on the plate and rubbed his face. "God, this is messed up. Somehow, all of this boils down to Kerri's death and what happened to my sister."

A weird urge to comfort him fell over her. This was getting freaky, because she wasn't the comforting type. For some reason she acted on the urge, touching his arm and giving it a reassuring rub.

He lifted his head and studied her. Yeah, this was out of character for her. Hell, she wasn't the cuddle type after sex, usually letting him get his fill of snuggling up to her but never reciprocating. Something had snapped inside of her. It was the only explanation. In the hospital hallway with Hillary Peterson, the instance when she, Lila, had acted like a caring, comforting person—that had been the moment. Now look at her.

For God's sake, this was Kyle. The man she'd grown fond of. Reliant on. If she was frank, even a bit infatuated with. Ugh, she was such a sap.

He gripped her hand and held it. She allowed it, not daring to pull away from him.

Through the fog of exhaustion, she recalled what happened at The Watering Hole. It was time to move on from Freya's troubles to their own.

"I found out something," she said, pulling her hand out of his and dug into her pocket.

She deposited all the gum wrappers on the table and pointed at them. "You said earlier that you had a theory on who gave the girls those phone numbers."

Kyle picked up one. "Yeah."

"Tonight, I found out two men chew the same brand and flavor of gum. And I called that number again. But I don't know who actually ignored the call."

He scowled. "What do mean?"

"I did it in the bar. I saw three people on their phones at the same instant the call connected."

"Who?"

"Sheehan, Fitzgerald, and Marnie."

Kyle sagged in his chair. "Marnie?" He shook his head. "Sheehan I can see being involved, but the other two ..." He stared at her. "Are you sure?"

"I'm not sure of anything. It could all be a coincidence. But it's just too damn convenient when the call ended at the same time they all seemed to ignore it."

He smoothed out the wrapper with the phone number and examined the writing. "I haven't seen any of their handwriting to know which one it could be."

"Wait a minute." Lila bolted from her chair and ran outside to her car.

She dug out the phone she found at Young's house, the one she had assumed was a burner Andrea used. Kyle was waiting in the doorway for her when she hurried back to the house.

She held up the flip phone. "Let's try this phone again and see if someone will actually pick up."

"Have you already done that?" He closed the door behind them.

"This morning when we found out Andrea was kidnapped." Lila activated the phone and pulled up the call history. She paused before hitting send. "Cross your fingers."

With the call on speaker, they listened. Three rings in, the line picked up. Lila's heart raced. Finally!

"You are supposed to have left town, Andrea," a distorted voice said over the line.

Kyle's eyes widened. He hadn't been at the office when Fontaine revealed the message left with Andrea when she was found.

"Leave. Or suffer the consequences."

CHAPTER TWENTY-THREE

Day 3: Saturday morning, Halloween

S HE SENSED A presence. Lila opened her eyes and stared into icy blue eyes framed by dark-green glasses.

"What are you doing in Kyle's bed?"

Lila jerked back at Freya's strident voice. It was then she realized she was alone in the bed, and she was wearing nothing but a T-shirt. Kyle had washed her filthy uniform and undergarments last night while she showered.

Freya scowled. "Deputy Dayne, why are you wearing Kyle's clothes?"

Swallowing, she dragged the blanket up to her chin. "Freya, there's a perfectly good explanation for this."

Kyle's sister stepped back from the bed, towering over Lila, and crossed her arms. Freya didn't look like she'd succumbed to fits of hysterics yesterday. This bright Saturday morning, she was glammed up in a pair of high-waisted dark-blue pants and a ruby-red blouse, her blonde hair pulled up in a decidedly '40s fashion.

"What's that perfectly good explanation?" she demanded.

The floorboards creaked behind her, and she spun around, snapping her arms down at her sides. Kyle, wearing his deputy's uniform, entered the room, holding Lila's freshly laundered clothing.

"Freya, I told you Lila was here," he said, setting Lila's uniform on the foot of the bed.

His sister glared at him. "You didn't tell me you were sleeping with her."

Lila's cheeks flamed hot. This was why she never stayed here. The exact reason Kyle spent nights at her place. Freya didn't have a problem with him being gone, but she had a huge issue with other people in the house.

He met his red-faced sister. "I'm how old again?"

Freya resumed her crossed-arm stance. "Just because you're older doesn't make it right."

"Who decided you were to be my moral compass?"

Freya pointed a red-lacquered nail at Lila. "If you're going to screw her, you should at least marry her."

Lila's entire body flushed. *Someone wave a wand, say abracadabra, and make me disappear.* To her amazement, she wasn't the only one. Above his carefully trimmed beard, Kyle's cheeks turned ruddy.

"Freya," he croaked. "Go downstairs."

After tossing a fierce glare at both Lila and Kyle, Freya stormed out of the bedroom and slammed her way down the stairs.

Lila flopped onto the bed and dragged the covers up over her head. "That went just fan-freaking-tastic," she growled.

Kyle yanked down the blanket, looming over her, an amused twinkle in his eyes. "At least we got her confrontation about it out of the way."

She pushed at his chest. "It's not funny." Lila groaned. "What's ironic is we didn't even have sex."

Chuckling, he sat on the edge of the bed. "Maybe we

should. She already thinks it happened."

"You shouldn't antagonize her like that."

"That's what big brothers do. It's in our job description, didn't you know? Rule number forty-five, thou shalt tease and torment your little sister and or brother."

"Seriously, you're an ass."

"Ha, you should see me when I really get going." He wagged his eyebrows. "There's a clause in our contract to do the same to our girlfriends and wives."

Lila jabbed a finger at him. "Don't you dare."

His smile made her stomach quiver. Ornery as all get out, but damn, it made him look hot.

"Oh, I dare."

She tried to kick him, but he grabbed her leg and pinned it to the bed. Before Lila could react, he crawled up on top of her and tickled her. She screeched in laughter as she tried to squirm from his hold.

"Stop it." She gasped.

"Oh. My. God! Stop already!" Freya yelled from the bottom of the steps.

Kyle leaned his forehead against Lila's as he laughed. "I think she means it."

Lila flicked his ear. "Ya think." She shoved at his heavy weight. "Get off me, you Viking oaf."

He did as she ordered and left the bed. "At least she's not thinking about what happened yesterday."

Lila scrambled out of the bed and grabbed her underwear. "Seems to have done the trick for you, too." Underwear on, she removed his T-shirt from her body and reached for her bra.

"I still think we should tell Ellie about the phone and the warning," he said, grasping her hands as she worked the sports bra down her chest, then pulled them away so he could explore her breasts.

"Kyle, let me get dressed."

He bent down to nuzzle her neck. "No."

Rolling her eyes, she smiled as he nipped at a sensitive point on her neck. "You do realize if we told the sheriff about the phone, the number, and the caller, we both have to explain where that all came from."

He pulled away and looked down at her. "We can't keep it hidden forever. We need to update everyone. Should have done it last night."

She sighed and slipped free of his arms. "I needed sleep. *You* needed to chill before you did something rash." She finished dressing, leaving her uniform top unbuttoned. She sat on a chair he kept in the room and slid into her boots. "In the light of the day, I still stand by what I said last night. We find out who the actual owner of the phone number is and then we tell Elizabeth."

"I don't like it," he groused.

Boots laced up and ready to go, she stood. Patting his chest, she smiled at him. "Too bad. You'll think twice the next time you get the bright idea to circumvent protocol."

Stomping feet coming up the stairs put a halt to their conversation.

Kyle turned to the door. "Freya, we're busy."

The blonde fury barged into the room, holding up both of their ringing phones. "Answer your stupid phones." She slapped their cells in his hand and then stomped out of the room and back down the stairs.

Grumbling something under his breath, he handed Lila her phone and then answered his.

Lila did the same. "Deputy Dayne."

"Lila, it's Georgia. We've got a situation. Sheriff wants you and Deputy Lundquist on site A-SAP." Georgia rattled off the location.

"On my way."

Kyle lowered his phone and ended his call. His features were twisted in confusion.

"What?"

"The address. It's the O'Ryans'."

Lila winced. "Think something happened to them?"

"I think we need to get there and find out. I'll have to ride with you. My unit is still at the sheriff's house. Her place is on the way. I can pick it up, because I'm going to need my gear."

They headed downstairs.

Freya stood guard in the doorway separating the kitchen from the rest of the house. "I'm not staying here alone," she said matter-of-factly.

Kyle stopped and frowned at his sister. "You're perfectly safe here."

"No, I'm not. He came for me here."

He went to move toward his sister, but Lila grabbed his arm and stepped in front of him.

"He who? Who was it?" she asked.

Freya stared at Lila with narrowed eyes and kept her flawlessly red-painted lips sealed.

"We don't have time for this," Kyle said. "Go to your

café if you don't want to stay here. It's public, and no one will do anything to you there where others can see it."

Fear flashed over Freya's face, turning her from a pinup girl into a weeping war widow. "Kyle, please."

The crack in her voice broke Lila. She'd heard that same sound rip from her lips in the past. She pushed Kyle back before he could step around her and moved to stand in front of Freya. Lila held out her hand and offered it to Freya. The fear that swiftly consumed the younger woman fled. She gaped at the outstretched hand a moment then slipped her chilled one into Lila's.

"Kyle's right. Go to your café, it's safer there. I'll follow you there to make sure no one does anything on the road."

"Nowhere is safe as long as he's out there."

Lila clasped Freya's trembling hand between hers. "Who is it? If you tell us, then we can stop him."

Freya looked everywhere but directly at Lila. Behind her, Lila sensed Kyle's tense body at her back. She held steady. Freya was on the verge. To keep Kyle from pressing her too hard, Lila touched her foot to his leg and pushed her boot into his shin to keep him back.

Finally, as if she'd come to a revelation, Freya's features turned stoic, and she met Lila's gaze. "*He* is Bre's killer."

The antique grandfather clock ticking away the seconds was the lone sound in the house.

Kyle dragged in a ragged breath. "You know who killed Bre? How do you know that?"

Freya freed herself from Lila's hold and fled into the kitchen.

Lila spun around and halted Kyle. "Hold it."

"If she's known that … all this time …" He plowed his fingers through his high and tight. "What the hell. She was just a kid when Bre died. How does she know who did it?"

The screen door cracked shut, jolting them both. They rushed through the kitchen and on to the porch in time to see Freya disappear into the garage.

"She's running," Kyle said and jumped off the porch.

By the time he reached the garage, Freya drove out and was racing past Lila's car.

"Shit!"

Lila hopped off the porch and jogged to her car. "If we hurry, we can hopefully catch up to her."

"Don't bother." He let his head fall back and he stared at the sky. Letting out a furious yell, he snapped his head back down. "Damn it!"

Lila checked her watch. "We need to go anyway."

They climbed into her car, and Lila followed the same path Freya had to the road. Kyle muttered and shook his head.

"Where would she go?" Lila asked.

"She could be going to the café."

"I hear a *but* in your voice. Where else would she go?"

He stared out the windshield, his features taking on a fierce mask. "She wouldn't."

"Wouldn't what?"

He glanced at Lila. "Go to Marnie."

CHAPTER TWENTY-FOUR

THE BODIES WERE displayed like scarecrows in the field adjacent to the O'Ryans' house. Erin had spotted them from a spare room on the west side of the house and sent Rick out to investigate. A note pinned to one of the men declared: YOU'RE WELCOME.

Here Elizabeth stood, feeling marginally better than she had the day before but getting increasingly frustrated. Elizabeth had spent part of her night documenting what Andrea had told her and the rest of it trying to sleep, of which she managed to sneak in a few hours. She had wanted to go over her notes and speak with Andrea again this morning to clarify things, but that wasn't happening.

Not when she had to deal with two bodies trussed up like scarecrows in a field, while Olivia examined the victims.

Who was the note directed at? The O'Ryans? Had to be. *You're welcome?* Welcome for what? *That we rescued your daughter from these men, then killed them?* Maybe the message was meant for Elizabeth and the rest of the Eckardt County Sheriff's Department. If it was, then what was the underlying meaning? *Hey, look! We can do a better job than you at catching criminals and inflicting our own brand of justice.*

Elizabeth's head ached with each new conundrum.

"It's a miracle in and of itself that Rick hadn't bothered

the bodies," Olivia said as she circled the men strapped to makeshift crosses. She paused and looked at the harvested bean field. "Using this flattened field means no visible tracks."

"We can't find drag marks. Rafe thinks multiple people carried the bodies out here," Elizabeth said.

Olivia stood behind the crosses and looked at the ground. "I can see indentations in the remaining stalks where the boards were on the ground."

"I know. My guess is, whoever did this laid the crosses out first, strapped the bodies onto the boards, and then hoisted them up into the holes they'd previously dug. It would be the easiest way to do it. In the middle of the night."

Olivia stared up at the backside of the bodies. "Ellie, did you see this?" She beckoned for Elizabeth to join her.

She cautiously rounded the crosses.

Olivia pointed up at the larger of the two men. "Under the hairline, right above the collar."

Elizabeth squinted at the man's thick neck. What was Olivia noticing? "I just see the back of his neck."

"There are red blemishes."

"You can see that?"

"I think I can. Once I get that mask off and he's on my autopsy table, I'll be able to see it better." Olivia glanced down at the ground, then stepped over the indentations closest to her and planted herself between the crosses. She inched closer to study her finding. "It could be urticaria."

"Laymen terms, Doc."

"Hives. The red, itchy welts on the skin."

"On a dead body?"

"Very possible if he was exposed to something that he was highly allergic to right before he died." Olivia shrugged. "Who knows. Maybe he died from anaphylaxis." She looked toward the road. "Wish Kyle and Lila would get here."

A voice hailed Elizabeth. Rafe was waving an arm and then pointing at the gravel dust rising to the east. Hopefully, this was her detective and her evidence man. The cars pulled off the road and onto the field, and the gravel dust parted, revealing the two deputies' squad cars.

"Looks like you get your wish, Liv."

"Ellie." Olivia stopped her before she could take a step to greet the arrivals. "These are the men who abducted Andrea, aren't they?"

With the Halloween masks on, there was no clear identification. Going by the physical descriptions Deputy Young and Andrea had given, it was a strong possibility these were the same men who abducted Andrea.

"I think the note gives it away," Elizabeth said. "Until you give the a-okay to take off those masks, we won't be certain."

The sound of slamming car trunks echoed over the fallow field. Elizabeth watched her crime scene techs, loaded with their gear, hike across the field. By the way the two walked close together, Elizabeth surmised they had truly kissed and made up. It would've still been nice to know what stupid mistake Kyle had done to cause the argument between the two. Eventually, one or both would admit the reason. She hoped.

Lila let out a whistle after she took a good look at what

they were summoned for. "They looked like actual scare-crows from back there."

"Someone has a sick, twisted sense of humor," Kyle remarked as he circled the scene. "You're welcome?"

"Are these the guys who abducted Andrea?" Lila asked.

"Strong possibility," Elizabeth said. She pointed behind the crosses. "We've got markings in the ground back there we need analyzed."

Olivia moved out of the two deputies' way to let them work. Elizabeth noted the dark circles and the tiny red line through the whites of her friend's eyes.

"Everything all right?" Elizabeth asked low enough that only Olivia could hear her.

The ME glanced at her then resumed her vigil on the deputies as they worked. "I'm fine. Just tired."

The lie bordered on the edge of truth. Elizabeth wouldn't call her friend out on it, but she sensed there was a deeper reason to Olivia's being tired, and it didn't have anything to do with work. It was a sensation she'd gotten off and on over the last year when she spent time with Olivia outside of work-related situations. After they wrapped this current homicide investigation, then she would press Olivia for the truth.

"Sheriff!"

She jerked around, regretting her hasty movements. Meyer jogged across the field. Behind him, Elizabeth saw a gaggle of people gathering around Rafe. Some shoved recording devices in his face.

"Damn it. Who the hell told them about this?"

Olivia looked back. "You've got a bigger problem than

the media."

Behind Elizabeth, she heard both Lila and Kyle swear. Thundering flames of fury rolled through Elizabeth at the sight of three men looming before Rafe, the leader of the group flapping his gums.

Meyer held out a sheet of notepaper to her as he came to a halt. "You need to see this before you go over there."

Elizabeth held up the note. She scowled at the words then looked at Meyer. "You're certain?"

"Like a heart attack."

Lila took the notepaper from Elizabeth. "What's this?"

"The person who sent a text message to Orville Patterson to tear down the camp," Elizabeth said between clenched teeth.

Lila looked to the three men now harassing Rafe. "That man has got some balls showing up here." She handed the note to Kyle as he joined her. "Want me to handle this?"

"No. You two finish what you need to do here so Olivia can get those bodies to the morgue. I'll take care of those asshats."

Meyer moved to join her as she walked away.

"Brent, you better stay with Dayne and Lundquist."

"I'm not letting you go over there alone with my father standing there."

Elizabeth stopped and brought her young deputy to a halt. "And I'm not letting you get into a pissing match with your father in front of those reporters. It's one thing for me to confront that trio and be recorded, quite another if you're in the mix. Hang back. Help them." She peered at the landscape behind the two dead men and her crime scene crew. "I bet anything someone will try to come up from the rear to get better footage of our scene. Keep watch for that."

"You're sure about this?" he asked.

"Like a heart attack," she parroted.

He gave her a half-cocked smile then turned to rejoin his fellow deputies.

Elizabeth took a deep breath and marched on. Despite the seeping on her surgical areas last night—which should have been a warning to not do it, but who was she to regard any warnings—she had worn her duty belt today. The weight tugged at her midsection, but she was done wandering about the county without her sidearm for protection. As she drew closer to the melee, she drew her authority about her like a cloak. Silence spread through the ranks of reporters, and yet they lingered near to catch any juicy tidbit liable to fly that would land them in good standing with the boss.

The leader of the three accosting Rafe shut his trap when she joined her undersheriff.

"Mayor Abbott. Mr. Meyer. Judge Spenser," she said.

Each man was on Jim's list of visitors to the campsite, each representing some position of power in the county. Judge Spenser had been the county attorney when Bre died. She narrowed her eyes. The same man who backed the now-dead sheriff and the kowtowed former coroner in ruling Bre's death an accidental overdose leading to hypothermia.

"Why are you here at my crime scene?"

Pratt's gaze slid to Abbott. Even Spenser chanced a glance at the ego-bloated mayor.

Abbott tipped his chin a bit higher. "The O'Ryans asked me to come. I felt it prudent to include Mr. Meyer and the judge."

If Erin and or Rick called Abbott, Elizabeth was going to wring their necks. She was getting sick and tired of people like those two circumventing her authority and bringing in yahoos like these three where they didn't belong. Two years on the job and she still hadn't broken the old mindsets that everything in regard to the law would involve politics or corruption. So much for handling the O'Ryans with kid gloves.

Elizabeth swept aside her jacket to settle her hands on her hips, her fingers brushing the grip of her service weapon.

"I suppose I have you to thank for the media?" she shot back.

Abbott kept his features schooled. "I had nothing to do with that. Perhaps it's a good thing they are here. Will keep everyone in mind that poor Andrea O'Ryan is missing."

Elizabeth gave him a cruel smile. "Straight for the kill." She shook her head. "Should have known Erin would blow our investigation and you would come waddling in like some glorified savior. Give some hyped-up story to the press to paint me as the incompetent female who should be at home convalescing from her surgery instead of out here investigating why two men were murdered."

Her words piqued the reporters' attention. They wanted a show. She was going to give them one.

"Now, Sheriff, that's not what's going on here," Pratt interjected.

"Bullshit! That's exactly what's happening. You're here as an upstanding citizen in the community. Spenser is here because he's the only willing judge who doesn't have ties to the criminal cases coming across his desk." Elizabeth's sneer landed on Abbott. "And he's here because it means he can have a hand in finding out what's going on to spin it to make his reelection look good." She leaned toward the men. "Or kill the story before the truth gets out."

Pratt scowled. "What story?"

Abbott's dark beady eyes twitched. He glared at Elizabeth but kept his mouth shut. An amazing feat for someone who loved the sound of his own voice.

"I want you off this property," Elizabeth said.

"We have a right to be here just as any other community member," Spenser rebutted. "Especially if we have permission by the landowners."

"Last I checked, Judge, this isn't the O'Ryans' property. The farmer who owns this ground has not given you permission to be here." She pointed at the line where the field ended and the O'Ryans' huge yard began. "If the O'Ryans want you here, get on their property. If you set foot over here again, I will have Deputy Fontaine arrest you for trespassing, disorderly conduct, and tampering with my crime scene. Would you like me to go on with the list of charges I can bring against the lot of you?"

This made Spenser's face turn red. "None of those would hold up."

"Maybe not, but they'd certainly make your life a living hell to get out of them. And tarnish your bids for continued public office."

Elizabeth stepped closer to Abbott, her hand easing down over the butt of her weapon. A threatening move, one her well-trained deputies and former military members had always warned her against doing in public. But damn it! She didn't care. She was done with this crap.

"Get. Off. My. Crime. Scene."

Fear flashed through Abbott's eyes. She had always suspected his bloated behavior hid a secret fear of women in power. Knowing what she did about his frequent visits to that out-of-way campsite and its suspected use, it did not surprise her in the least Abbott would cower. Given her extensive studies on psychological behavior, she'd pegged him as a narcissist, one who had been getting away with his misdeeds for far too long. His gig was up.

Judge Spenser took hold of Abbott's arm and tugged him away. "We're going, Sheriff."

"Oh, Judge," Elizabeth called out before they could get too far along. "I'd like for you to pay a visit to my office in two hours. I have some questions for you."

The man pursed his lips, his face taking on a pale hue just like Abbott's. With her request out there for all to hear, in order to save face, he'd have to show up. Then she'd nail him with the questions as to why he had ordered Orville and Jim to tear down the camp.

The two men pushed a path through the reporters, ignoring the recorders and microphones thrust into their faces. Pratt remained, studying Elizabeth. She returned his scrutiny with her own. He inched closer to her.

"What do you know, Elizabeth?" he asked in a low voice.

"Out of respect for your son and our ability to set aside differences in the past in the name of the greater good, I highly suggest that if there's something you need to clear the air about before things get truly ugly, I'd do it sooner rather than later."

His gaze widened. Without a word, he turned on his heel and escaped.

Rafe came to stand beside her, watching the trio part ways and the reporters chase them down. "Good deflect."

"Now to start dragging every single person on the list into the office. Get Meyer and Young on it."

"Young's hand is still giving her problems. Regular pain meds aren't strong enough."

"Have her make the calls. If someone gives her lip, send Meyer to pick them up. You and I will personally handle those three when it's their turns. Let's save them for after we're finished here."

Rafe nodded and took a step forward, then stopped. "Any luck figuring out who those two are out there?"

She shook her head. "Olivia will unmask them here as soon as Dayne and Lundquist are finished and we can get the bodies down."

A single reporter, a woman who worked for the local newspaper, someone Elizabeth had a good professional rapport with, separated from the pack of blood-thirsty jackals and headed back toward her. Alissa Rhinehart made a point to always shine a fair light on the sheriff's office, and Elizabeth respected her for it.

"Sheriff Benoit, are you able to relay any information at this time about the current situation?" Alissa asked.

"Unfortunately, it's too early into the investigation to give any information. Thank you for asking."

With a dip of her head, Alissa turned and walked away.

"Rafe," Elizabeth said after the reporter was out of earshot. "I want you to take special interest in Abbott's life behind closed doors. Do not let on to your snooping."

"Any particular reason?"

"Last night, Andrea told me the reason behind all those young women being at that campsite. Seems Abbott was fond of picking certain ones and gifting them with lavish souvenirs."

Rafe frowned. "In exchange for what?"

Anger, red-hot and fiery, seeped through Elizabeth's veins. It had taken an enormous amount of effort on her part to control the urge to track the bastard down and beat him to a pulp after Andrea admitted the purpose behind the camp and the gifts.

Abbott was not that far away. She could unleash holy hell on him.

"Elizabeth," Rafe said gently.

She blinked, the red haze filling her vision seeping away. The breath she hadn't realized she'd held squeezed free.

"Do you need to remove yourself from this case?" he asked.

"No." She turned her back on the bevy of reporters still following the three men. "He's been using the young women of our county as his personal escorts. That's putting it nicely."

An ungodly sound rumbled in Rafe's chest before he let loose with an uncharacteristically nasty curse. "Why didn't you arrest his ass on the spot?"

"Because all I have is the say-so of a traumatized woman. He's a slippery son of a bitch—he'd get out of it. No. I want all the fireproof evidence we can get to throw his ass in jail for good." Elizabeth started walking toward the trussed up scarecrows. "Let's get going on the groundwork."

"Yes, ma'am," Rafe called out.

Elizabeth had a gut feeling this whole thing was coming to a violent conclusion. Possibly the bloodiest one this county had ever seen. Whether it be metaphorically or literally, heads were going to roll.

She returned in time to see Kyle and Brent pull down the crosses. With the bodies laid out before Olivia, she squatted between the two men.

The ME peered up at Elizabeth. "Ready?"

"As I'll ever be. Let's see who these poor saps are."

Using a pair of sharp scissors, Olivia cut along the sides of the rubber masks. Then carefully peeled the first mask from the man on her right. Kyle and Brent swore. Olivia glanced at Elizabeth before removing the second.

Seeing their faces hit a hard place in the back of Elizabeth's mind. "Son of a bitch."

"Who are they?" Lila asked.

Of course she would not know them. She had not grown up here, had lived in Eckardt County for only shy of two years. Had yet to encounter every single person who resided in the county, even in the remotest sections.

"Deputy Dayne, I introduce you to Duane and Dale Jones. Two of the rottenest brothers to have ever run afoul of common decency," Elizabeth said.

"Now the 'you're welcome' makes sense," Kyle said. "Did Andrea mention if they had assaulted her?"

"Nothing more than snatching her from Deputy Young's home, tying her up, and blindfolding her." Elizabeth eased down and took a knee across from Olivia. "Her rescuers got to her in time before they could act on any urges. Or they were under strict orders to keep their dicks in their pants."

"By whom?" Lila asked.

"That would be the million-dollar question."

Olivia met Elizabeth's steady gaze. "This one for sure"—she pointed to Dale, whose face was covered in large, red rashes, his eyes swollen shut, and his lips enlarged—"died of anaphylaxis shock. Anyone know what he was highly allergic to?"

"Not a clue," Elizabeth answered. "No one from the Jones family was known for proper medical care. Hell, they thought doctors were voodoo priests and government con artists."

"I don't think a single one was ever born in a hospital," Kyle added.

"Guess we'll hope toxicology will help us figure that out." Olivia focused on Duane. "This one looks like he died of fright if his facial expression is any indication."

"Is that even possible?" Lila asked.

"Very, if he had a severe heart defect or some other medical condition. Nothing jumps out at me as a clear-cut cause of death. Autopsy should verify this." Olivia stood. "I'm not even going to hazard a guess on time of death. I've got my data for now. I'll get into detail during the autopsy."

Elizabeth rose. "Let's get these two out of here before some numbskull gets the bright idea to use a drone to capture images of this."

CHAPTER TWENTY-FIVE

FINISHED WITH THE crime scene, Lila dragged Kyle to her car and angled her body so none of the others could hear her.

"You need to find your sister."

"Don't you think I was considering that?" He glanced around, then bowed his head closer to her. "I overheard Meyer talking with the sheriff. She has some list of names."

Lila cocked her head to the side. "List of names for what?"

"Maybe you should find that out. I'm going to drop off the evidence box in my lab and get in contact with DCI. I'll go check for Freya in the expected places."

"If she's with Marnie as you suspect?"

"I don't know why I thought it. There's no way she'd ever go there." He rubbed the back of his neck. "Yet I never expected her to call Marnie when she was being threatened." He jerked his hand down at his side. "Who the hell is the guy after her she claims is Bre's killer?"

"You're asking the wrong person that question." Lila gripped his hand. "Go find her. I'll come up with a cover story if the sheriff starts asking where you are."

He looked at her hand in his, smoothing his thumbs over her knuckles. "Let me test the pill and the patch to see if I can come up with what drug it is."

"I don't know if it's a good idea. If we try to use it as evidence, we're going to open a whole slew of problems we don't have good answers for."

"We don't have to tell anyone about it. I want to know what drug it is simply because you exposed yourself to it."

She poked her finger into his vested chest. "If I let you do it, you can't say a word about where you found it."

"Fine. But would you reconsider telling the sheriff about the phone and stuff?"

"Yeah, that's going to look good on my part. Let's accuse the sheriff's sister of nefarious acts of the unknown."

"Could still be a fluke that she happened to look at her phone at the same instant. So many people are hardwired to their cells in this day and age, it's not impossible. The other two are more closely connected to the number than her if you consider the gum wrappers it was written on."

Lila scrunched her nose. "I just don't think it's the right time."

"Bad enough I blew it with chain of evidence. We can't keep hiding this from her. If it could become key evidence in the case against Sheehan—"

"I'm gonna stop you right there. This will never hold up in a court. I've been down that road, and it was ugly. Not me personally, but a fellow detective. She lost her job and seven years' worth of cases she'd worked were brought under scrutiny. There were crooks who got out of jail free because the key evidence prosecution used in nailing them for their crimes was found to be circumspect because she was the one who found it."

"This isn't Chicago."

"No. It's Iowa." Lila sighed, placing her free hand on his chest. "I know you mean well. And you're willing to own up to your mistake. But, Kyle, we're trying to prevent the very thing the sheriff has spent the last two years cleaning out of the county."

"Are you hearing yourself? You're actually arguing for a corrupt measure."

She shook her head. "It's not corruption if you don't make up a story and lie to use it to our advantage." She fisted his shirt and gave it a shake. "If we even hint at something that could implicate Sheehan, the sheriff is going to run straight down that rabbit trail and forget what she should really be doing."

Eyes closed, he nodded. "I can't argue with that."

"Hold steady. Somehow this will pan out. If it doesn't, we don't worry about it."

"Still concerns me what that person on the other end said. Only Andrea's rescuers knew about telling her to leave town."

Lila released his shirt and in an uncharacteristic move smoothed the wrinkles she'd created. "I'm worried about it too. But we don't have time to analyze it. Go find your sister." She pushed him toward his car.

"You be careful."

"I'm always careful."

He guffawed before folding his body inside his vehicle. Once he pulled away, Lila headed for her next target. Sheriff Benoit.

The lady herself was standing in front of her SUV, staring at the landscape before her. Lila took a spot next to her and leaned back against the cow-kicker.

"I should go visit with Hillary Peterson." Elizabeth resettled her crossed arms. "I'd like to go over Kerri's childhood bedroom if Hillary hasn't done anything to it."

"Are you asking me to come along?"

"If you wouldn't mind."

"Shouldn't you be letting the Jones family know their sons are dead?"

Elizabeth smiled at that. "There's no one left to tell."

"Don't they have any family anywhere?"

"Maybe a long-distant cousin who wouldn't claim them if they wanted." Elizabeth pushed off the metal bars protecting the vulnerable part of the SUV. "No one would be able to recall if they knew where anyone from the Jones family now resided. Best to let the dead lay dead in this case."

"What are we going to do with the bodies then?"

"Probably bury them next to their father. Not that he or they deserve the place of honor."

Lila, following the sheriff around to the driver's side of the SUV, frowned at Elizabeth's acidic words. "Who was their father?"

"Willard Jones, the sheriff Sheehan disposed when he took over all those years ago."

Blinking at her boss, Lila grappled with something to say and came up empty.

"Yeah. What a shithole our little county used to be. Get into your car, Deputy Dayne, and follow me."

LILA PARKED ALONG the street behind the Interceptor. She'd spent the whole drive to the Peterson house trying to piece together what the sheriff had told her. Trying to connect the dots was making her head hurt.

She gave Elizabeth a few moments to gather herself and exit the SUV before she exited her unit. The sheriff waited for Lila to join her on the multicolored pavers making up the sidewalk. They were in the residential part of town where well-maintained Victorians mingled with turn-of-the-century Craftsmans and Cape Cods. This was a part of town those with money, or pretended to have money, lived.

Hillary Peterson kept a neatly landscaped lawn, allowing the bright yellowed leaves of the maples to blanket the grass for that quaint Halloween feel. Topping off the charm were the cute *Peanuts The Great Pumpkin*-inspired decorations. Nothing spooky or scary for this yard. Seated on a wicker rocker, a happy-go-lucky pumpkin-head scarecrow waved to passersby from the porch. The white with dark red trim Craftsman home appeared to have been meticulously renovated in the last few years to keep up the aesthetic appeal of the street and its historical value for the town.

Lila did a bit of a double take as Elizabeth marched up the front porch steps. Not once this morning did the sheriff appear to be slowed down by her recent surgery. Apparently, bleeding surgery sites be damned, because Elizabeth was carrying her sidearm.

"You doing okay, Sheriff?"

Elizabeth held open the old-fashioned wood screen door and knocked on the interior red door. "I'm perfectly fine, Deputy."

"Just checking."

They waited a bit, then Elizabeth knocked again.

"Hillary, it's Sheriff Benoit," she called out.

Lila backed from the doorway and wandered over to the right-hand side of the porch to the driveway. She hadn't seen a vehicle parked in the drive. Farther down the paved lane sat a single-car garage, the door down.

Once again, Elizabeth knocked harder and called out to Hillary.

"She might not be home," Lila said over her shoulder.

"Would you check the garage for her car?" Elizabeth closed the screen door. "I'll try the back entrance."

Together they headed down the steps and around the house. Through a line of precisely trimmed hedges, Lila made out the top of a dark gray, painted fence. She parted from Elizabeth to find the door to the garage, while the sheriff entered the fenced-in backyard through the gate situated between the hedges. Lila was able to access a side entrance via a path between the Peterson property and the next-door neighbor. It was positioned on the far corner of the garage, tucked behind a pair of large waste receptacles. She heard Elizabeth knock as she grasped the door handle.

Locked.

Leaving the door, she headed back to the front side.

"Sheriff, is there another access point to the garage over there?"

It didn't make sense to have two doors on a garage, along with the door for the vehicle access, but stranger things were known to happen.

"There is."

Lila entered the backyard and came to a hard stop to gape at the elaborate pergola with hanging flowerpots, and climbing vines decked out in their autumn dresses. A paver patio extended from the wooden pergola to encompass a stone fire pit surrounded by Adirondack chairs.

"What does this woman do for a living?"

Elizabeth abandoned the back door. "She was an architect designer for some bigwig company out of the Quad Cities until two years ago."

"She gave it up?"

The sheriff shrugged. They headed to the second side entrance to the garage and discovered this door locked as well, but it had a glass pane. Lila cupped her hands around her eyes and peeked inside.

"No car."

"I'll give her a call."

Lila left the garage and headed for the back door while Elizabeth made the call. The paver-design patio met up to a small deck. Lila peered in the back door, noticing that it entered the kitchen. There was a window high up to her left, probably over the kitchen sink. To her right was another window, set at a lower level. She glanced over her shoulder. Elizabeth was still on the phone.

Lila looked in past the gauzy curtains framing the window. A spare room appeared to be set up as a craft/sewing space. She started to pull back from the window, but something caught her eye. Pressing flush to the glass, she stared hard at the narrow table lining the wall to the right. There, sitting on a stack of what looked like colorful cardstock, lay a familiar object.

"Sheriff."

"She won't answer her phone."

Lila reeled back from the window. "Look in there and tell me what you see."

Elizabeth returned her phone to its pocket as she moved up to the door. "What do you mean?"

"Look."

The sheriff mounted the single step to the deck and joined Lila by the window. She dipped her head down and copied what Lila had done to see into the room. Slowly, she pulled away. "The pendant on the table ..."

"Right side of the room against the wall," Lila finished for her.

"I really can't tell if it's the same style."

Lila touched the windowpane. "It's on a black velvet choker."

"We don't know that."

"Then we get inside and find out for certain."

"That's not going to happen without Hillary here to let us in. And we have no reason to go into her craft room."

Lila crowded the sheriff's personal space. "Then tell me this. Was Hillary here when Bre died?"

Elizabeth's head snapped back at the question. After a moment of thinking, her features slackened. "I don't know. I think so."

"How old is Hillary?"

"She's the same age as ... Marnie and Seraphina."

"Seraphina who?"

"Seraphine Russell, Denise Russell's younger sister." Elizabeth wandered away from Lila and stood on the edge of the deck, staring at the backyard. "All three of them were in the same class, but they didn't run in the same circles. Bre and Denise were my age. We three were friends." She wheeled around. "Come with me."

Lila chased after the sheriff. "Now where are we going?"

They were halfway down the drive when the squeal of tires on the street pulled them up short. A silver Buick SUV sped away, dodging a car backing out of a drive across the street.

Lila jogged to the end of the drive and tried to catch the plates, but the car was too far along.

"Who was that?"

Elizabeth's pinched features turned red. "I think that was Hillary."

"Why would she run when she spotted us?"

"Good question." Elizabeth grabbed Lila's arm and tugged. "Follow me."

"Okay, but where are we going this time?"

"Into the past."

CHAPTER TWENTY-SIX

ELIZABETH HADN'T BEEN kidding when she told Lila they were going into the past. Nothing about the Russell residence had changed in the last thirty years. In fact, Seraphina had done a bang-up job making sure time and weather hadn't destroyed the wheelchair ramp or anything else with the ranch-style home. That hadn't always been the case. For a few years, after Denise's death, things went to ruin.

Standing at Elizabeth's side as she knocked on the door, Lila studied the area. Unlike Hillary Peterson's part of town, Caroline Russell lived in an area that in post-World War II went through a fleeting boom as people moved out of farming the homestead and into industries and businesses. A lot of the old factories were now defunct, and businesses moved on or shut down. The prefabricated homes were left to fall in or turned into public housing for the poorer residents of Eckardt County. Elizabeth understood why Seraphina wanted to move her mother out of the area.

The interior door gave a little rattle as the locks were disengaged, then glided open on quiet hinges. From her chair, Caroline beamed. "Elizabeth, what brings you way out here?"

"I stopped by to say hi and see if Seraphina is here."

"She left early this morning to meet up with Marnie, I think." Caroline dragged the door open farther. "Why don't you come in for a spell. I've got a fresh pot of coffee."

Elizabeth glanced at Lila. "Sounds nice. We could always use a cup of coffee."

She and her deputy entered the house. They meandered into the living room and were greeted by a tail-wagging golden retriever wearing a wide collar with bold white lettering stating SERVICE DOG.

Elizabeth knelt, and the retriever wiggled his way into the circle of her arms. "Hello, Bono."

"Still like it black?" Caroline asked from the kitchen around the corner.

"That I do."

"And your deputy?"

Elizabeth glanced back at Lila, who was planted in front of a wall of framed pictures. "She takes it black as well."

She gave Bono a good ear scratching before joining her deputy. Family photos from happier times and not-so-happy ones hung on the wall in a wayward puzzle.

Lila tapped the black-framed photo of an adult Seraphina from a party of some kind. "I saw her in the bar last night talking to Marnie."

"She's here visiting." Elizabeth's gaze shifted to the senior picture of Denise, the last professional photo of her old high school mate. "I think she tries to come back every year at this time because she knows what her mother goes through."

"Do you think anyone has told either of them what's happened this week?"

"I'd rather Caroline find out from me than some vindictive person."

The clatter of cups on a tray greeted them as Caroline returned to the living room.

"Here you go," she said handing up the steaming red ceramic mugs. "It's pumpkin spice. Some blend Sera gets for me from someplace. I don't remember where. But it's good."

"That'll work for us." Elizabeth sipped the coffee. It was good.

While Lila remained standing, Elizabeth took a seat on a newer sofa. Caroline, with her own mug of coffee, wheeled herself into a spot left open for her chair.

"I'm glad you stopped by." Caroline frowned. "Should I be calling you Sheriff?"

"You can call me by my given name."

Caroline smiled. "Seems so strange seeing you in this official capacity when I recall the years you spent running around my yard swinging from the rafters."

From the corner of her eye, Elizabeth caught Lila's upraised eyebrow as her deputy regarded her. *Oh, yes, Deputy Dayne, your pulled-together sheriff was a wild child.* A girl who had been expected to be a well-behaved, eldest daughter and was everything not good and well-behaved. For every biting aside, every verbal jab to be the opposite of who she was, Elizabeth fought back the best way she knew how—defiance. Probably why she had been dead set on flying out of town on Joel's kite tails and taking on the world as she had.

"Those were the days." Elizabeth leaned back into the sofa and managed to get her left leg crossed over her knee. "Feels like forever ago."

Caroline looked into her mug, a brief bout of grief falling

over her. "I do miss those days."

The squeak of duty belt leather had the older woman looking up. Weathered features and wrinkled skin, dotted by dark spots spoke of too much time spent in the sun. The strawberry-blonde hair her daughters had inherited from her had gone silver. Elizabeth had forgotten that Caroline was in her late sixties, nearly seventy, just as her own parents were.

"How are your folks doing?" Caroline asked, as if she could read Elizabeth's thoughts.

"Living it up in Arizona." She chuckled. "Most people flee to Florida. Not my folks. Nope. They'd rather brave blazing hot desert temps and sandstorms than hurricanes and an invasive species of python."

Caroline chuckled. "They always were the type to buck trend." She sobered, looking Elizabeth dead in the eye. "I heard a rumor."

Tension took over the room. Remaining in her nonchalant position, Elizabeth waited for Caroline to go on.

"It's happened again. The same thing that happened to my girl is happening all over again."

"Where'd you hear this rumor?" Elizabeth pressed.

"Does it matter?"

Elizabeth glanced at Lila, who was hiding her face behind her mug but keeping a close eye on Caroline. Sensing that she was about to learn something she hadn't before, Elizabeth slid her foot to the floor and leaned forward.

"You have a secret to tell?" she asked.

Slowly, Caroline brought her mug to her lips and took her time drinking the coffee, then at a snail's pace set the mug down on the table next to her chair. She stared at the items scattered over the small tabletop, brushing her fingers against a white crocheted doily.

"You remember those years after the car accident?" Her hand continued to stroke the tightly woven threads. "How we struggled with my disability and the loss of my husband and his income?" Her fingers ceased their motions. "The way the girls suffered." Caroline looked at Elizabeth. "The way I suffered."

Elizabeth set her coffee mug aside and took Caroline's still hand in her own. The tensile strength in that warm grip came from countless years of maneuvering her chair around in daily life and using mostly her upper arms to transfer her body in and out of the chair.

"I remember. I've never forgotten how my family and the Fontaines did everything possible to help you out."

"Something I was forever grateful for but so ashamed to accept." Caroline's voice cracked. She pressed the fingers of her free hand to her lips. Once she settled, she clasped Elizabeth's hand between her own. "It just wasn't enough for Sera."

Elizabeth sensed Lila shifting from her position near the wall, but she didn't avert her gaze from Caroline.

"Ever since the day Denise was killed, Sera has been paying penance. For what, I have never fully understood. She claims it was her fault Denise died out there that snowy night." Caroline's eyes watered. "And it was because of her that Bre died."

"Did she say how exactly it was her fault?"

Caroline shook her head. "If I bring it up, she shuts me down." She waved her hand about the room. "All of the upkeep. The renovations. Keeping me comfortable. This is how Sera pays penance. She insists I need to move in with her, get away from here. But I can't. Too many memories are wrapped up in this home. Good memories. For her, they're only bad."

A buzzing sound came on the heels of Caroline's words. Elizabeth felt her phone vibrate again. Lila stepped forward and held out her hand. Elizabeth retrieved her phone from her jacket pocket and held it out to her deputy, who walked outside to answer it.

Left alone with the woman she had once upon a time thought of as the aunt she never had, Elizabeth scooted to the edge of the couch cushion to be closer. "Caroline, I never came to you after Denise was killed. When I came home for Bre's funeral, I was so wrapped up in my own rage and grief, I didn't once think of you. I'm sorry for that."

"You have more than made up for it since then, Ellie. There's no need to apologize. We were all struggling to understand."

"Did you ever figure out why Denise was out there that night?"

Caroline shook her head. "Sheriff Jones gave me some piss-poor excuse about an underage drinking party gone wild."

"Did he tell you who was there?"

"Claimed he couldn't get anyone to admit to being there. And if they did, they were underage, and law stated he couldn't release their names."

Elizabeth frowned. "Was Sera there?"

"I don't know. She wanted to spend the night with

Marnie. They were planning to crash the trick-or-treating after the little kids were done. I remember because Sera begged me to let her go. She was a senior in high school at the time, and I just couldn't understand why they wanted to do such a childish thing."

The door handled clicked. Elizabeth glanced back as Lila reentered the house. A grim line to her jawline spoke of bad news.

Seeming to sense the shift, Caroline squeezed Elizabeth's hand, pulling her attention back. "Listen to me. Sera has been behaving strangely since she got here Thursday night. Normally, when she visits me, she doesn't leave the house. I've barely seen her. And last night …"

"What about last night?"

"She thought I was sleeping, but I heard her speaking to someone. A voice I didn't recognize. Another woman."

"Did you hear what was said?"

"I only heard snippets because I was trying very hard not to eavesdrop. It didn't make any sense to me." Caroline drew in a sharp breath. "Something about the lane. I heard rope. And payback."

Elizabeth met Lila's troubled gaze. Whatever the phone call had been about might have something to do with what Caroline was saying.

"Was there anything else?" Elizabeth asked.

"Not that I can recall. I heard the door close when they left. I fell asleep shortly after. Sera was here this morning when I woke up. Had breakfast made for us and told me she was going to meet up with Marnie."

The infernal buzzing started again. With a sigh, Lila

stepped back outside to answer Elizabeth's phone.

"I'm right," Caroline said. "Another girl is dead. It's why you're here. Why you're asking about Denise. And Sera."

She released Elizabeth's hand then dug into a colorfully crocheted bag hanging inside the wheelchair's armrest. Her hand came free of the bag, and Elizabeth's heart stopped. Caroline grabbed Elizabeth's hand and pressed the object into her palm.

"I've been hiding this from Sera for years. I found it in her bedroom a week after Denise's death."

Elizabeth clenched her hand around the pendant attached to the black velvet choker.

"The symbol in the pendant," Caroline said. "It's a Viking rune. It has several different meanings, but the one that stood out to me, the one that made sense, was possession."

Scowling, Elizabeth lifted the pendant to examine the symbol. "How did you figure that out?"

"I've had twenty-five years to figure it out."

The door opened again, and Lila stepped inside. "Sheriff. We need to go."

Elizabeth flipped the pendant back into her palm and fisted it, then stood. "Caroline, thank you for the coffee."

"Ellie, you find the person who did this." Fire burned through Caroline's eyes. "Make them pay."

CHAPTER TWENTY-SEVEN

FOLLOWING LILA'S ORDERS, Elizabeth trailed the deputy vehicle back to the department with no explanation. Once they were both parked in the lot, Elizabeth stopped Lila before they walked up the sidewalk.

"I waited long enough. What were the phone calls?"

Lila held up a finger. "One was from Meyer, to let you know he's not having any luck with this list of names." She wagged her finger between them. "You and I are going to talk about this list and why I've not been told of its existence. Second call"—her middle finger joined the pointer—"was from Olivia. She can tell you exactly what killed the Jones brothers but wants to do that in person."

"Why are we here instead of at the morgue?"

"Because this list deal is more important." Lila headed for the sidewalk. "Olivia said she'd meet us here."

Heaving the biggest exasperated sigh she could muster, Elizabeth hiked after her deputy detective. They entered the building. A quiet building. The conference room where Andrea was supposed to be camping out was empty. Where was she?

Elizabeth and Lila rounded the corner at the end of the hall and discovered the reason for the silence. Two people were left in the bullpen.

Georgia stared at the space where they were now standing. Meyer was doing the same from his desk. Bentley, having heard Elizabeth enter, scuttled out of her office and over to greet her owner.

"Where is everyone else?" Elizabeth demanded, patting her dog's head.

"Andrea is in your office, sleeping again. Rafe took Deputy Young to look for our wayward and missing," Georgia quipped.

Elizabeth gave Bentley a final pat before the collie trotted back into her office, slinking through the gap wide enough for her sleek body. "Who is wayward and missing?"

"Fitzgerald has not reported in. And he's not home." Georgia pinned her gaze on Lila. "When was the last time you saw or spoke to him, Deputy Dayne?"

"Last night at Marnie's bar. We parted ways from there and that was the last time I saw him."

"Alexis said he never checked in with her last night," Georgia said.

"He hasn't missed a check-in before. Where would he go?" Elizabeth demanded.

Those left of her team stared back at her with questioning looks. How would they know where Fitzgerald had gone? She was such a dunce.

"He's not the only one missing," Georgia added. "Deputy Lundquist isn't answering his radio or his cell phone." Once again, she pinned a hard stare at Lila. "Care to answer that one?"

Lila threw back a sassy expression. "Deputy Lundquist is out looking for his sister. She ran off this morning like a bat out of hell."

"Why would she run off?" Elizabeth asked then held up her hand. "Wait, this has something to do with what happened with her yesterday."

"Something like that. We think she knows who killed Brendette."

Elizabeth's body turned frigid. "Come again?"

"At least, that's what she alluded to before she ran. Kyle was hoping to find her before *he*—whoever *he* is—finds her first and finishes whatever he planned to do to her yesterday."

"She said she knew who killed her sister?"

"Sheriff, I don't know if she knows or not. This is Freya we're talking about. She was pissed to find out about me and Kyle."

Meyer made a choking sound, bringing attention on himself from all three women. He cringed at his faux pas.

"Where would he think she'd run off to?" Elizabeth pressed.

Lila shrugged. "He thought maybe she went to Marnie's. Which is a ridiculous idea," she rushed the last bit. "By now, he would have been there and learned if she'd gone there or not. We told her to go to her café."

"Brent," Georgia said with a such mothering tone it made even Elizabeth straighten up. "Tell the sheriff."

The look of regret he gave Elizabeth made her chest seize. "Marnie's not home. The back door to The Watering Hole was wide open and Luna was running around outside, yowling."

Elizabeth had to grip the back of a chair and lock her

knees to keep from hitting the floor. "You checked the place over?"

"Yes." Meyer swallowed, glanced down at the stack of files on his desk, then back up at her. "I've called Marnie several times. She's not answering. Her phone goes straight to voicemail like it's turned off."

"Why were you there in the first place?"

"Looking for Sheehan." He grabbed up a few sheets of notepad paper. "I learned some things in my research on that list, and I decided talking to him was better than guessing. If he would have said anything to me."

Meyer rose from his desk and brought over the sheets of paper. The top sheet was Jim's list with certain names circled in red. "I've called about half of the list. No one is answering, or when they did, they hung up on me right away."

Elizabeth shifted through the pages, skimming what he'd written, until a name caught her eye. She shuffled the page to the top and read thoroughly.

In July of 2013, a parent who demanded to remain anonymous called Sheriff Sheehan to report inappropriate behavior with this anonymous caller's daughter on the part of a certain individual in an official capacity. When Sheriff Sheehan learned the young woman was of a consenting age, he stated there was nothing he could or would do about it unless the young woman pressed charges for harassment. The report states nothing after this.

She shook the sheet at Meyer. "Did you find a name of this individual in official capacity?"

Meyer shook his head. "I went through the reports from that year, the year before, and after. Found nothing. This report was scarce on details, and I didn't find any others like it." He went back to his desk and picked up a file, bringing it back to her. "I did, however, find these."

Lila moved to stand at Elizabeth's shoulder.

Lila took the handwritten notes and list. "Who gave you this list?"

"Jim."

"This list is a who's who of men in this county." Lila's gaze narrowed as she moved to the next sheet with the names of all the young women who had been there over the years. "What the hell? Was the camp some kind of brothel? This looks like a damn prostitution ring."

Elizabeth scowled. "Quiet. One of those poor women is sleeping in the next room. She feels bad enough about being used in that way. We don't need to rip the wounds open further."

Lila closed her eyes and drew in a breath as her way of acquiescing. She remained silent as she strode over to the dry-erase board, turned it over to the side with all their information, and tacked the lists to the side with magnetic clips.

Elizabeth flipped open the file Meyer had given her and shuffled through the pages of reports on disturbance calls made over the last twenty-five years in the general area of where they'd found the encampment. If Sheriff Jones had taken the complaint, nothing more was done. If Sheehan took them after he assumed office, he managed to make a few public intoxication arrests in the area, but other than that there was nothing more significant than misdemeanor counts.

"This is why you went to look for Sheehan?" she asked Meyer.

"I was tired of making speculations. I was really hoping he'd be honest with me. Figured he was at Marnie's since he spends half of his life there."

"Not necessarily," Lila added. "For some god-awful reason, he owns shares in the Dew Drop Inn. Maybe he's there."

"You know this how?" Elizabeth asked.

It would explain why she and Rafe had spotted Sheehan there on certain occasions over the last year.

"Fitzgerald took me there yesterday when we went looking for Orville and Jim. Sheehan was inside. Admitted to being part owner."

Lila moved back to the dry-erase board, this time picking up a marker. "We've got bigger issues at hand." She started writing, adding in the discovery of the Jones brothers' corpses and Freya's revelation. "Two separate things are going on here."

"Hold up," Elizabeth ordered, looking at the clock. "Georgia, get on the horn and tell Judge Spenser to get here. I gave him orders to visit me—his two hours are up and he's not here."

Georgia got to it. Elizabeth shifted her focus to Meyer.

"Did Rafe say anything to you about looking into Mayor Abbott? Whether he learned something new?"

"If he did, he didn't relay any information to me. I think that was who he planned to go visit when he and Deputy

Young left here."

"How long ago was that?"

He looked at the wall clock. "Maybe an hour before you and Deputy Dayne arrived."

Georgia hung up the phone, her brows furrowed. "Judge Spenser's wife said he left the house early this morning and hasn't returned. She hasn't heard from him all morning, and she's tried calling his phone and he's not answering. They were supposed to be at a birthday party for one of their grandkids."

"Start writing these names down," Elizabeth told Lila. A thought hit Elizabeth and cold dread washed over her. "Seraphina Russell was supposed to be meeting up with Marnie this morning."

"You know this how?" Georgia asked.

"Russell's mother told us this," Lila said. "You think ..."

The office door creaked. Elizabeth stepped around the chair she'd been using as support as Andrea, with Bentley at her side, exited the room. The young woman's gaze bounced from person to person, landing on Elizabeth as she approached.

"Sheriff?"

Elizabeth gripped Andrea's shoulder. "What is it?"

Andrea's eyes were wild with fear, her face pale. She stepped out of the office doorway and staggered toward Elizabeth. "Sheriff, there's something else I need to tell you," she said softly. "Something I ... I wanted to tell you from the start. But he warned me to keep my mouth shut."

"What, Andrea? Who told you to not talk?"

"They said I couldn't. If I squealed, Allegra would be in

trouble." She choked on a sob. "Or worse. I'm sorry. It got out of hand. It wasn't supposed to happen like this."

Elizabeth looked to Lila for answers. The deputy only shrugged.

Elizabeth gave the young woman a reassuring squeeze and caught her teary-eyed attention. "Andrea, I don't understand. What do you mean, Allegra would be in trouble? Who is he? Who are they?"

After taking a few deep breaths, Andrea plowed forward. "Kerri, Allegra, and I were helping Kelley Sheehan."

This brought Lila wheeling around. "You were what?"

Elizabeth gaped at the girl. "Explain."

"He asked us to help him shut down that camp. He'd been trying to do it for years, but none of the girls he approached before would help. We were the only ones who would do it."

She could now connect Sheehan with the camp, with the whole sordid affair. But not as she expected. *Damn it!* The old codger was proving himself every bit the antihero in the whole scenario. He was the Severus Snape to her Harry Potter.

"Andrea, what did Kelley ask you girls to do?" Elizabeth asked.

The young woman trembled under Elizabeth's hold. Beneath them, Bentley whined, sensing the terror taking hold of everyone in the room.

"We were to get close to all those men. Report back to him and his partners what was going on. He didn't know if Allegra would be taken in since she's Black, but a few of them didn't care."

Elizabeth placed both her hands on Andera's shoulders. "What really went on in that camp?"

Her features crumpled and a sob escaped. Elizabeth dragged her into her arms and held Andrea as she wept. Through the blubbering, Andrea hiccupped her confession. They, along with three other young women from the county, had been prostituted. It had been going on for decades.

Elizabeth closed her eyes against the red haze filling her vision. These men, starting with the one who orchestrated this whole setup, were going to burn for their depravities.

Gently, she pried Andrea out of her arms and cupped the young woman's face. "Andrea, dear, why in the world would you ever agree to something like that? Especially with a man like Kelley Sheehan."

She gulped, her stricken features going impossibly pale. "He blackmailed us."

Once a son of a bitch, always a son of a bitch.

"With what?"

Closing her eyes and lowering her head, Andrea shuddered. "He caught Kerri and Allegra selling drugs."

"That explains the fentanyl patches I discovered."

Andrea startled out of Elizabeth's arms at Olivia's clipped voice.

"That's what the patch was?" Lila asked.

Olivia scowled, stalking toward Lila. "How do you know about a patch?"

Lila blanched. "How do you know about the patch?"

"I found several of them on the Jones brothers. When I did a closer examine on Kerri's body, I found two on her lower back. I missed them in my previous exam because they're colored the same skin tone as hers. Now explain yourself, Deputy."

"Kyle and I found a pill and a patch in the girls' apartment."

"What the hell are the two of you talking about?" Elizabeth broke into their back and forth.

Andrea was now cowering behind Elizabeth.

"Okay!" Georgia hollered, coming around her desk and entering the middle of the fray. "We've got too many things going on at once."

"I'll say," Meyer remarked.

"You three," Georgia pointed to the women. "Sheriff's office. You hash out your evidence and timeline there. Andrea, you're going to sit with me until the county attorney arrives. We need some lawyers around here. And Deputy Meyer." She zeroed in on the lone male deputy. "You get on the horn and start talking with Deputy Fontaine. We've got a mess a'brewin' and not enough help for it."

When no one moved, Georgia clapped her hands. "Get!"

Elizabeth trailed Lila and Olivia into her office, pausing in the doorway to look back at Andrea. "You write down everything, Andrea. Everything."

Shutting the door behind her, Elizabeth faced the other two. "What the hell is going on in my county?"

CHAPTER TWENTY-EIGHT

"FIRST THINGS FIRST," Olivia said and squared up with Lila. "The fentanyl patch you found. Give it."

"It's in my car. Hang on." Lila bolted out of the office through the side door.

Head spinning, Elizabeth stumbled over to her desk and dropped into the chair. "Liv, I mean it, what the hell?"

When she took over the position of sheriff, Elizabeth spent many a free moment going over the reports, the evidence, the trail—what little of it there was—and got nowhere. There was a cover-up, it was plain as day, more so now than in the last twenty-five years. At first, her suspicions had circled around the sheriff's department as the culprits, but as pieces were dropping into place this go around, it looked like the corruption was far reaching into every aspect of everyday life.

"Ellie, I'm going to be blunt here, but this is what you expected when you took office. Your friend's death was your catalyst." Olivia crouched down in front of Elizabeth and took both her hands in her own. "This whole ordeal has been a rumbling volcano for decades and it's erupting. Don't you quit now."

Elizabeth just stared at Olivia, studying every wrinkle, every plane to her friend's face. Closing her eyes, Elizabeth drew in a deep breath, bowed her head, and exhaled. Out in the bullpen, Andrea's conversation with Georgia drifted in through the open door.

Through the chaos in her mind, a phrase screamed to the forefront. Andrea's phrasing. Elizabeth snapped her eyes open and bolted from the chair, startling Olivia.

Mumbling a quick apology, Elizabeth bypassed her friend and hurried to the door. She grabbed each side of the frame and leaned out.

"Andrea."

The young woman swung her startled gaze Elizabeth's way. "Yeah?"

"You said partners. Sheehan had partners?"

Andrea nodded, then glanced at Georgia.

"Who are they?"

Behind Elizabeth the side door to her office closed. Lila was back.

"They won't be in trouble?" Andrea asked.

Elizabeth's grip on the wooden frame tightened. God, in her experience, no good news ever came from someone when they asked if another person would be in trouble. "As long as they have not done anything illegal, no, they won't be in trouble."

Andrea wrung her hands. Elizabeth did her best to beat back the impatience roaring in her body. The girl needed time to accept her word.

Finally, Andrea lifted her chin and looked Elizabeth dead in the eyes. "It was Marnie. And Deputy Fitzgerald."

Had she not been holding onto the doorframe for dear life, Elizabeth would have collapsed to the floor.

"Holy shit," Lila uttered behind her.

"That's it?" Elizabeth forced out.

Andrea nodded and said nothing more.

Gentle hands pried Elizabeth from the doorway and guided her to the nearest chair.

"Sit," Olivia ordered.

Lila's mantra continued as she paced the floor. Elizabeth watched in stunned silence.

This was not happening. She did not just hear a girl implicate her sister in illegal activity. No! It was a lie. Sheehan and Fitzgerald she could see pulling off something like this. Not Marnie. Never Marnie.

Burying her face in her hands, Elizabeth bent at the waist and began breathing hard, rocking. Every inch of her protested. Every fiber of her being wanted to scream. To beat someone to a bloody pulp. First on the list was Kelley Sheehan. He did this. He was the cause of all of this.

Marnie's plea yesterday morning broke through the white noise. She'd begged Elizabeth to never stop loving her. This was what prompted the unexpected statement. This was what Marnie had been hiding for years. Why she tolerated Sheehan's presence at the bar. All this time she'd kept this secret from Elizabeth. What else was she hiding?

Dragging her hands down her face as she lifted her head, she wiped the frustrated tears dripping from her eyes. Olivia and Lila stood there, waiting.

They needed a plan. Something to keep them hot on this trail. But what?

"Sheriff," Lila said. "It's time you saw this."

Her deputy stepped forward and held out a small flip

phone and three wads of gum wrappers.

"What is this?"

"Fairly certain this is how Andrea and the others were able to stay in contact with Sheehan."

Elizabeth took the phone and opened it, seeing that it had made a call last night. "You've had this the whole time?"

"Only since yesterday morning. Andrea left it in Young's house. The wrappers with the phone numbers we got the night before."

"We?"

"I found one in Kerri's room." Lila's features pinched. "Kyle found another in Allegra's."

"Why didn't you say anything before now?"

Sighing, Lila's eyes rolled heavenward for a few moments. "Because Kyle did an unauthorized search of Allegra's room. I didn't want to get your hopes up. It's a mess, okay." She tapped the phone in Elizabeth's hand. "Last night, I tried the number again, and someone picked up. They warned Andrea that she was to leave town or else."

"Or else what?"

"Don't know, they hung up."

Elizabeth scrutinized her deputy. "You're not telling me something. What?"

After a bit of lip gnawing, Lila straightened. "While I was at The Watering Hole last night, I tried that number again on my own phone. I witnessed Sheehan, Marnie, and Fitzgerald doing something on their own phones at the same exact time. I couldn't tell if it was just a weird coincidence that they all answered a text or call or ..." Lila held out her hands and shrugged. "Now with Andrea's revelation ..."

"How would one phone number be connected to three different phones?"

"It's possible," Meyer said from the doorway. He slipped into the office. "There's an app that could handle doing it. If those three had it on their phones, it would link a single phone number to theirs. It takes on the conference call aspect then."

Elizabeth shook her jumbled head. "I don't understand why my sister would be involved with something that's in essence an escort service. My God! She's a freaking pimp."

"I doubt that's what Marnie would say she was," Lila interjected. "Andrea told us Sheehan was trying to shut down the whole encampment."

"Doesn't matter. He blackmailed them into helping and in the end forced those girls to have sex to get information." Elizabeth banged the back of her head against the chair rest. "He turned my sister into freaking Ghislaine Maxwell."

"Jeffery Epstein he is not," Olivia countered. "You've got that backward. The men who created the whole camp and its reason for existence are the ones we should be focused on."

"Liv is right," Lila added. "There has to be a legitimate motive for Marnie's involvement."

The radio crackled to life at Georgia's desk, and Rafe's voice broke through asking for Lila. The deputy detective left the office and returned Rafe's summons.

"Lila's right, Ellie. Marnie had to have a damn good reason to do whatever it was she did with Sheehan."

"He has to be blackmailing her. He did it to the girls; he's doing it to my sister." Elizabeth groaned. "It's the only feasible excuse for her to have anything to do with him."

"What would he blackmail her for?"

Lila poked her head back into the office. "We need to leave. Now."

Elizabeth bolted upright at Lila's strident tone. "What happened?"

"We have an officer down. It's Fitzgerald."

Elizabeth balled her fist so hard her knuckles cracked. A chilled hand grabbed her elbow. She glanced over and met Olivia's concerned gaze.

"What happened?" Elizabeth managed to squeeze past her tight throat.

"I don't know for sure. Fontaine said he's in a bad way and EMS is on the way."

"Where are they?"

"At Wailing Lady Lane."

"I'm coming too," Olivia said. "Best to have a doctor on site in case Fitzgerald's injuries are severe."

"I don't care. We're going now." Elizabeth slapped her keys to the Interceptor into Lila's hand. "You drive." She turned to Meyer. "Did you attempt to contact your father?"

He shook his head. "Still holding to your orders to hold back and let you handle him."

"I'm rescinding those orders. Go to his home and see if he's there. If not, seek out him, Abbott, and Spenser. Those three were together this morning, they still have to be. Maybe they went to the encampment and that's why no one can contact them."

He nodded, but before he could leave, Lila grabbed his arm.

"Rookie, be careful. Do not approach them if they're

there. Call us."

Meyer stared at his sometimes partner. Elizabeth sensed he still had a thing for Lila but knew she was with Kyle and wouldn't ever come between them. He'd been through a lot over the last two years himself.

He gripped Lila's hand then exited to do his sheriff's bidding.

Elizabeth pushed her deputy forward and the three women left her office, Bentley scurrying after them. Elizabeth turned to command the collie to stay, but something in her made her stop. Changing her mind, she allowed the dog to come.

"Georgia, hold down the fort. Get Deputy Lundquist to meet us out there," she ordered as she passed the dispatcher's desk. "Andrea, stay here with her. If you need more police presence, call Ed and ask if he can send over one of his officers."

"Sheriff, wait." Andrea jumped up from her seat and rushed over to Elizabeth, slamming into her, and hugging her. "Be careful."

Elizabeth met Georgia's worried gaze. Wrapping her arms around the young woman, she returned Andrea's hug. "I always am. Besides, I have some of the best law enforcement officers working for me."

Andrea bit her lip. Without another word, the young woman released her and backed to Georgia's desk.

Before Lila left the bullpen, she unlocked the gun safe and withdrew a shotgun, a rifle, and boxes of ammo for both. She handed the rifle to Elizabeth. "We're going nowhere without extra firepower." She relocked the safe.

"I don't think these will be necessary, Deputy."

"I'd rather hope not, but I'm not taking any chances. Especially if we end up going into the woods."

Olivia gave Elizabeth a sidelong look then dipped her chin in agreement. Elizabeth wanted to argue, but Lila had a point. After her own abduction and fight for survival in the woods of Eckardt County without a weapon, she had every reason to want backup firepower.

Elizabeth wished that niggling feeling in the back of her mind and in her gut was nothing more than stress and recovery from surgery. Because God forbid any more blood was spilled in this battle to clean up Eckardt County.

CHAPTER TWENTY-NINE

LILA DROVE LIKE a bat out of hell, lights flashing, siren blaring, straight for the juncture of the gravel county road and Wailing Lady Lane. She had only been out this way once with Kyle when they were responding to a tractor accident. After the incident was cleaned up and reported, she'd learned about the story of Wailing Lady Lane. Never the superstitious type, Lila shrugged it off as local lore.

Now? Now with Halloween, her least favorite holiday of the year, hours away and the chaos expanding in the last two days, Lila was reconsidering her lack of belief in the supernatural.

Georgia had contacted them two minutes ago to relay that she was unable to get in touch with Kyle. Elizabeth had commandeered Lila's phone and tried to hail him. Lila made every effort to focus on the road and not let a niggling of panic set in. He had to be with Freya.

Lila glanced in the rearview mirror to check on Olivia. The ME was fiddling with her phone.

"Doc, what were your findings on the Jones brothers? We never did get around to that," Lila asked.

From her position in the passenger seat, Elizabeth brought her head up, ceasing her efforts to call Kyle so Lila could drive. "That's right. What did you learn?"

"Both men had injection sites in their thighs. It could have been a powerful painkiller, like oxycodone or fentanyl, and lots of it. When I got their clothes off, I found their arms, legs, and torsos sliced to ribbons. Whoever did that to them wanted to disrupt their pain receptors to get maximum damage to them. Except Dale died from anaphylaxis shock. All of his wounds are post-mortem. It's possible his killer or killers didn't know or didn't care that he was dead."

"And Duane?" Lila asked.

"Between the torture and the drugs, his heart gave out."

"Why didn't we see any blood at the scene?" Elizabeth asked.

"Wherever they were initially tortured was where they bled. They were reclothed before transporting them, blood should be in the vehicle. Some seeping happened, but the cuts weren't deep enough for them to bleed out and die from those wounds. I also found rope burns on their ankles and wrists like they were restrained."

Lila drove the Interceptor off pavement onto the gravel road. Dust billowed behind the vehicle, coating the back window. She had another mile and half to go before they reached the meeting point.

"If there was oxycodone or fentanyl in their system, where the hell would the killer get access to it?" she asked. "When Fontaine went to fill the sheriff's prescription after her surgery, he literally had to sign his life away to make sure it was going to the correct person."

"It's very likely the killer or killers have access to it because they're in the medical field, whether in a hospital or a pharmacy," Olivia said. "Let's not kid ourselves. It's still easily gained illegally."

Which was exactly how Kerri and Allegra got access to theirs. Andrea didn't elaborate where the girls were getting the drugs or the patches—which screamed medical field, because the patches were used on patients with serious to terminal illnesses.

Elizabeth made a choked sound. Lila glanced at her, pulling the wheel in the same direction and nearly causing an accident.

"What?"

The sheriff shook her head. "Nothing."

"Oh, don't give me that nothing crap. It's something or you wouldn't have had a choking attack."

"It's just not possible. She wouldn't do that. Couldn't."

"She who?" Olivia pressed.

Ahead, Lila made out the flashing lights of the bus and Fontaine's Charger.

"You've got two seconds to tell us what you're talking about," she said, slowing the SUV.

"Seraphina Russell." Elizabeth blew out a breath. "She's a pharmacist."

"Which would give her full access to a whole slew of drugs." Lila pulled the Interceptor behind Fontaine's car, parked, and left the engine running. "And she'd have motive for going after the Jones brothers if they had a hand in her sister's death."

Elizabeth shook her head. "They weren't old enough. Duane's a year younger than Marnie and Sera, and Dale is three years younger. The only thing connecting them to any of this was Andrea's abduction. Why would Sera go after them for Andrea? She was never friends with Erin or Rick."

"What about Hillary?" Lila asked.

"That makes even less sense."

Olivia huffed. "You need to stop thinking about how this should connect and start reconsidering everything you've ever known about these people. Especially your sister."

Lila spotted Fontaine coming their way, and she held up her hand. He came to a stop and scowled at her. Elizabeth's features morphed between confusion to anger and finally resignation.

"The only way we're going to get straight answers is to ask Ben." Lila reached over the console and took her phone from Elizabeth. "I'm going to keep trying Kyle."

"Don't bother. We're in a dead zone out here," Elizabeth said and pushed out of the SUV.

Lila checked her cell service and groaned. Sheriff was right. No Gs. No bars. "I really hate parts of this county," she grumbled as she turned off the engine.

"Radios," Elizabeth said as she headed for Fontaine.

Bentley tore after her owner while Lila and Olivia hung back.

"This is already bad on so many levels," Olivia said in a low voice. "Top among them is the fact she's rushing around only days after surgery."

"You aren't going to be able to sideline her. She's got the bit in her mouth and she's running hell-bent for leather."

Irony being what it was in this new life of hers in the rural areas of Iowa, Lila was thrown for a loop when they passed the ambulance and saw the horse trailer and truck.

"Isn't that interesting," Olivia muttered.

"Able to get back there unless we ride," Fontaine was telling Elizabeth.

"Wait, what?" Lila demanded. "Ride horses? Where?"

"You ain't ... got a ... choice," a voice rasped behind Fontaine.

Fontaine stepped aside to reveal Fitzgerald propped up on a stretcher. Horror slammed into Lila. She and Olivia swarmed the gurney.

Fitzgerald's swollen face was covered in bruises, gashes along one eye and his bottom lip split wide open. Cuts crisscrossed his shirtless torso. An air cast encased his left leg.

"My God, Ben," Lila sputtered. "Who did this?"

He tried to swallow, but the effort must have been painful. "I don't know." He panted. "Left me ... for ... dead."

Olivia gently took Fitzgerald's wrist and examined it. "Were you tied up?"

"No." He lifted to point at his face. "Hit me ... back of head. Put a hood ... over ... Beat me." His hand flopped on his chest. "Broke leg." He rested his head against the pillow.

Lila grimaced. "How the hell did you get out here?"

"He dragged himself to the road," Fontaine finished. "Had Young and I not come along on a hunch, God knows what would have happened."

The tap of steel horseshoes against the gravel made Lila turn. Young, her bandaged hand tucked to her chest, rode up on a dark gray horse. Wearing her uniform and a black ball cap, her long, dark hair a plait tossed over her shoulder, she looked comfortable astride the horse.

"Sheriff, if we're going in, we need to go now before we lose daylight," she said.

"Should she be doing that?" Lila asked, looking at Olivia.

"She," Young snapped, "has ridden with far worse damage to her than a cut hand."

"Deputy Young is right. We need to go. Now," Elizabeth said. "Rafe, we've brought an extra shotgun and rifle. Are there scabbards on the saddles?"

"Yes. I'll grab the guns. Young has already loaded up my extras from the car."

Lila turned to the sheriff. "You do know I've never ridden."

"You'll be fine. It's like riding a bike."

"Except it has a mind of its own and will buck you off," Young added, turning her horse to face the trailer.

"Corey, we don't need any fearmongering," Elizabeth chided as she walked past the horseback deputy.

"You really shouldn't be riding, Ellie," Olivia called after her and gave chase.

Stiff as a board, Lila stayed rooted in place next to Fitzgerald's stretcher. What the hell was she doing? She'd never been on the back of a horse in her entire life. Why couldn't they use ATVs? Now that was something she could handle.

"Why aren't we using the four-wheelers?" she asked Fontaine as he passed with the weapons.

He paused and glanced at her. "Because the underbrush is bad in there. You can't see a damn thing unless you're on the back of a horse."

"We can't stay on the road?"

"For three quarters of a mile, maybe. After that it's gone. It's a dirt road, Dayne, which means everything grew back in place." He continued forward to the trailer. "You'll be fine."

It was a dirt road, in a heavily wooded timber, with a history of haunts and spooks, and she was a woman who had barely survived being hunted down like prey by a twisted psychopath in a similar setting. Yeah, this had all the hallmarks of a great idea. *Not!*

"What's back there?" she asked Fontaine.

A hand fell on her wrist. Fitzgerald's eyes, what little of them she could see through his swollen lids, burned.

He tugged her closer to him. "They have Kyle and Marnie."

Lila's heart flew into her throat. Pressing against the gurney's steel braces to get closer to him, she grappled to take his hand from her wrist and gripped his. "How?"

"Freya." He tried to shake his head but winced instead and sank against the upright stretcher.

"Deputy, we really should get him to the hospital," one of the medics said.

Lila laid Fitzgerald's hand on the white-sheeted pad. "Go." She stepped out of the way for the two medics to move the stretcher. "Send another bus or two this way," she told them.

Just in case I fall off a horse and crack my head open.

The one who took lead gripped the brim of his ball cap in acknowledgement. When they had wheeled the gurney to the back of the ambulance, Lila headed for the horse trailer.

They, those sons of bitching *they* had Kyle and Marnie. Who else did they have? How did Freya fit into this? How did Fitzgerald know they had those two but not know who it was who beat him?

Lila stumbled up to the left side of the trailer to find four saddled horses and the owner speaking with Fontaine. She leaned into the huge steel trailer and hugged her body. Everything about this whole damn case—the homicides, the prominent men using young women for sex, and the secrets that flew like flies everywhere—was a nightmare. She'd thought the serial killer case she'd worked in Chicago, provoking the man to attack her not once but twice, had been a convoluted mess.

This whole thing was worse.

A year ago, Kyle had been hurt when he came between her and the killer who'd stalked her. Now he was in the clutches of a faceless assailant who had already killed two men, severely injured another, and was working up to something big.

Lila pushed off the trailer. *Screw it!* No way was she going to allow a bit of psychological warfare on her part get between her and doing her job. No way in hell would she allow her fears to prevent her from protecting someone she loved. Yes, she did love Kyle, in a weird, complicated way.

Elizabeth parted from the horse she'd chosen to ride and approached Lila. "I know it's bad, but we need all hands on deck. These horses are the best and the safest. You'll be fine."

"Fitzgerald told me they have Kyle." She worked saliva into her mouth then swallowed. "And Marnie."

The blood drained from Elizabeth's face. Lila's hands shot out and grasped her boss's arms before she buckled.

"Who the hell are they?" Elizabeth ground out.

"I don't know, but they sure as hell are going to get what's coming to them."

CHAPTER THIRTY

Wailing Lady Lane spread before them like a path in a horror movie. A path only the crazy, addle-brained slasher-flick fan would dare to run down, believing they could outrun the chainsaw-wielding killer. Elizabeth adjusted her seat in the saddle, gritting her teeth against the twinges coming from her healing abdomen. Riding would take different, unused muscles, and she'd regret every minute of being on the back of a horse, but right now she didn't care. Somewhere, deep in the middle of this untamed land was her sister and one of her deputies. Nothing was stopping her from finding Marnie.

Olivia had tried to put up an argument to come with them, but Lila's insistence that this required people with proper weapons training ended the argument. Olivia promised to stay put with the owner of the horses, waiting for Meyer and the extra ambulances Lila had ordered to show up. Though she promised to stay, it didn't mean it stopped the ME from pacing the length of the truck and horse trailer.

A series of sharp barks tugged on Elizabeth's heart. She'd had to shut Bentley inside the Interceptor to keep her from following them. The collie was frantic. A part of Elizabeth knew the dog sensed danger. But there was no way she'd risk her dog's life, whether it be at human hands or the wild animals willing to prey on the domestic one.

Facing forward, Elizabeth put her friend and her pet out of her mind. They needed to pick up the pace. The shadows were growing fast in the east. Once the sun was down, they would be at the mercy of whoever waited for them.

"Ellie." Rafe rode to her right, sitting tall in the saddle, looking the part of a Wild West sheriff. He and Joel had grown up riding horses, even did a stint during high school on the rodeo circuit as team ropers. "We need to book."

"I know." She glanced over at Lila, riding between her and Young. "Lila, sit forward in the saddle, don't squeeze your legs, and hold onto the reins."

The woman's panicked eyes flicked her way. "Why?"

Behind her head, Elizabeth caught Young's wide grin. She half-expected the woman to let out a war whoop when they moved into a canter.

"Because we're gonna run," Young said.

"Oh my God, seriously?" The trepidation in Lila's voice did a lot to mask the fear for her lover that she had done a pitiful job of hiding.

Not that Elizabeth had any room to speak when she was scared out of her damn mind for her sister.

"Burning daylight," Rafe said and with a smooch, he drove his dark bay into a lope.

Elizabeth took two seconds to admire the man's backside as he rode. That was enough.

Young clicked her horse into gear. Both riders shot ahead. Elizabeth's sorrel quivered, wanting to run.

"Lila, just breathe. The horse will do all the work." And with that bit of wisdom, Elizabeth gave her mare her head and took off.

In her wake, Lila let out a caustic curse and then shrieked. If they weren't heading into a hellish landscape, Elizabeth would find humor in this. She held the mare back until Lila's gelding caught up. Like every inexperienced rider before her, Lila hunched over the saddle horn, holding on to it and the reins for dear life.

"Sit up," Elizabeth ordered.

"To hell with that. I'm falling off."

"He's got the smoothest lope out of all of these horses. Sit up."

Lila managed to do as she was ordered. The farther they rode, the more confident she grew until she wasn't clinging to the saddle horn.

Three quarters of the way down the lane the dirt turned to weed-infested grass. They slowed the horses to a trot. A little over a mile in, they had to return the horses to a walk as the weeds reached the horses' bellies.

"Where did Fitzgerald say he was ambushed and left?" Lila asked as she navigated her horse through the chest-high underbrush.

"He didn't," Young answered. "He was so disorientated. We couldn't find where he dragged himself from either."

"Where are all their vehicles?" Elizabeth asked. "Each of them would have driven out here, and I don't see the cars."

"We couldn't find those either," Young said.

"Maybe our infamous *they* hid the vehicles somewhere back here," Lila suggested.

"It's possible," Elizabeth said. "But we should see signs of that."

Rafe fell back to her side. He kept a constant sweep of their progress.

"How close are we to the old farmstead?" Elizabeth asked in a low voice.

"First place is less than a mile up. Trees and bushes have taken over the yard and fields." He reined his horse closer to hers. "I haven't seen signs of anyone having come this way. I don't think our suspects took the vehicles elsewhere."

"Wasn't there another road on the far eastern edge of the property lines?"

"Going north and south, yeah. Hunters still use it to get back into the fields. It's possible whoever is back here used that way to get in. Could be hiding out at the second homestead."

"That's almost a mile from the first place." Elizabeth peered up at the darkening sky. "Night comes too fast this time of year."

"Do you smell that?" Young asked, her chin tilted up.

Sniffing the air, Elizabeth stiffened. Wood smoke. Faint.

"Where's it coming from?" Lila asked, doing her own sniffing.

"The wind is dispersing it," Rafe said. "It could be coming from anywhere at this point."

Far ahead, Elizabeth could just make out the pointed top of a structure. "Rafe, look."

"What the hell?" He checked his watch, a gift from his brother with a few extra features besides telling time that the Delta Force operators typically used when in the field. He twisted around in his saddle to look back. "We haven't gone far enough to be at the first farmstead."

"Are you sure?" Elizabeth reined her horse around to face their path they'd just taken. "We veered off the road a long while back."

"The trees aren't thick enough." He swung his horse south. "What used to be the road should be a hundred yards over."

She examined the area. The landscape was densely populated with small trees, bushes, grass, and weeds. It was impossible to tell how far they'd come and how far they'd gotten from the lane.

"Rafe, I think we're farther along than we realize."

"Shit," he spat.

"Uh, Sheriff."

Elizabeth wheeled her mare about.

Lila pointed at a gap in the shadowed underbrush. "I see light."

After ordering everyone to dismount and hobble the horses, Elizabeth and Rafe gathered with Young and Lila. Shadows were lengthening with each passing minute.

"I don't like this," Lila muttered.

"No one does." Elizabeth stared at the small patch of red light coming through the dying foliage. "It's too steady to be firelight."

"I can't tell if it's a house or a barn." Rafe parted the bushes, shining his flashlight into the hole. "A lot of crap to get tangled up in going this way."

"Get the rifles and shotguns," she told Young and Lila. She pointed to their left. "We'll have to go around. If someone is in the structure, they had to get to it somehow, and this way wasn't it."

"Should we split up?" Young asked as she handed Elizabeth one of the rifles, keeping the other for herself.

"I don't like that idea." Elizabeth slung the rifle strap over her shoulder. "Rafe?"

"Neither do I. In case we have an instance of friendly crossfire." He pocketed extra shotgun shells in the front of his tactical vest. "We don't have NVGs and we're not trained for this. We stay together."

"Wish we had those things and a K9," Lila groused.

"I'll be sure to bring that up in the next budget meeting," Elizabeth sniped.

"Ellie, we don't have time for this," Rafe admonished.

Lila rotated her ball cap backward. Young and Rafe did the same. Elizabeth decided against doing it.

Rafe took point, Lila to his right, Young and Elizabeth trailing a few feet back off to his left.

"Watch out for the multiflora rose. It's all over out here." With that warning, he started forward.

The path was obstructed by all manner of foliage, a lot of it snagging and tearing at their clothing. Elizabeth dreaded the thought of the slew of ticks she'd be covered in after this excursion. The damn things loved to hang out in places like this.

Even cutting a wide arch around the structure, they still hadn't found an easier way to get closer. Darkness completely covered the whole area. With the thick undergrowth, it felt darker than it should. The sliver of the moon showing did nothing to help with light.

Rafe slowed as he got to a point where they should be behind the structure. He removed his ball cap and scratched his head. "Damn it."

Elizabeth moved closer to him; Lila continued on a few more feet.

"We keep moving. There will be a hole somewhere," Elizabeth assured him.

"Found it," Lila said.

An ungodly high-pitched screech rent the evening air. They all jolted. Another ghastly noise followed on its heels.

"What the hell is that?" Lila muttered.

"Sounded like a wicked spirit," Young said, making the sign of the cross. "The Wailing Lady is here."

"Stupid nonsense." Rafe pulled away from the group and shoved through the gap Lila had discovered. "It came from the building." He looked back. "It's a barn."

A breeze filtered through the brush, bringing the acrid bite of wood smoke. Stronger. Closer. Elizabeth peered through the void between the tops of the bushes and the bottom tree foliage still clinging to the limbs. Behind the pointed roofline she spotted a plume of smoke not masked by darkness.

"Something is burning behind the barn."

"We're going to have to move—" Lila was cut off by a man's pain-riddled shout.

Elizabeth went stone cold at the god-awful sound. It continued for a few seconds more then cut off.

"If that's Kyle, I'm going to kill whoever made him do that," Lila fumed.

"Let's move, now," Rafe ordered. He grabbed Elizabeth's arm. "Stay with me. Dayne, Young, you circle left. We're going right. Weapons ready."

Elizabeth grasped his sweat-slicked forearm. "We need to radio Meyer first. I want troopers and DCI out here ASAP. Have them wait with Olivia until we give the go-ahead."

Another drawn-out yell joined the first. Swearing a blue streak, Rafe dove froward, dragging Elizabeth with him. Behind her, she heard Lila radio back to Meyer and dispatch, ending the transmission for them to not follow, to stay put until they next heard from one of them.

The rush across the weed-choked yard made Elizabeth's blood surge. More sounds, along with the red light, leaked out of the warped wood slats as they closed in on the barn. The four parted at the southeast corner of the building. Elizabeth stayed on Rafe's heels, trying to peek through larger gaps in the wood. Moments of bright, strobing light would burst through, blinding her.

"Like a haunted house," she commented.

"More like the house of a butcher," Rafe said.

A rickety side door brought them to a halt. Rafe examined the padlock. It was new, along with the hinges and the lock.

"There's probably another way in." Rafe dug out his folding knife and flicked it open. He slid the blade between the lock hinge and the disintegrating wood and pried it out, along with the screws. Once freed, he pushed the hinge aside and carefully swung the door open.

"Quiet."

They stepped into a wash of red light. It came from an array of red string lights adorning the exposed support beams and encircling the entirety of the barn. Moans and wails joined distorted voices from the center of the building. That part of the barn was walled off by paneling of some sort.

Rafe keyed out some kind of message to Lila and Young on his radio but kept silent. He tapped his shoulder and then beckoned for Elizabeth to follow.

Around the paneled walls they went, catching snippets of sounds coming from within. Something brushed against Elizabeth's right cheek, and she jumped back from the flutter of tattered cloth. Sighing, she continued on behind Rafe.

A few steps farther they found what looked to be a door of some kind. It was blocked off by a waist-high gate falling apart.

"We move that and they'll hear it," Rafe said.

Soft, rhythmic clicks over their radios gave them pause.

"What is it?" Elizabeth whispered.

"Dayne and Young found a door on the other side and are inside."

"Should we wait?"

A new scream shattered the silence, this time female. Elizabeth's bowels turned watery.

"That was Marnie." She moved past Rafe. "We're not waiting."

CHAPTER THIRTY-ONE

T HE SIGHT THAT greeted Elizabeth when she and Rafe came through the door set her back on her heels. Red lights mingled with strobing white lights were strung from every available plastic skeletal limb, board, or nail. Decapitated doll heads with grisly lines painted bloodred from their eyes and mouths were nailed to wood posts or the walls. Skeletons wearing bloody and blackened sheets floated about. Axes and knives hung from the ceiling among chains that rattled and clanked. Dangling in a corner, but not hard to miss, was an effigy of a female pirate. From where she stood, Elizabeth could make out the details of the mannequin.

It was a version of Bre as a rotted corpse. Meant to terrorize the man who'd hastened her death. She swallowed back the bile in her throat.

"Someone had way too much time on their hands," Rafe uttered.

Elizabeth agreed. "This was meant to be psychological terror. Who the hell would know how to do something like this?"

She spotted movement from the opposite side then Lila and Young appeared, gaping. Lila bumped into another dangling effigy; the dummy rotated to her and let out a witchy shriek. Lila slapped a hand over her mouth; Young grabbed the mannequin and flung it aside.

The hideous thing landed at Rafe's boots. Elizabeth could scarcely believe what she was staring at. A zombie bride. Wearing the same damn costume Denise wore when she was struck and killed.

"This is completely sadistic," she said over the sounds of audio-generated banshee screeches.

"Imagine what a mind drugged with a hallucinogen would do under all of this." Lila shuddered as bits of pulled batting made to look like cobwebs billowed out and caught on her hand.

Rafe tapped Elizabeth's shoulder then pointed up and down. "We've got a ladder to a loft and a cellar."

"We'll go up," Lila said and she and Young parted for the ladder.

Swallowing her trepidation, Elizabeth followed Rafe to the ancient stone steps. The real-life screams joined in the audio-generated ones bombarding them from all directions. The god-awful sounds echoed throughout the entire structure and in Elizabeth's head, giving her a massive headache. As they crept down the steps, the strobing lights intensified. Elizabeth switched between closing and opening each eye to avoid the nauseating effect of the lights.

At the bottom of the steps, they hit a dirt floor. Voices came from a back room. Elizabeth shifted her weapon from her two-handed grip to her right hand, grasped Rafe's arm with her left, and allowed him to lead them to the room. Each step closer brought the voices into focus and put the strobing lights behind them.

"Admit it, bitch! You should have done something. But you didn't!"

"Go to hell!"

Marnie. That was Marnie. Her comeback was rewarded with pain as she let out an earsplitting howl.

Elizabeth dug her nails into Rafe's arm. Marnie's scream faded into a raspy cry.

"All these years you've been hiding behind a façade. Pretending to be something you're not. Because you couldn't face what you had done. What you made us all become."

There was a stifled whimper and the disjointed shuffle of feet.

"Look what it turned her into. A terrified child."

Rafe paused next to the opening to the room where the speaker was standing. Elizabeth peeked inside, but all she saw was a stone wall. If she had to guess, this room might have been the well room. On the floor above would have been a pump and possibly a trough to water the animals once housed in the barn. The dirt floor beneath their boots was damp and churned into mud.

"Then there's you." A male grunt answered the speaker's taunt. "The disinterested deputy. The future corrupt sheriff. Thought you could outsmart those bastards. Outsmart me!"

Rafe popped his head around the corner and jerked back. He lifted his face to the barn floor and grimaced.

"What do you have to say for yourself, Kelley?"

For a flash of a moment, Elizabeth felt a pang of satisfaction to know Sheehan was getting some comeuppance. Then guilt pinged her conscience. Kelley might be a pain in the ass, but he was her pain in the ass to deal with.

From deep inside the room, Sheehan chuckled. "You really think your torture games will break me, girl?"

The girl answered with her own laugh. "I don't have to break you. Just kill you."

There was a horrific yell from Sheehan. Rafe shoved Elizabeth away from the door when she made a move to enter.

Elizabeth jerked Rafe close and pressed her mouth to his ear. "We can't wait."

"It's ugly in there, Ellie," he replied into her ear. "Just be prepared."

She nodded. He gave her a quick kiss to the cheek, then tapped his nose and pointed for her to move across to the other side. Holding his hand up, he counted down with his fingers, closed his fist, and moved. Elizabeth darted to the other side as he ran into the room.

"Seraphina! Stop!"

Three mostly naked bodies suspended from a beam by ropes, bloody, weeping cuts inflicted across the limbs and torsos on two of the victims. Elizabeth wanted to hurl. Curled in a tight ball on the floor against a wall, just behind her unconscious brother's suspended body, Freya rocked, sobbing. Centered among the carnage stood Seraphina Russell, clothed in a black grim reaper robe covered by a clear plastic poncho, the black velvet choker dangling from her neck. She wielded a bloodied knife.

The hate in her eyes burned a hole through Elizabeth's chest.

Shouts and gunshots from two floors above jolted everyone in the room. The brief distraction gave Sera her chance, and she bolted behind the towering well wall.

Rafe moved to go after her.

"Rafe, no!" Elizabeth yelled. "Take care of them." She ran for the opening. "I'll get her."

She was in the pitch-black passage before he could stop her. Ahead of her, she heard Sera's labored breathing. Something fluttered back at her. Elizabeth tried to dodge it but got a face full of bloody plastic. Ripping the damn thing from her, she kept running forward. Faint light ahead gave her pause as she made out Sera's silhouette.

"You shouldn't have come, Elizabeth," she said and darted into the barnyard.

Elizabeth holstered her sidearm and switched to the rifle before giving chase into the darkened forest yards from the barn. Overhead, she heard shouts and the scuffle of a fight. She couldn't help Lila and Young. Just as she turned away from the barn, a woman's scream pierced the night air.

Elizabeth whipped back in time to watch a body slam into the ground, right into a burning fire pit. She looked up and saw Young hanging by a hand from the edge of the open hayloft. Lila appeared in the gaping maw and grabbed her fellow deputy, dragging her into the loft. Elizabeth's gaze shot to the fire and the unmoving woman.

"Shit!" Elizabeth ran to the pit.

She skidded to a halt at the edge of the fire, setting the rifle aside. Oh God. A piece of wood was thrust through the woman's back. Risking the chance of burning her hands, she slapped her way to grab the facedown female's arms and dragged her from the fire. She rolled her onto her side then looked away.

It was Hillary Peterson. She was dead.

A yelp came from above. Elizabeth looked up to see Young and Lila were no longer in the hayloft opening, and the sounds of a new struggle drifted below. There was another person up there?

"You never could leave well enough alone."

She rotated on the balls of her feet, staying low. Her hand dropped to the rifle's stock.

Seraphina emerged from the edge of the trees. Dressed like the wailing specter she wanted to be, her jaggedly cut sleeves rippled in the breeze. The bloodied knife glinted firelight as she rotated it.

"I knew I should have waited another day. Sent you running in circles." She took two steps forward. "But Hillary wouldn't be deterred. Wanted him to pay for taking her daughter."

"That gave you the right to abduct my sister and my deputy?"

Seraphina laughed, a cold, witch's cackle that made Elizabeth's skin crawl. "She never told you the truth. Why doesn't that surprise me?"

Elizabeth rose, leaving the rifle on the ground as she did. The fire's heat penetrated her uniform, making her sweat. She wouldn't step away. Needed its bright light to disorient Seraphina.

"Whatever deal Marnie had with Sheehan obviously wasn't important enough to include me."

"Why would she dare include you? To tell you the truth would turn you against her."

"Because she wanted to right a wrong? I wouldn't have changed my mind about my sister just because she went about it in the wrong way."

"You poor, dumb, deluded woman. You really don't know." Seraphina cocked her head to the side, taking a few more sauntering steps forward. "Ever ask Marnie the reason why Denise and Brendette died? Did you ever stop to wonder why she never talked about it?" She dipped her chin down and glared at Elizabeth. "Because your sister is nothing more than the whore she turned all of us into. Ain't that right, Marnie?"

Elizabeth tensed as her sister stepped in line with her. Marnie, listing to her left and holding her left arm where Seraphina had cut open her forearm, didn't look at Elizabeth.

"It had never been my idea, Sera. I told you it was Denise's."

"Liar!"

"Marnie, you better tell me what is going on," Elizabeth ground out.

"No!" The shriek startled everyone as Freya ran in front of Marnie and Elizabeth and stood between them and Seraphina. "No more!" She pointed at each person. "Too many have died. No more will die," she sobbed.

"Freya, get out of the way," Seraphina barked.

Stomping her foot and slapping her arms at her sides, Freya faced off with Seraphina. "You've done enough. He's the one who should pay. Not her."

"Who the hell is he?"

"This is he," Lila said as she came around the far side of the fire pit and shoved a naked man to the ground in front of everyone.

Freya shrieked and jumped back from the man.

Elizabeth straightened. "I should have known."

Randall Abbott lay on his side, staring at Elizabeth, his entire body twitching. His torso, arms, and legs were covered in deep cuts, the cuts especially vicious around his genitals. Someone had attempted to castrate him.

"He's doped up," Lila said. "And so are the other bastards up in the loft."

"How many are up there?" Elizabeth asked, noticing that Rafe hadn't joined their little fray. If she knew him, and boy did she know him, he was circling around behind Seraphina like the hunter he was. They needed to keep her preoccupied until he could spring his trap.

"We've got five more. All sick perverts who were on the list," Lila replied.

Freya clutched her tattered shirt in one hand and pointed at Abbott with the other. "He. He did it. He killed them." She backpedaled from the frothing man.

"All three of them," Seraphina stated. "Denise, Bre, and Kerri. And ruined the lives of countless other young women for his own twisted, sexual pleasure."

Abbott's twitching turned to convulsions.

"What did you give him?" Elizabeth demanded.

"Just a dose of his own medicine." Seraphina gave a wicked smile, and Elizabeth reached for her sidearm. One bullet would end this living nightmare for all of them. "Just like Bre."

Abbott had killed Bre. *The sadistic, perverted twat deserves everything he has coming to him.*

Elizabeth shoved the ugly thought aside and slowly loosened her grip on her service weapon. "Damn it, Seraphina! What is he on?"

She leaned forward. "By the time you get the counter active, he'll be gone."

"Fentanyl," Lila uttered.

Seraphina clapped her hands, the knife bouncing about. "A plus for the deputy from Chicago."

"Sheriff!" Young yelled from the hayloft. "These guys are dying."

Lila moved, but Seraphina thrust her knife toward her.

"Leave them. All those rapists deserve it."

"Lila. Pratt isn't up there, is he?" Elizabeth asked.

"No," her deputy gasped.

One tiny miracle.

"Sheriff?" Young called again.

"I radioed Meyer before I dragged Abbott down here. He's on his way with the cavalry," Lila said.

Two miracles.

"Deputy Young, do what you can," Elizabeth called up. "It's going to be too late for all of them."

"Then we make sure Sera pays," Marnie said weakly, and she sat hard on the ground. "Do it, Ellie."

Elizabeth pulled her sidearm and leveled it at the knife-wielding woman. "Seraphina Russell, drop the knife. You're under arrest for murder."

"No." Seraphina brought the knife to her throat.

Before she could slash herself, Rafe burst from the trees and tackled her, knocking her knife hand away from her throat. They slammed into the ground in a tangle of limbs. Seraphina let out an ear-piercing shriek and pummeled and scratched Rafe like a demented cat.

Elizabeth ran, but fire ripped through her side, and she slowed. Lila, moving faster, got ahead of her and managed to get in the middle of the fray. When she pulled Seraphina off of Rafe, the maniacal woman planted a fist into Lila's face. Free, Seraphina scrabbled after the knife, coming face-to-face with Elizabeth's boot. She wheeled backward and flopped to the ground, dazed by the kick to the head. Standing over her, Elizabeth trained her weapon on the crazed woman's torso.

"Don't make me take you out, Sera."

Seraphina lay there, panting, staring up at Elizabeth, blood trickling from the corner of her mouth. "You were always a Goody Two-shoes."

Staring at the woman, Elizabeth didn't see Seraphina but Denise. Her statement, her wording, a favorite nickname Denise had given Elizabeth. It stole the breath from her lungs.

For decades, Elizabeth had been driven by Bre's death. What she'd forgotten, what she'd allowed to be buried in all the grief and the drive, was that she'd lost another friend that night. But she hadn't been the only one to lose someone close to her. Sera had, too. She had lost her only sister. The young woman she'd looked up to, relied on to get her through life, was violently ripped from her life forever. In Seraphina, Elizabeth saw her own grief, only bitter and rotten. Sera had tortured and killed to get the vengeance that she wanted, where Elizabeth sought justice by the law.

Elizabeth lowered her sidearm and squared her shoulders. "Being the Goody Two-shoes never failed me before."

Lila grabbed Seraphina's arms and hauled her onto her

feet then cuffed her. "Let's go."

Elizabeth holstered her weapon and helped Rafe to his feet. "Are you okay?"

"Fine." He gingerly touched his face and jaw. Sera had left wickedly jagged claw marks along his left cheek. "She fights like a girl."

His quip made Elizabeth smile.

"Thank you for stopping her. If she'd …"

He tugged her into his arms and crushed her to his chest. "Don't think about that. We've had enough of that tonight."

"God, Caroline's going to be devastated."

"Worry about that later." He released her and pulled her around. "I had to leave Sheehan in the cellar with Lundquist. He's bad off."

"Kyle?"

"No, Sheehan. Lundquist will be fine, he was just knocked out."

Elizabeth put her brakes on, jerking Rafe to a halt and dragging him to her. She took hold of his face and stared into his eyes. "Is this really over?"

"Some of it is. The real problem is just beginning."

CHAPTER THIRTY-TWO

Day 4: Sunday morning, two a.m.

LILA SAT ON the tailgate of a side by side someone had managed to get back here, with Freya leaning into her, watching Kyle, who, despite a concussion, was aiding the DCI techs. He'd argued vehemently to be allowed to help, against the EMS and Lila's protests. No damn concussion was going to stop him. Too grateful that a knock to the head was all he'd suffered at Seraphina's hands, Lila ceased her protests and let him be.

Somewhere in the midst of the fray of state criminal investigators, Undersheriff Fontaine was barking orders. He'd stayed behind to man the operation so the sheriff could go to the hospital with her sister and the ailing Sheehan. Olivia was busy doing her duties as medical examiner with the crime scene crew as well. Meyer and Young had taken Seraphina into custody and were working with the county attorney on the charges being brought against her.

Lila, feeling a bit out of place here, decided she was best needed as support for Freya, who refused to leave without her brother.

Freya shifted then lifted her head. Her hair was a dirty, debris-ridden mess, her makeup smeared, and her clothing tattered and filthy.

She blinked at Lila. "Is it really over?"

Reaching around the young woman's shoulders, Lila tucked her close to her body. "It looks like it."

Freya relaxed. It was a reaction that caught Lila off guard, after the years this poor woman had spent as a wound-up, anxiety-riddled mess. After her tantrum the day before catching her and Kyle together, Lila had been certain Freya would never trust her. Looked like things were going to be different.

"Lila?"

Lila rested her head on Freya's. "Yeah?"

"I'm sorry I never told anyone about what happened to Bre."

Frowning, Lila closed her eyes and tightened her arm. "Why didn't you?"

"I was scared. They threatened to do the same thing to me if I ever said a word."

"They who?"

Freya stiffened and sat upright. She dragged her knees to her chest and hugged them.

Lila glanced at Kyle, assured that he was absorbed in his duties. "You can tell me. Nothing bad is going to happen by telling me the truth."

Freya's shattered gaze slid to Lila and held. "Promise?"

"Seraphina killed most of them. What can they do?"

After a few moments of staring off in space, Freya sighed. "Not all of them." She shoved her knees back over the edge of the tailgate. "Bre really did die of a drug overdose because Randall Abbott forced her. He blamed her for Denise's death."

"How do you know this?"

"I was where I wasn't supposed to be." Freya hung her head. "I was a stupid child determined to spend time with my big sister. The night Denise was killed I snuck into Bre's car. Kyle had a football thing, and my parents were gone, so no one saw me. From the car, I saw everything."

"Oh, God, Freya, I'm so sorry."

"Me too. Randall found me before Bre died, and he made Sheriff Jones drag me home. Jones threatened to do the same to me if I ever said a word about what happened." Tears rolled down her cheeks. "Bre saw me before I was shoved into the sheriff's truck. I was screaming for her to save me, but she couldn't."

Lila sensed another person. She glanced over and found Kyle standing next to them.

"I'm sorry, Kyle, I couldn't save her."

He reached out and grabbed his sister's hands, pulling her sobbing form into his arms. "It's not your fault, Freya. You were a kid." His gaze met Lila's. "None of it was ever your fault."

Lila ran a hand through her hair, bringing her hand to a stop at the nape of her neck. Kyle was saying it for his benefit as well as Freya's. And underneath, just a tiny bit was directed at Lila, too.

"Was Randall the one who showed up at the house?" Kyle asked a moment later when Freya had pulled herself together.

"Yes." Freya's response muffled by his chest. She drew back and slumped on the tailgate. "He thought I was the one who told Kerri about Bre."

"You weren't," Lila supplied. "That's why you called Marnie out there." She caught Kyle's attention. "Did you hear any of what Seraphina was grilling Marnie about?"

He shook his head. "She made sure I was knocked out. Sheriff is going to have to get her sister to tell her the truth." He beckoned Lila to join him. "Freya, are you going to be okay sitting here for a few?"

She watched Lila scoot off the tailgate, and for the first time since Friday morning, Freya smiled. "Yeah."

They didn't get too far from her, just enough to be out of earshot.

"What happened with Hillary? DCI thinks they have it figured out, and without Young here to confirm what occurred up there …"

Lila held up her hand. "We need to tread carefully with Young. She's shaken pretty badly by what we found in that loft."

"What did you find?"

Swallowing hard, she checked to make sure Freya was staying put. Lila crossed her arms. "Hillary had already force-fed all of them with fentanyl, and some of them were already on the verge of death from the overdose. She'd taken vicious delight in slicing up Abbott." Lila shuddered at what she'd seen up in the hayloft. "Young startled her when we showed up in the loft. Hillary was about to hack off his … junk."

Kyle grimaced. "Why?"

"Maybe because he was the one forcing some perverted sexual encounters on Kerri." Lila squeezed herself. "Or he'd done the same to Hillary back in the day. Either way, she was rabid. Young beat me to her, and they got into a struggle over the knife. The fight pushed them to the edge of the loft. Before I could stop them, Young flung Hillary around, but they were too close to the opening and Hillary fell, dragging Young with her. How she caught the edge of the loft, I have no idea. I helped her up."

"Doc says Hillary died on impact. Other than the burning stick that penetrated her body, the fall snapped her neck."

Lila couldn't stop the second round of shudders. "She didn't deserve to die like that."

"It might have been a mercy, considering how her victims died." He grasped her hand and tugged her to him. "You and Young are going to need a long heart-to-heart together."

"She's not going to talk to me."

"Don't discredit your experiences. She's never encountered horrors like this. Or killed someone. She'd going to need a sympathetic ear."

Lila looked up at him. "What about you?"

"I've got Freya to worry about."

"Kyle."

He leaned over and pressed a kiss to her forehead. "I need to get back to work." With that, he released her and strode toward the melee of crime scene techs working under the spotlights.

Hugging herself once again, she watched him go. Freya was still huddled on the back of the side by side. Her revelations about Bre's death reopened those seeping wounds, and both would be bleeding out. Kyle would shove all of this in a tiny box and lock it away.

Lila dreaded the repercussions to come.

"SHEEHAN'S BAD OFF, but the old snake is going to be fine," Dominic told Elizabeth. "He's going to have to stay overnight."

"Lucky bastard," she muttered. "What about Marnie?"

"She lost enough blood to make her light-headed, but she'll be fine, too." He gripped her elbow and escorted her down the hospital hall. "Is Olivia okay? I heard she was out there when this was all going down."

"She's fine. We didn't allow her anywhere near the area until after it was secure." Elizabeth patted his arm. "Nothing to worry about. She's doing her thing with DCI."

He seemed relieved by her assurances, but the angry look in his eyes didn't settle with her. Elizabeth shrugged it off as her mind still coped with the revelations that occurred this night. She was seeing conspiracies where there were none.

"What's the word on Ben?" Redirecting the conversation seemed best.

"He's going to be tricky. He's concussed and his leg was shattered."

"How long are you keeping him?" Elizabeth asked.

"At least twenty-four hours. I still haven't decided if I need to bring an orthopedic surgeon in on his case. I want the swelling to ease first."

She frowned. "Should you be telling me all of this?"

Dominic cleared his throat and clasped his hands behind his back. "Uh, didn't you know that he has you and Marnie as his emergency contact and are approved family members?"

"I'm what?"

"Um." Dominic rubbed his cheek. "You might want to talk with Marnie. Ben's sleeping." Giving her a forced smile, he exited the conversation.

What in the name of all that was holy was going on? Elizabeth about-faced and marched to Sheehan's room. She should ignore him and go to her sister, but something was nagging her. And he held the answer.

With Kelley Sheehan, there was always a payout of sorts. So what was his motivation in shutting down that camp, stopping Abbott, Jones, and all their cronies? It had to be about what was in it for him. Why drag her sister into this? What was he holding over Marnie's head to get her to cooperate? He was going to fess up. They were going to lay this whole damn sordid affair to rest.

This was his moment to prove once and for all he was someone she could trust explicitly. Because, damn it, she was so damn tired of trying to loath him.

As she approached the room, a searing fire rippled through her right side, bringing her to a gasping halt. Elizabeth gripped her abdomen with one hand and placed the other against the hospital wall. Teeth gritted, she breathed through the pain, feeling her head grow light. When the fire ebbed away, she remained in position for another minute, until she was certain she wouldn't tip over. Then Elizabeth took a cleansing breath and stepped back from the wall.

Tilting her right hand off her abdomen, she gulped at the bright, red stain on her palm. She fisted her hand and glanced around. None of the hospital staff within eyesight paid any attention to her, going about their duties. Elizabeth spotted a laptop cart with hand wipes on a shelf. She snatched a few and cleaned her hand.

Her uniform top was soaked with blood in the exact spot her hand had been. She zipped up her jacket to conceal her misdeeds. The soiled wipes stashed in her pocket, she continued into Sheehan's room.

Unfortunately, the old coot was passed out, probably from the painkillers Dominic had prescribed for the myriad sutured cuts on his chest and arms.

Elizabeth watched him sleep for a moment then moved to Marnie's room a few doors down. Due to her injuries, she'd been admitted but not in the ER taking up a room.

Her sister was curled up on her bed, the blue blanket balled up under her bandaged arm, which she cradled on a pillow. The nurses had managed a cloth bath to help clean her up, but Marnie needed a good, long hot shower to wash away all traces of the horror that had befallen her.

Marnie lifted her head, made eye contact, then let her head flop back on the uselessly thin pillow. "Did you know you were bleeding?"

Elizabeth glanced down, the blood now staining her jacket. She shrugged. "It'll heal."

She shuffled around the bed and took the chair beside it. Her body sighed in relief. But the dampness in her midsection was sliding south. The fire from a few moments ago was returning.

No way was she going to let some torn sutures deter her.

Her sister stared, her gaze filled with weary caution. The

hospital gown covered the cuts and gashes on Marnie's torso, but Elizabeth couldn't unsee the damage Seraphina had inflicted in that torture room. Closing her eyes, she bowed her head.

"Ellie, it's going to be okay," Marnie whispered.

She lifted her head. "It's never been okay. Has it?"

Marnie gnawed on her bruised lips. Elizabeth leaned to the side, taking pressure off, and gently took her sister's right hand. Sitting there, holding her, was the right thing to do.

"How long have you and Ben been married?"

A pained smile crossed her sister's face as a lone tear streaked from the corner of her eye. "I don't know if you'd call it married per se."

"Did you speak vows? Exchange rings? Sign a paper?"

"Yes, yes, and yes. We just don't really live together."

Elizabeth smoothed a blood-tipped white lock from her sister's face. "Doesn't matter, you're still married. Do you love him?"

"Have for a long time. We just never wanted anyone to know." She rolled her eyes. "Except Kelley. Sneaky bastard managed to find out."

"He used that as leverage to get the two of you to help him?"

"No. We'd been doing that long before we got married." Marnie's hand twitched. "It was my idea."

"I doubt the blackmailing was your idea."

Marnie shook her head. "That was all Kelley."

Elizabeth sighed. "You have a lot of explaining to do. It's going to have to be you, because Kelley ain't going to speak a word of truth about this whole operation."

"Andrea tell you everything?"

"Of what she knew. We'll have to track down Allegra King and get her side to this as well." Elizabeth hunched down to her sister's level. "Why? Why couldn't you tell me what was going on? What happened to Bre and Denise?"

Marnie's face crumpled. More tears leaked from her eyes. "Because I blamed myself." She sniffed. "I wasn't lying out there. The whole thing had been Denise's idea. She was desperate for cash because her mother was bad off. It was supposed to be a few times and nothing more than us just giving a few of the old rich men some attention." She shuddered, wincing when it bothered her injuries. "Randall and Jones took it too far."

"Was Kelley ever part of the …?"

"No." Marnie swallowed. "I was the one who told him what Jones was doing. It was months later. And only after … I found out Randall was raping Denise and Bre. The chokers. It was his way of marking them as his."

"Seraphina had one on. Lila and I found one at Hillary's house."

"Sera found one of Bre's; she'd had two. She was never part of his conquests. Hillary …" Marnie took a shuddering breath. "Hillary was his replacement after Denise and Bre were killed."

"Were you?"

Marnie blanched. "Never. I never allowed any of them to use my body that way. But …"

Elizabeth wanted to throw up. She leaned back into the chair, her hand slipping from Marnie's. Her energy was draining quickly. Elizabeth didn't know how much longer she'd be able to ward off passing out. The sisters stared at each other.

"How many girls?" Elizabeth asked.

"I don't know. After Hillary managed to break free and move away, I stayed out of it. But Abbott and Jones continued it. Kelley let it leak during his run against Jones for sheriff that the man was a sadistic perv, and I think there was a break for a few years, during his time as sheriff anyway. Randall started it back up before you took office."

"That's when you, Ben, and Kelley decided to take him down." Elizabeth shook her head. "How does Ben fit into all of this, other than being your husband?"

"Being my husband and a deputy. That's it."

Elizabeth felt every minute of her waking life in the last three days. Her brain hurt. She was sick. Sick from the pain. Sick from the prolonged grief. Sick of everything.

"All this time, you let me think Kelley was corrupt?"

"Oh, he is. He's just kept himself off your radar."

"And The Watering Hole?"

"Joint venture. I needed funds. He had it and was willing to let me run it. Only concession, I had to stock the bar with his favorite whiskey and bourbons." Marnie blinked. "He's not all that bad, Ellie. Just a byproduct of his environment." A yawn followed up her statement.

Elizabeth had to stifle her own. "I'll let you sleep."

Marnie thrust her good hand out. "Stay with me."

Unable to say no, Elizabeth scooted the chair closer to the bed and clasped her sister's hand in hers.

"Marnie, you do realize what you three did was illegal?"

"In a way, maybe, but what the girls did is on them. Ellie, we never told the girls to have sex with the bastard. Knowing Randall, he probably forced himself on them and then manipulated them into believing it was what they deserved. He used that same tact on all the others."

"So why kill Kerri?"

"Because he figured out what she was doing. Or she got mad and let it slip. It's what happened with Denise. He was so furious with her because she finally had enough of his bullshit and cut him off. He chased her through those woods and in front of that truck after attacking her."

"And Bre?"

"Blamed her for what he did. But I think it was because she witnessed the whole thing and he had to get rid of the eyewitness. All these years, I suspected he was really behind it, but I didn't have the proof. Had I known about Freya … Ellie, believe me, I would have never put another girl in his line of fire. I should have realized that with Hillary being one of his conquests, he went right after her daughter."

"And turned Hillary into a murdering avenger." Elizabeth sighed. "Marnie, there'll be repercussions from this."

Her sister studied her. "How much are you willing to bargain with your position as sheriff to prevent a sister charged with a crime?"

"That's not …" What Marnie was referring to struck Elizabeth. "No one would believe me. Will they?" She rubbed her eyes with her free hand. "I'm so over this."

"It's over now. For good."

"Is it?"

Marnie yawned again, this time triggering Elizabeth's response. They smiled at each other but didn't speak another word. As she stared at her sister, Elizabeth's vision began to grow dark at the edges.

"Ellie?" Marnie's voice sounded like it was in a tin can.

Elizabeth felt herself sliding but couldn't gather up the gumption to stop it. She welcomed the embrace of the dark warmth.

"Sheriff? Sheriff, open your eyes."

She peeled one eyelid open. A blurry figure loomed over her.

"Oh, Elizabeth, you should have listened to me."

"Doc, I listen to no one."

From somewhere off in the distance, she heard, "Let her sleep. She'll be back at it here in a week."

Elizabeth tried to smile at Lila's declaration. Her deputy detective was right.

Her county was in dire need of her after the fallout. She would sleep off this setback. Start fresh again next week.

THE END

Want more? Check out Elizabeth and Lila's latest adventure in *Hush, My Darling*!

Join Tule Publishing's newsletter for more great reads and weekly deals!

ACKNOWLEDGMENTS

First, foremost, and always, honor goes to the One who gave me this talent and drive.

There are days I can't believe I get to be an author and with such a fantastic crew like Tule. It's such a privilege to be an author for Tule. Thank you Jane, Meghan, Cyndi, and Nikki, and to all of the unnamed people behind the scenes that do such a wonderful job. Hats off to Lee Hyat for a scary, freaky cover! Lee, it's like you crawled inside my head and pulled it out. *Magnifico!*

I will scream it to the ends of the earth: I have one of the best editors in the biz. When things in my family took a scary turn into the unbelievable, I knew I could go to Julie for support. The mark of a great editor/author relationship comes in the fact that the editor can read her author as well as Julie reads me. I'm so glad we continued working together at this level. Julie, you're da best! We need a weekend to just gab.

My beta readers, Rachel and Jenn, are the sounding board all authors should have. I can't do any of this without either one of them. Rachel takes the role of rah, rah, I'll haunt you if you don't write faster. And Jenn is my first round of Julie. She knows how to delve into the mystery, suspense side and make sure I see first what Julie will catch later. Both are my closest friends and brutally honest readers.

If it won't work, or I went too far off the deep end, they get me back on track. Love ya both!

Ha! I don't know if they'll see it, but many thanks to my coworkers for letting me escape work early for a few extra hours at home to write so I could make this deadline. I truly do enjoy working where I do, even if we have a few kooky characters call in with some of the weirdest questions or requests.

My family has grown up, yet they're still here. When I started this journey, they were babies. Now I have young adults out there making me proud to be their mom. I love you all.

Then there is my partner in this crazy thing we call life. My husband was more than willing to run off with me to some Iowa State football and basketball games this past year, all the while doing the driving so I could write or work. We've been through hell and back again, and here we still stand as husband and wife. Love you, Shawn.

If you enjoyed *Straight for the Kill,*
you'll love the other books in the…

BENOIT AND DAYNE MYSTERY SERIES

Book 1: *The Killer in Me*

Book 2: *Hush, My Darling*

Book 3: *Straight for the Kill*

Available now at your favorite online retailer!

ABOUT THE AUTHOR

Winter Austin perpetually answers the question: "were you born in the winter?" with a flat "nope," but believe her, there is a story behind her name.

A lifelong Mid-West gal with strong ties to the agriculture world, Winter grew up listening to the captivating stories told by relatives around a table or a campfire. As a published author, she learned her glass half-empty personality makes for a perfect suspense/thriller writer. Taking her ability to verbally spin a vivid and detailed story, Winter translated that into writing deadly romantic suspense, mysteries, and thrillers.

When she's not slaving away at the computer, you can find Winter supporting her daughter in cattle shows, seeing her three sons off into the wide-wide world, loving on her fur babies, prodding her teacher husband, and nagging at her flock of hens to stay in the coop or the dogs will get them.

She is the author of multiple novels.

Thank you for reading

STRAIGHT FOR THE KILL

If you enjoyed this book, you can find more from all our great authors at TulePublishing.com, or from your favorite online retailer.

TULE
PUBLISHING